DEATH BY PUMPKIN

The door to the room was open. Pumpkins were laid out as if the room was meant to be a pumpkin patch straight out of someone's nightmares. Some of the pumpkins were carved so that they looked sinister. There were no friendly smiles on these jack-o'-lanterns. The walls of the room were painted in shades of dark orange and blue that was reminiscent of dusk. Guarding the pumpkins were a trio of scarecrows, their jack-o'-lantern faces grinning evilly down at where the body of Marilyn Monroe lay.

Gasps echoed through the crowd, and I heard Margaret Yarborough's name whispered more than once. I'd eased my way to the front with Will, so I could see that it wasn't the older woman's body, but rather, one of the younger Monroes I'd seen earlier.

Her head was turned at an unnatural angle and smashed through a pumpkin . . .

Death by Pumpkin Spice

Alex Erickson

KENSINGTON PUBLISHING CORP.
http://www.kensingtonbooks.com

KENSINGTON BOOKS are published by

Kensington Publishing Corp.
119 West 40th Street
New York, NY 10018

All Kensington titles, imprints and distributed lines are available at special quantity discounts for bulk purchases for sales promotions, premiums, fund-raising, and educational or institutional use. Special book excerpts or customized printings can also be created to fit specific needs. For details, write or phone the office of the Kensington Special Sales Manager. Kensington Publishing Corp., 119 West 40th Street, New York, NY 10018. Attn: Special Sales Department. Phone: 1-800-221-2647.

Kensington and the K logo Reg. U.S. Pat & TM Off.

ISBN-13: 978-1-61773-755-8
ISBN-10: 1-61773-755-0
First Kensington Mass Market Edition: October 2016

eISBN-13: 978-1-61773-756-5
eISBN-10: 1-61773-756-9
First Kensington Electronic Edition: October 2016

10 9 8 7 6 5 4 3 2 1

Printed in the United States of America

3361405774 65561

1

The pleasing aroma of fresh-baked pumpkin cookies filled the room as I removed the pan from the oven. Halloween was one of my favorite times of the year because that was when the world turned into a pumpkin lover's bliss. I leaned in over the pan and breathed in deep. It was a challenge not to give in to temptation and sample the cookies as I carried them to the front to place within the empty display case.

"Some have just come up!" Lena Allison said from her place at the register. She held up two fingers and gave me a relieved smile as I slid two cookies into a bag.

Death by Coffee had been buzzing since we'd started selling pumpkin items. The cookies were gone almost as fast as I could bake them, and the various coffees were constantly in need of refills. It was running me ragged, but it was worth it.

As Lena rang up another order, I finished filling the display case and carried the cooling cookie sheet to the back. I deposited it in the sink where it would need to be washed before I could use it again, then headed back out front to make a coffee of my own. I filled the cup three quarters of the way full, added some pumpkin spice flavoring, and then plopped in one of the recently baked cookies.

"Ugh." Lena turned up her nose as she leaned against the counter. The line was gone for the moment, giving her a few seconds to breathe. "I still don't see how you could drink that. I hate pumpkin."

I took a sip and grinned at her over the rim of my cup. "Yum."

She laughed and shook her head, causing her purple hair to bounce around her ears. Her chin was clear of scrapes, though her elbow had a pretty nasty scab that she'd covered with a pair of Band-Aids. Her skateboard was parked in the back room, and it looked just as beat-up as she often did.

Still, I wouldn't trade her in for anyone else. Since Lena started working at Death by Coffee, she'd made my life a whole lot easier. She's a smart girl, and friendly to boot. She was saving up to go to college, and I privately hoped she would stick close to home when she did leave. I'd hate to lose her.

The bell above the door jangled and in came Rita Jablonski, bundled in a coat lined with fur I hoped was fake. She was a short woman, on the plump side, and was the biggest gossip in all of Pine Hills.

"It's getting windy out there!" she said, coming straight to where I stood. "They're saying we could see some pretty serious storms over the next few days."

I glanced out the window, and indeed, the leaves were blowing around as if a tornado were itching to come roaring down out of the cloudy sky. The reds and yellows were beautiful, but I'll admit, I did miss the warm sun and full green of mid-summer, though I wasn't a fan of the sometimes oppressive heat.

"I hope it won't be too bad," I said. If the power went out, there'd be no more cookies or coffee. And that meant no more business.

"Well, as long as it spends itself before this weekend, I'll be happy." Rita glared out the window as if the rain could hear her and comply. "The church is having our annual Trunk or Treat, and I for one plan on being there, rain or shine. We are participating this year, just like the last, and I won't let a little wet weather ruin it."

I narrowed my eyes. "We?"

She looked surprised for a moment before smiling. "The book club, of course! We talked about it during our last meeting." She paused and a look of understanding passed over her face. "That's right, you weren't there." She leaned forward, pressing against the counter as she spoke. "We're holding it at the church on Sunday evening. Cars will be parked in the lot, trunks filled with candy. The kids walk around and trick-or-treat like they normally would. It's safer than going from house to house and the costumes are a little less . . ." She grimaced.

"Scary?"

"Disgusting, more like. You can't imagine what some of the teenagers dress up as when left to their own devices."

Oh, I could imagine all right. I'd lived near a college campus for a few years. Halloween was always a lesson in the perverse, especially since most college kids took any opportunity they could to drink and party. Add in costumes dreamed up over a drunken weekend, and let me tell you, it didn't take long before I made sure not to be anywhere near the campus on Halloween.

"I do hope you get the night off," Rita said. "We start at six."

"I'll check with Vicki," I said. "But it should be okay. We aren't open much later than six anyway."

"You do that."

I was surprised to realize I was actually excited about the event. It sounded fun, and Vicki was always pressuring me to get out more. It might give me a chance to meet more people in town, and maybe advertise just a little.

The door opened and I glanced up just as Will Foster walked in. He paused just inside the door, looking as uncomfortable as any man could, before his eyes landed on me. He strode across the room, right past Rita, and came to a stop in front of me.

"Krissy." He coughed to clear his throat. "Could we talk for a moment?"

I was so flustered, I almost didn't answer. Will was a dream to look at normally, yet today he seemed to positively glow. His dark brown eyes, his near-black hair, and skin the color of a creamer-rich coffee was enough to cause me to break out into an instant nervous sweat. His coat was one of those long, black, button-up jobbies that all the stylish men seemed to wear on magazine covers. I couldn't see his shoes from where I stood, but I was pretty sure they'd be polished to a shine.

"Krissy?" he asked. "You okay?"

"Huh? Oh! Yeah." I hurriedly set my coffee down before I spilled it. "I'm just surprised to see you." The last time I'd seen Will, he'd left thinking I was seeing another man, not knowing the man he'd seen me with had been a suspect in a murder investigation. The guy had hit on me and made a scene, but I'd never even considered going out with him. I hadn't had time to explain what really happened before Will was gone.

He flushed a little and looked down at his hands. They looked strong and manicured. "Well, I . . ." He cleared his throat and looked around me like he was afraid looking me in the eye would cause me to start yelling at him.

As hurt as I was about him vanishing like he had, I let him off the hook. "Let's go upstairs so we can talk privately." I glanced at Lena. "You'll be okay for a few minutes, right?" She nodded with a grin. I turned to Rita. "I'll be back soon. Feel free to order and take a seat."

I stayed behind the counter as I headed upstairs to where my best friend and co-owner of Death by Coffee, Vicki Patterson, was showing our newest hire, Jeff Braun, how to ring up a book sale. He was a slow learner, but I had no doubt he'd get it eventually. Vicki glanced toward where Will was walking up the stairs across the room and then raised a delicate eyebrow at me.

I shrugged and tried to hide my grin as I walked past her; I didn't know, either. I strode around the counter and went to where Will was waiting between a pair of book-shelves.

"What did you want to talk to me about?" I asked.

"First, let me apologize," he said. "I was stupid. I jumped to conclusions and didn't let you tell me your side of the story. I'm an idiot."

"No, you're not," I said. His apology had my insides jumping up and down for joy so much, I felt sick.

"No, I am." He took one of my hands and clutched it

in both of his. "I shouldn't have walked away like that. And then with what happened after . . ."

"It's nothing," I said, willing my glands not to over-react. His hands were so warm and strong and yet soft at the same time.

Will sighed and smiled. "I don't know how you can forgive me so easily. I should have come before now, but was afraid that after I'd made such a fool of myself, you wouldn't want to see me."

"That's silly," I said. "Of course I want to see you."

A gleam came into his eye. "I know that now." He laughed. "But you know how things are. I felt stupid, was afraid you'd call me on it the moment you saw me, and with work being so hectic lately, I used it as an excuse not to come see you."

"But you're here now."

"That, I am."

It was as if a hole had opened in the roof and a beam of pure sunlight had washed over me. I felt warm all over and had an intense desire to squeal in joy.

"You didn't need to apologize," I said, doing my best to contain my excitement. "I should have been more up front with you about what I was doing in the first place."

"You didn't owe me anything," he said. "We'd barely had a chance to speak, which was my fault entirely. If I'd given you more time, then maybe I wouldn't have let my imagination get carried away with me. It's a fault, I know."

He didn't need to tell me about it. My imagination had a tendency to get me into more trouble than I cared to admit. It was a wonder it hadn't gotten me killed yet.

Will let go of my hand and cleared his throat again.

"Now that that is out of the way, I have something I'd like to ask you."

"Okay." It came out as a little squeak.

"Because I was such a knucklehead, I'll completely understand if you say no."

"I won't." I forced a nervous smile. "I mean, I won't say no just because of that."

That caused him to laugh. "All right then." He cleared his throat yet again. He appeared almost as nervous as I felt. "I would like to make up for my ignorant actions by taking you to a party."

"A party?"

"A Halloween costume party, to be exact." A devious smile crooked the corner of his mouth. "Unless you are frightened."

"I . . ." Fear clenched at my core. I might love Halloween, but I'd never been one to dress up in a costume. Any time I tried, it was always an unmitigated disaster. Pieces would fall off constantly, or I'd end up wearing the same thing as a dozen other people. Then there was the one time when I'd worn a rubber nose that caused me to break out into a horrible rash that spread over half of my face.

A look of worry crossed Will's eyes. "If you aren't interested, you don't have to go," he said. "I have an invitation and thought it might be the perfect way to say I'm sorry."

"No!" I said, worried he would take it all back and leave, never to return. "I want to go. I'm just not sure I have anything to wear."

Relief washed over his face. "That's okay. The party isn't until Friday night. You have a couple of days to find something appropriate." He reached into the pocket of his coat and removed a folded piece of stationery. "Here," he said, holding it out to me.

"What's this?" I asked, taking it.

"It's my number. My cell, actually. In case you have any questions."

"I . . ." It was my turn to clear my throat. "Thank you."

He looked amused as he said, "It's no problem at all. And if you wouldn't mind, I have my cell on me and can input your number now in case I need to contact you before the big night."

"Of course!"

Will whipped out his phone and handed it to me. It was one of the really nice ones that cost a fortune. I always opted for the free phones that came with a two-year contract, promising myself I'd eventually upgrade to something better, but never actually going through with it. I mean, how can you beat free?

I typed in my number. Once it was in, I saved the contact and handed him his phone back. He was grinning as he glanced down at his screen, before shoving the phone in his pocket. He then checked his watch and frowned.

"I need to get back to work," he said. "I'll call you tomorrow sometime so we can work out the details."

"Okay." It was about the only thing I could manage.

He turned and started to walk away but stopped. "Is he supposed to be doing that?"

I followed his gaze to the upstairs table where people could sit to read. The black and white store cat, Trouble, was standing on his hind legs, front paw reaching into the eye socket of a jack-o'-lantern, trying to bat at the light inside.

"He'll be fine," I said. "The candle is fake." Though

the pumpkin wasn't. If he were to knock it off, I'd end up having to clean it up.

"Ah." Will watched the cat a moment longer before chuckling. "I'll talk to you soon." And then he was gone.

I floated over to Trouble and picked him up. He meowed in surprise as I gave him a quick hug, before he started squirming to be put down. I carried him across the room and deposited him on top of one of the four-foot-tall bookshelves, where he glared at me before lying down to wash. I patted him on the head before going back downstairs to where Rita still stood, eyes focused on the front door Will had just exited. She turned to me with a surprised look on her face.

"Well, well," she said. "William Foster now, is it?"

I couldn't keep the stupid grin off my face as I answered. "He asked me to a costume party."

Rita's eyebrows tried to leap from her face. "Really? You?"

I was too happy to be miffed. "Yep. Me!"

She made a sound that was part incredulous and part impressed. "There are quite a few women who would kill to go somewhere with him." She paused, eyes widening. "Did he say what party?"

"No," I said, wondering what all the fuss was about. "He said he had an invitation and he wanted to take me."

Rita looked as if she might keel over right then and there. "Oh, Lordy Lou! He's taking you to the Yarborough party! I can't believe you of all people get to go!" She paused. "You did tell him you'd go, now didn't you?"

Annoyance started to seep into my voice as I answered. "I did. And how do you know which party he was talking about?"

She rolled her eyes. "Everyone who is anyone always

goes to the Yarborough party. It's by invite only, you see, and I'd wager it is the *only* one someone like William Foster would go to."

My gut clenched. "I didn't think it was all that big of a deal."

Rita's eyes widened. "Not a big deal? Where have you been? It's a huge deal!" She leaned onto the counter and lowered her voice. "I'm just surprised they are having it this year after . . . you know."

"No," I said. "I don't."

"The party was always Howard Yarborough's baby," she said, keeping her voice down as if she was sharing some deep, dark secret. "He was an architect, you see. He designed his house for this very occasion. He loved Halloween, did Howard, and he made sure to show it."

I noticed the past tense. "He's passed?"

"Just a few weeks ago, if you can believe it." Rita shook her head sadly. "He was a strange man, believe you me, but he was always kind. His wife, Margaret, never was big into the costume parties, but Howard loved them, so she put up with them. I can't believe she's going to continue on the tradition without him, especially after what happened."

Some of the air went out of me then. What I'd thought of as a chance to get to know Will better was now starting to sound more and more like it might end up being a somber affair where Howard's wife and friends would lament his passing by holding the party he'd held so dear. I would feel like I was imposing, not having met the man.

Rita leaned forward even more, so that she was only a few inches from my face. "And let me tell you something about William Foster . . ."

I held up a hand before she could go on. "No," I said, taking a step back. "Just, no."

"No?" She said it like she'd never heard the word before. "No, what?"

"I don't want to hear it." I picked up my cooling coffee and took a sip, shaking my head all the while.

"I don't know what you could mean?"

"No gossip," I said. "No secrets. I want to discover these things on my own."

Rita stepped back, looking mildly offended. "I don't gossip!" Someone sitting at a nearby table snorted. She glared over her shoulder at him. "Well, I don't."

I knew for a fact that Rita spent most of her life gossiping about the people of Pine Hills, but I decided not to press the issue. It would get me nowhere but on her bad side, which in turn would turn me into a major target of her gossipy wrath.

"Well, I should run," Rita said, hand going to her hair. She'd recently curled it, though with the coming rain it was starting to sag. "You *must* tell me how the party goes."

"I will," I said, knowing I wouldn't have any choice. I'd either tell her everything, or she would find someone who would. At least if I told her, I could make sure everything she heard was true.

She gave me a simpering smile before walking away.

"Party?" Vicki asked, startling me. Apparently she'd come downstairs at some point during my conversation and was standing behind me. "What party?"

I turned away from Rita, and with a grin that nearly split my face in half, I told Vicki all about it.

2

"This is going to be amazing! I can't believe we're both going to be there."

Vicki beamed at me as we entered the costume shop, Halloween Queens. We'd both gotten up early so we could be at the store just as it opened so Vicki could get to Death by Coffee and start her shift. Lena was opening today, which was a big deal for her. Usually, either Vicki or I was present when the store opened and closed, but not today. We both trusted her to do a good job, even if she was going to have to train Jeff in some of the basics by herself.

"Mason's invite came because of Raymond." The elder Lawyer and all-around jerk. "He didn't want to go, but when he told me about it, I insisted. I mean, it isn't every day you get to go to a big Halloween party! It's been so long since I've been to anything this large, I'm kind of nervous."

Vicki had definitely been to her fair share of parties, and mostly under protest. Her parents were both small-time actors, but they were still able to attend quite a few cast parties since they held a few minor roles here and there. They'd dragged her along, kicking and screaming, not caring if she wanted to be there or not. Even though she got to meet quite a few famous people at these events, Vicki just wasn't interested in the lifestyle. It was part of the reason she'd moved to Pine Hills in the first place. The only acting she wanted to do was on the small stage, in front of friends and neighbors; not on the television or movie screens.

Not many people understood her choices. I, for one, was glad for them.

"I'm worried," I told her. "I won't know anyone and I'm sure I'm going to look like an idiot."

"I'll be there," Vicki said, glancing around the shop. It had opened its doors only a week ago and would be gone by the end of next week. "Mason will be there. And of course, Will." She winked at me and grinned.

I sighed, unable to get into the spirit of things. "Yeah, well, there will be a lot of other people there, too, many of whom won't want me there."

"You'll be fine." Vicki patted me on the arm. "You're just nervous. It'll pass."

"Yeah, I guess."

"Trust me." She gave me a winning smile and then turned to start poking through the aisles.

Halloween Queens was full of costumes and decorations fit for the holiday. There were the requisite gravestones and giant spiders, along with a battery-powered witch's broom that swept the floor all by itself while it cackled madly. Screams and moans filled the air, all mechanical, and all a bit tinny. I breathed it in, hoping to regain some of my love for the holiday, but I just couldn't manage it.

It wasn't that I didn't want to go to the Yarborough

party with Will, because I did. It's just that I'd never felt comfortable around a large number of strangers who might expect me to be social with them. Stick me behind a counter, and I'm fine. Put me in public with others, and I turn into a scaredy-cat of the highest order.

I think the reason I was so frightened was because Rita had told me how big of a deal the party was. If it's so important, did that mean the mayor of Pine Hills would be there? What about out-of-town guests; people with money and social standing? Why would they let someone like me into a place like that? I would stick out like a sore thumb.

"What do you think?" Vicki drew my eye, saving me from more self-deprecating thoughts. She was holding up one of those sexy fairy costumes that always left so little to the imagination, it made me wonder, why bother?

"It doesn't really cover much, does it?" It consisted of what looked like a green bra, green panties, and strap-on wings. Oh, and the tiny little wand with glittery streamers on it. Couldn't forget that.

Vicki replaced it on the rack and laughed. "You're right. Why can't women's costumes be a little less . . ."

"Revealing?"

She nodded.

There was no way I was going to a party of any kind, Halloween or otherwise, dressed in a sexy anything. I didn't have the figure for it, and while I'm not obese, I was pretty sure I'd look twice my size the moment some ultrathin sexpot strutted up next to me in her sexy she-devil outfit. It was best I stuck to something a little less exposing, and a whole lot more concealing, like maybe a full-body wardrobe, mask and all.

"I'm not sure what I want to do," I said, eyeing a

naughty policewoman outfit. I'm pretty sure no officer worth her salt would ever wear a midriff–exposing shirt pulled that tightly.

"Find something that catches your eye," Vicki said. "Mason told me to choose something I feel comfortable in and not to worry about anything else. He's going as a gangster, if that tells you anything."

I raised my eyebrows at that. "His dad got him the invite, so I'm assuming Raymond is going, too?" I wasn't Raymond Lawyer's biggest fan, nor was he mine. I doubted he would tolerate his son dressing in something that put him in a bad light.

Then again, he didn't tolerate much of anything now that I thought about it.

"I think so," Vicki said. "Mason said he was going to try to get his dad to go as one of the *Godfather* characters so they'd match, but Raymond balked at the idea. I don't know if that means he's not going, or if he's going to go dressed as something else." Her eyes widened. "Oh!" She scurried over to a rack full of fake guns, wigs, and gangster outfits. "Maybe I should get something that matches!"

"You should," I said.

As she started poking through the rack, I wandered off to find something for myself. While the gangster outfits were far less revealing than what I'd seen so far, I didn't want to ride on Vicki's coattails the entire night. I should have called Will and asked him what he was wearing. Maybe it would give me an idea what to look for. We could match, just like Vicki and Mason.

There were only a handful of people in the shop, mostly college age. I figured once school let out, the teenagers would be in full force, throwing plastic eyeballs at each other. I could call Will without anyone overhearing.

No, Krissy. I was a big girl; I could find something on my own. I didn't need to go running to a man every time I was unsure about something.

I glanced at a rack of horror movie character costumes. Would Will have a problem if I went as Jason from *Friday the 13th*? The mask would give me something to hide behind, as would the baggy overalls. The machete had fake blood inside that sloshed around when you moved it.

I started toward it, thinking I'd give it a few swings, when another costume caught my eye. The red twine wig and the red and white socks would surely draw the eye. I picked up the blue polka dot dress and checked the size. There was nothing sexy about Raggedy Ann, and it wasn't as manly as Jason. With the face paint and wig, I might not be easily recognized. It might save me from embarrassment the next day if I made a fool out of myself at the party.

The costume looked like it would fit, but the thought of going as a character that was more appropriate for little girls curdled my stomach. I shoved it back onto the rack and continued to search.

And then I saw it. The costume was in the men's section, but I thought I could pull it off. I took it from the rack and held it up to my chest to see if it would fit.

"It's perfect!"

I turned to find Vicki grinning at me, her chosen gangster costume folded over one arm. She was wearing a cheaply made fedora pulled down low over one eye.

"I don't know," I said, loving my choice, but worried about it at the same time. What if Will didn't like it? "It's for men, and it's, I don't know, a little too on the nose, don't you think?"

"Will it fit?"

I double-checked the size, though I'd just held it up and knew it would be fine. I picked up the hat that went with it and tried it on. Perfect fit. "Looks like it."

As soon as the hat was on, Vicki pulled a plastic gun from somewhere and pointed it at me. "You're not going to take me in, Holmes," she said in a surprisingly good British accent. "Not this time, you won't."

I laughed but refrained from attempting a Sherlock Holmes impression, knowing how badly it would go. I considered the costume a moment longer and then walked over to Vicki. "I guess it's decided then."

We carried our wares to the counter and paid for them. I wondered if I told Will what I'd chosen, if he would go ahead and be my Watson. Matching outfits could be cliché, sure, but I was positive we'd make a cute couple. The more I thought about it, the more, I don't know, romantic it seemed.

We left the shop and started the short walk back to Vicki's car. Would Will be offended if I recommended a costume to him? I doubted it, but I wasn't sure I could bring myself to ask. The party was only a few days away, so I was pretty sure he'd have a costume picked out by now, anyway. It was probably best I didn't make things more difficult than they needed to be.

A police cruiser rolled past and vanished around the corner, causing me to pause midstride. It wasn't until Vicki spoke that I realized I'd been staring after it like some sort of lovesick fool for a good thirty seconds.

"Hear from Paul lately?"

I grimaced and shoved my costume into the backseat

of her car. "Not since he saved me from my would-be murderer." I got into the passenger seat and waited for Vicki to get in behind the wheel. "I think that ship has already sailed."

"Good thing you have Will to take your mind off him then."

"Yeah, maybe."

She started the car but didn't put it into drive right away. "You aren't interested in him?"

"I am, but . . ." But what? He was good looking, had a stable, well-paying job if his appearance told me anything. And he genuinely seemed to be interested in me, despite my shortcomings. So what was I so hung up about?

"Look, Krissy." Vicki turned in her seat to face me. "Don't pass up on a good thing just because you are scared."

"How do I know if it is going to be a good thing or not?"

She gave me a flat look. "How else? You take a chance, put yourself out there. You'll never get anything you want if you don't try." She gave me a sympathetic smile. "We all go through the what-ifs. 'What if he doesn't really like me?' 'What if I scare him off?'"

I gave her a skeptical look. I couldn't imagine Vicki ever worrying about what a man thought about her. She was physically perfect and had the personality to boot.

"Me too," she said, holding up her hand as if swearing on it. "I'm always afraid I'm going to trip over my own two feet, or drip sauce all over my shirt when I'm with Mason. I get over it. You will, too."

"But what if he runs screaming in the other direction after getting to know me?"

"Then he's not the right man for you."

I was beginning to wonder if there *was* a right man for me. "It's just . . ." I heaved a sigh and spilled my guts. "Will's great, but what if he turns into another Robert? I've always had a knack for choosing real 'winners.'" I framed the last word with air quotes. "He already left when he saw me talking to another man. He never even let me tell my side of the story."

"But he came back, right?"

"Well, yeah."

"And he apologized, right?"

"I suppose he did."

"Men do stupid things all of the time," she said. "We all do. He realized his mistake and came back to you and admitted it right to your face. Not all men do that. Just think about how Robert handled the situation."

Oh, boy. My ex was like a sore that wouldn't go away. He kept popping up, insinuating himself into my life, even though I'd much rather forget he ever existed. And never once, not during any of those conversations, had he ever sincerely apologized for his actions.

"It'll work out, Krissy, I promise you that."

I nodded. Vicki was right; she always was.

She turned and put the car in gear with a look on her face that said she thought she'd proved her point. And I guess she had. I was letting the doubts win, and it was going to ruin my chance at a real relationship. Why was I always so hard on myself?

I checked my phone at least a dozen times on the ride back home, hoping Will would suddenly call. I wanted to hear his voice in the worst way, as well as ask him about my costume. If he didn't like it, I'd still have time to go back and get something else, even though I wasn't sure what that might be.

We pulled up in front of my house a few minutes later. "Do you want to come in for a few minutes?" I asked, checking the time. Vicki still had an hour before she needed to be at Death by Coffee.

"Can't. I'm going to meet Mason before I go in to work." She just about purred his name.

"It sounds like you two are getting serious."

Her eyes gleamed. "I think he might be the one." She looked just about ready to burst from excitement.

"That's great!" I said, and I meant it. Vicki deserved to find someone nice, and despite the rocky start to our relationship, I thought Mason very well might be it.

Vicki's gaze moved past my shoulder. "You have company coming, anyway," she said. "I'll see you tomorrow."

I glanced back to see Jules Phan walking across the lawn between our houses, his white Maltese, Maestro, in his arms. Jules owned the local candy store and, as far as I could tell, was the only person to work there. I was surprised he was here now.

I got out of the car, grabbed my costume bag, and waved as Vicki backed out. I turned just as Jules reached me.

"Is everything okay?" I asked him, worried. "Has something happened to Lance?"

Jules looked surprised. "No, I hope not!" He laughed, dispelling my anxiety. "I thought I'd pop on over to say hi since I rarely get to do so so early in the day."

"Who is working at Phantastic Candies then? Are you closed today?"

"Oh no. Lance decided to give me a day off and is working in my place. I check in every hour to make sure he isn't getting overwhelmed. Once school lets out, I'm thinking of stopping in and helping him. The rush can be brutal when you're not used to it."

I reached out and ruffled Maestro's soft fur. He licked my hand and gave a happy little yip. "I'm glad everything's okay."

"It is." Jules's eyes went to the bag in my hand. "A Halloween costume?"

"Yeah." I held up the bag, though he couldn't see what it contained. "I'm going to a party with Will Foster."

His eyes just about popped from his head. It seemed to be a common reaction when I told anyone about the invite. "The Yarborough party?"

I nodded, my trepidation coming back. I was starting to feel as if the party was too big for me, that I'd made a huge mistake in saying I'd go. "Should I cancel on him?"

"Oh, Lord, no!" Jules just about shouted it, which caused Maestro to bark in surprise. He lowered his voice as he went on. "It's a huge event. Lance and I are going this year. Normally, we never get invited, which is understandable; we don't really fit in with the usual crowd. But Lance got us an invite thanks to a friend, so . . ." He shrugged as if that said it all.

A big part of me relaxed, glad to know I'd know at least two other people. "I'm worried I won't fit in, either."

Jules patted me on the hand. "You'll be fine. They'll all love you just as much as the rest of us do."

If only I could be as sure of that as Jules. "I don't know the woman who is holding the thing at all. I think her name is Margaret?"

Jules nodded. "Margaret Yarborough. Used to be a McAllister, if you can believe it." He said it like I should know what that meant. "She's . . . an interesting one. Her husband, Howard, was pretty eccentric, but since she married him, it made her even stranger."

"Strange how?"

Jules shrugged. "Their house is like a funhouse. Or maybe one of those haunted houses you walk through this time of year, but it's like that all year-round. It's like *The Addams Family* come to life."

"Sounds intriguing."

"Oh, it is that, if nothing else. I've always wondered what it is like inside, and now I'll get to see it. It is a shame about Howard, though. He was the one who was the most enthusiastic about the parties." He glanced at his watch. "I best get back. Lance will be expecting my call."

I wanted to ask him more about the Yarboroughs but thought it best to let him make sure Lance wasn't getting overwhelmed by enthusiastic toddlers. "I won't keep you."

He gave me a startling white smile. "See you at the party!" He lifted Maestro's paw and made the little dog wave before he turned and walked back to his house.

Curtains in the house on the other side of me fluttered as I turned toward the front door. My nosy elderly neighbor was at it again, watching me like she expected me to do something horrible at any moment. I smiled in her general direction, fished out my keys, and let myself into my house where prying eyes couldn't see.

My orange cat, Misfit, was asleep on the couch. He glanced up at me as I walked in, then went right back to sleep, which was fine by me. I wanted to try on my costume and it would be much easier if he wasn't weaving in and out of my legs, begging to be pet the entire time.

I loved my cat, but he could be a handful when he wanted to be.

I made it halfway to my bedroom when the phone rang. I immediately dropped the shopping bag and fished it out of my purse. Without looking at who it was, I answered with a near-out-of-breath, "Hello?"

"Krissy? It's Will."

"Hi, Will!" I tried not to sound too eager. "I'm glad you called. I just got home after buying my costume."

"Don't tell me what it is!" he said quickly. "I want to be surprised when I come to pick you up."

That took a little wind out of my sails. "Okay. Are you sure you don't want to know, just in case it doesn't fit in with what everyone else will be wearing?"

"It'll be fine. Don't worry yourself over it."

As if I could stop myself. "My friend Vicki is going to be at the party, too. Do you remember Vicki? She was at the bowling alley when we first met. Well, she co-owns Death by Coffee with me and is going with her boyfriend, who I didn't like at first, but now I do, so I'm going to know a few people there. Oh! And my friend Jules will be there, too. He owns the candy store down-town. Do you know the one?" I stopped, realizing I was rambling.

"That's good," Will said, humor in his voice. "I'm glad you'll have someone there, other than me. Carl and Darrin will be there, so if you get sick of me, I'll have someone to talk to."

"I'd never get sick of you."

"Good." He paused and then heaved a sigh. "I only have a few minutes before I need to get back to work."

"Oh, okay."

"The party starts at eight, but most people will start

arriving by seven thirty. I can pick you up at your house at seven if that works for you?"

"Seven is perfect."

There was a short stretch of silence before he said, "I'll need your address."

"Oh!" I flushed, thankful he couldn't see me. I gave him my address, giddy. "I'll leave the outside light on for you."

"Thank you."

"And beware of my next-door neighbor. She's a bit of a snoop and will watch you the entire time you're here."

"Noted." He laughed.

All my words dried up. I was really going to do this! I felt like a teenager again, and unlike most of the time when I felt that way, it was a good feeling. I couldn't stop grinning.

"Well, I best get going. Work calls."

"Okay." It came out sounding a little sad.

"I'll see you on Friday, seven p.m. sharp."

"Can't wait."

"Me either."

And with that, the date was made.

3

I frowned at myself in the bathroom mirror as I
adjusted the deerstalker cap on my head. The Sherlock
Holmes costume was plaid gray, very cheap, and very
ugly when you got right down to it. It didn't help matters
any that I didn't have a pair of shoes that matched the
outfit.

"What am I going to do?" I asked, glancing toward
Misfit, who was lounging on the bed, watching me with
detached interest. "Will is going to be here any minute
and I look like I tripped and fell into an old man's
closet!"

The coat—and I use that term loosely—was made of
a flimsy material that wouldn't protect me from the rain
that was pounding the roof of my house with such force,
it made the windows rattle. It came with one of those
annoying short capes that only reached the middle of my
back and was a little too stiff, as if it was starched or
made of plastic. The cap was just as ugly and just as gray
as the rest of the costume.

The pants hadn't fit, so I swapped them with a pair of

black slacks. I added my white tennis shoes because when I'd tried my black flats, I'd nearly wept in embarrassment.

Did it match? Not entirely. But it was the best I was going to be able to do.

I picked up the magnifying glass that had come with the costume, considered it, and then dropped it into the trash. There was no way I was going to carry that thing around with me all night. If it actually worked, then maybe I would have found a use for it somewhere, but the "glass" was a cheap foggy plastic that was impossible to see through, making it utterly useless.

I left the bathroom feeling like I'd screwed up the evening before it had even gotten started. This was supposed to be my chance to impress Will, and instead, I looked like an idiot. Maybe I should have gone with the sexy detective outfit instead. I doubted it could have been much worse.

"At least I'll have pockets," I told the cat as I ruffled his ears. He closed his eyes and leaned into my hand, which reassured me somewhat. If the party was a disaster, at least he'd be here when I got home.

"Do you think I'll have time to find something else?" I asked, glancing toward my closet. There wasn't an actual costume tucked away in there anywhere, but I thought I might be able to cobble something together if given the chance.

I glanced at the bedside clock and, with a sigh, shoved my cell phone and a few other necessities into my coat pockets. This was going to have to do.

I sat down on the bed to wait for Will, stroking Misfit all the while. At least he was being good tonight, which kept my nerves hovering right around seven instead of blasting to eleven. He could be a terror sometimes, but I loved him anyway, especially when he was calm like this.

A knock sounded at the door after only a few minutes. I rose on shaky legs, gave Misfit one last ear rub, and then left the bedroom.

The knock came again just as I reached the door. I opened it to a deluge. Will was standing on the front stoop, holding a rather large umbrella. I blinked at him, blinded by his headlights spearing through the pounding rain. It was as black as midnight out there, and wet enough I was worried about flooding. I hadn't seen rain this hard in my entire life.

"Ready to go?" Will asked. He was dressed in a black suit, open wide in the front, revealing a white button-up shirt. He held a cane in the hand not holding the umbrella. A white mask hid half of his face, and his hair was slicked back from that.

"Oh my." My hand fluttered to my chest. He looked absolutely dreamy. This wasn't some off-the-rack costume he was wearing, either; the whole getup had to have cost him a couple hundred dollars, money I was finding to be very well spent.

Will smiled, obviously noting my appreciation, which was quickly turning to a horrified realization that I was going to be walking into a roomful of people I didn't know, right next to him, while wearing *this*.

"You look fantastic," I told him, swallowing back my uncertainty. This was no time to chicken out. "If I'd known it was going to be such an extravagant affair, I would have chosen something different."

"Why?" Will asked. "You look stunning."

I blushed despite myself. "You're just saying that so I won't go hide under the bed."

"No, really." His smile widened, which had the effect of causing his eyes to gleam. "It's perfect on you." He glanced back toward his car, which was still running. "We really should get going. The rain is going to slow us down."

I checked to make sure Misfit wasn't going to make a mad dash for freedom, then stepped out under the umbrella.

"Wet night," I said needlessly as Will led me to his car. He kept the umbrella firmly over my head the entire time. The canopy was large, yet I found myself walking so close to him, I could feel the brush of his clothing against mine. He opened the car door for me, careful not to let the umbrella slip, and then stepped aside as I slid into a luxurious interior. He closed the door with the faintest of clunks before hurrying around to the other side.

The inside of his car was like sitting in a spaceship. Lights lit up the dash, far more than I thought necessary in a car. A touchscreen display sat in the center of the console, telling me everything from the gas mileage—it was fantastic—to the air pressure of the tires. There were even Facebook and Twitter icons in the corner of the screen.

Will opened the driver's side door, slid in, and shook out the umbrella before closing it and tossing it on the floor in back with his cane. He checked the rearview mirror once to make sure his hair was okay and then put the car in gear. It was a standard, of course. I hoped he wouldn't drink too much at the party and ask me to drive him home. I'd be utterly lost, having never driven a standard before.

"It's really coming down out there," Will said. The

windshield wipers swished back and forth in a steady, pleasant rhythm, yet almost as soon as they brushed away the rain, it was back again.

"Storm of the century," I said, unable to look away from the side of his face, which was covered by the mask. I swear the thing had been molded for his specific facial structure. It was perfect in how it lined his cheekbone, curved around his mouth. It stood out in stark contrast to his darker skin.

"Phantom of the Opera, huh?" I asked.

He shrugged. "All I had to do was buy the mask. I already owned the clothes, so it was a no-brainer."

My eyebrows rose at that. The suit wasn't modern. The white shirt was the frilly type, but not so much that it looked silly. I had a feeling he had a pair of black gloves tucked away in one of his pockets. He looked as if he could have come straight out of the early 1900s.

"How do you know the hostess?" I asked, needing to talk about something other than how great Will looked. "I hear she's a little strange."

"That, she is." Will laughed. "But she isn't too bad, I suppose. I don't know her personally. I'd mostly dealt with her husband, though we also take care of Mrs. Yarborough when she comes in."

"We?"

He glanced at me before putting his eyes back on the road where they belonged. The dark skies and rain were making it hard to see more than a few feet ahead, which made me nervous. Anything could pop out of the night like a jack-in-the-box, deer most likely.

"Me, Darrin, and Carl," Will said. "We have a small practice in town with a few other doctors." He paused, checked the lane, and passed someone going about ten miles per hour. "The Yarboroughs, like nearly everyone in town, come to us whenever they have the sniffles. Anything major is taken care of at the hospital in Levington. We all rotate there."

A sinking feeling rushed through me. I took in Will's tailored clothing, thought of the expensive watch I'd seen him wear, and the car I was currently sitting in, and it all came together. No wonder everyone was so shocked I was on a date with him.

William Foster was loaded.

A low groan escaped my lips, which brought his eyes off the road again to check on me.

"Krissy? You okay? You're looking a little pale."

"Yeah," I said, not feeling okay in the slightest. "I'm just nervous."

"Don't be." His eyes returned to the road, as did his smile. "You'll do great."

People kept telling me that, but I was beginning to wonder. I could pull off hanging around people I knew, or even the people who came into Death by Coffee for a drink. How in the world was I going to play off being a rich man's date?

By now, we'd made it most of the way across Pine Hills and were actually in the hills themselves. Water ran down the road like a river, streaming by so fast, I was worried we might lose traction and get swept away. Will seemed to know what he was doing and hardly slowed as we took curves and hills fast enough to make my entire body tense. The rain was still coming down and showed no sign of letting up. It was as if it was intent on drowning every living thing and filling the Earth with water.

Might be time to break out the trusty Ark.

We turned into what used to be a driveway a few minutes

later. I could see lights on atop the hill, illuminating the house, but I was afraid to take my eyes off what lay in front of us. The driveway was a slick of mud and running water. As soon as the tires of Will's car hit it, they spun out. He shifted, gained traction, and carefully maneuvered us up the hill.

"Looks like Margaret is having some work done," Will said, voice tight.

Orange cones kept us from driving off into the yard. A big yellow machine of some kind sat next to a few lonely looking trees. There was a pile of gravel next to the driveway, and I wondered if it was supposed to have been lain before the party. By the *crunch* I periodically heard beneath the tires, I could tell there was some down there, just not enough.

"It was paved the last time I was here," Will said, apologetically. "But the grade had always been poor. I knew she was going to need to fix it at some point, but didn't know she'd started."

I nodded, almost too scared to speak. The driveway curved at too sharp an angle, back toward the house. Every now and again, Will's tires spun, throwing up more mud, which had to be coating his pristine car. I glanced at the steering wheel and noticed the Lexus insignia. I wasn't sure if the car had ever been so dirty, though the thought of Will standing outside, sans shirt, washing it was enough to get my blood pumping.

It was starting to get warm in the car as we bumped over onto concrete. My eyes widened as I took in the gigantic house that loomed out of the rainy night like the *Titanic.* Lights burned in many of the windows, candles in many cases, though I couldn't tell if they were real or not. A realistic-looking family of skeletons stood out front, bony arms extended toward the side of the house as if pointing the way. Will drove around, clearly knowing where he was going, and parked in a small parking lot.

He shut off the engine and glanced at me. "Ready?" he asked, eyes pinched from the near-harrowing drive.

"I'm not sure."

Seeing the mansion had brought all of my doubts roaring back. It was huge. Pumpkins lined this side of the house, some of them carved as jack-o'-lanterns. There were also a few little pinpoints of light hidden within them, as if there were tiny little monsters waiting to leap out and devour anyone who walked by.

"It's a lot to take in at first," Will said. "But I promise that nothing here can hurt you." He gave me a crooked grin. "Unless you count some of the stuffy old people we'll encounter once we're inside. They very well might bore you to death with their self-important stories if you let them."

I somehow managed a smile of my own. "I guess I'll stay close so you can sweep me away if one of them traps me in a corner."

"I hope so." His grin was infectious.

Maybe this won't be so bad, after all. I mean, I *was* with a good-looking guy who seemed to genuinely like me. There were quite a few people who would be jealous of me of all people! And who cared if a few stuffy old men were insulted by my presence. They could just get over themselves.

There were quite a few cars already parked in the lot, but no one else was making their way toward the house just yet. Will reached back for his cane and umbrella, and then in one fluid motion popped it open as he pushed out the driver's side door. I watched as he jogged around the front of the car, to my side door. He opened it with as low of a bow his umbrella would let him.

"Shall we?" he asked with a smile. He held out his hand for me.

With a grin of my own, I took it, feeling like a girl in a fairy tale.

Hopefully, this story would have a happy ending.

4

"Ah, Mr. Foster and . . ." A man dressed like Igor frowned as he looked me up and down.

"Kristina Hancock," Will provided. "She's my date this evening."

"Ms. Hancock." Igor smiled at me, but it never reached his eyes. "Right this way." He bowed and began to shuffle down the hall, back slightly hunched.

"Don't mind him," Will said. "He hates these things almost as much as the rest of the help does. They're in for a long, busy night without a chance for a break."

I nodded absently, distracted by the entryway into the Yarborough mansion. It was decorated like a movie theatre hallway with large, framed posters, lit from below by floor lights. Women with wide eyes gripped their hands close to their chests while giant monsters stalked toward them. Giant bugs, bloody murderers wielding weapons just as bloody, and hideous creatures were the order of the day, apparently.

"Howard loved his horror movies," Will said. "Fits right in with the Halloween theme."

That was an understatement. I hadn't seen over half of

the movies, and I never wanted to. I wasn't a total wimp, but the last time I went to a scary movie, I ended up "watching" it with my eyes closed and humming to myself so I couldn't hear the creepy music.

We were led to an open doorway. What appeared to be intricate runes were carved in the frame, as well as the two large open doors. Fake spiderwebs hung above the doorway, and I caught a glimpse of a very real-looking spider in the corner. Beyond, the party was taking place.

Igor bowed to each of us in turn before hurrying back to his place at the doors where another rain-drenched couple was coming in.

A handful of eyes turned our way as we stood outside the doors. Many of the guests continued on with their conversations as if we were beneath their notice. Apparently, the parking lot we'd gone to wasn't the only one because there were at least three dozen people milling about, if not more. Most of the ones who'd turned to see who had come in looked away when we didn't turn out to be interesting enough. A select few continued to stare as if waiting to see if we'd do a trick or two.

"Ready?" Will asked, holding out his arm. I took it gratefully, unsure I'd manage to keep from fainting without his support.

As soon as we stepped inside the room, a woman dressed in a '40s era waitress uniform took Will's umbrella with a smile that was practically painted on. "Enjoy the party," she said, shaking off the excess water into a vase before putting the umbrella in a container with a dozen more.

Will twirled his cane and tapped it onto the hardwood floor as we made toward the small crowd. Almost every costume I saw made me think of people with money. Many of the women wore extravagant dresses in place of a real costume. They compensated by holding masks up to their eyes every now and again. Only a few were actually wearing them. Some of the men looked as if they hadn't dressed up at all, choosing to go as a high-class socialite, if anything. I had a feeling it wasn't too far of a stretch for many of them. There were a few real costumes, but most of those involved dresses and suits with hats and fake mustaches to complete the outfits.

"Krissy!" I turned, pivoting with Will, as Vicki and Mason strode up to us, arm in arm. I just about collapsed in relief to see they'd both worn their gangster outfits. Vicki had somehow managed to make hers look as if it hadn't come off the rack in a Halloween store, while Mason's looked as if it had come straight off the set of one of the *Godfather* movies. They looked absolutely perfect together.

"Vicki! Mason! You don't know how relieved I am to see you." I let go of Will's arm and clasped Vicki's hands in my own.

"You look great," she said, eyes flickering to Will. "Care to formally introduce us?"

"Of course! Will," I said, stepping back to his side. "This is my best friend, Vicki Patterson, and her date, Mason Lawyer." I took Will's arm again. "Everyone, this is Will Foster."

"Pleasure to meet you both," Will said.

"Likewise."

The men shook and eyed each other in that way men have when they are sizing each other up. Vicki rolled her eyes and pulled me a few paces away.

"Can you believe this place?" she asked, looking

around. The room we were in could hold a good hundred people without feeling stuffy. A large chandelier hung overhead, crystals twinkling like little stars. Tables lined the walls, filled with finger foods and wines. There were a few punch bowls sitting off to the side, and I noticed not too many of the guests ventured over to them. Most of them were holding wineglasses that looked to be real glass, not the plastic ones you'd normally see at a party.

This isn't your usual party, now is it?

"It's a lot bigger than I expected," I said.

"Wait until you see the bathrooms!" She shook her head in wonder. "I can't even describe them. You'll have to check them out for yourself."

By the sound of it, I anticipated being impressed. "Have you seen anyone else?" I asked, scanning the crowd in the hopes of catching a glimpse of a few more people I knew.

"Mason's dad is here," Vicki said, pointing.

Raymond Lawyer was dressed like, well, Raymond Lawyer. In fact, I think he was wearing the same suit I'd seen him wearing the last time I'd seen him. He was red in the face, which wasn't much of a surprise if you knew him. The man had a temper, and he wasn't afraid to show it. In the brief amount of time I knew him, I don't think I saw him do anything but yell at or belittle his son.

"How did the Lawyers get an invite, anyway?" I mused. "Most of the people here are rich."

"Dad's new girlfriend," Mason said, coming up to stand next to Vicki.

I raised my eyebrows at him, firstly, surprised that anyone would date Raymond Lawyer, and secondly, by how it had come out sounding. Mason acted as if he wasn't thrilled about the idea of his dad dating, which I

supposed was natural. I don't think I would like it all
that much if my dad were to suddenly jump back into
the dating pool, though sometimes I thought he needed
it. Sitting home alone wasn't good for anyone. I should
know.

"Not a fan?" I asked.

Mason grunted a laugh and then pointed. "You tell
me. There she is."

I followed the direction of his finger and then gasped
in shock by who I saw. "No way."

"I could hardly believe it, either."

Standing over by the punch bowls was none other
than Regina Harper, mother to the widow of Raymond
Lawyer's late son, Brendon. I wasn't sure who she was
supposed to be, dressed in a severe tight skirt and blouse.
Maybe a well-dressed drill sergeant? High-paid lawyer
willing to glare the prosecution into submission? Either
way, she looked just as angry as she always did. I could
see the clench of her jaw from clear across the room.

"I thought they hated each other?"

"So did everyone else who knew them." Mason sighed.
"After Brendon's funeral, they spent quite a lot of time
together, dealing with the will and everything. It started
with a few afternoon meetings with all of their lawyers
there to keep the peace, but before long, those meetings
turned into late-night dinners that sometimes lasted into
the next day." He shuddered.

"Wow." As I watched, a young woman dressed as
Marilyn Monroe in the famous white dress picture, wig
and all, walked over to stand beside her. Regina looked
her up and down, grimaced, and then turned and walked
away, as if offended that the girl was sharing the same air
as her.

"Still frosty as ever, I see."

"You don't know the half of it." Mason looked pained as he said it.

My gaze went from the girl at the drinks to an older woman who was dressed in the same white dress. "Who's that?" I asked, thinking it had to be her mother.

Will was the one to answer. "That's Margaret Yarborough."

She had the figure to pull off Mrs. Monroe, and the confidence to do it, too. Her hair looked natural, but could very well have been a high-end wig. Unlike the first Marilyn, Mrs. Yarborough was wearing an expensive diamond necklace that caught the light and blinded anyone who was foolish enough to look directly at it.

She was talking to a man half her age, which put him no older than his mid-thirties. His eyes constantly scanned the crowd behind horn-rimmed glasses that were a little too thick for his face. He wore a fedora and a long trench coat, which concealed much of his features, though I got the distinct impression he was well-built.

"I'm not sure who she's talking to," Will said, sounding mystified. "But that is Terry Blandino walking up to them."

The man Will indicated looked to be in his fifties, dark hair graying naturally at the temples. He wasn't all that bad looking for a man his age, and it only helped that he appeared to be dressed as Clark Gable with the part in his hair and thin mustache. When he reached the two, he spoke harshly to Mrs. Yarborough before turning to level a finger at the man in the hat, before turning and storming off.

"Drama already," Will muttered in a way that made it sound as if this sort of thing happened all of the time.

I watched Terry go and then caught a glimpse of another man, standing against the wall. He was wearing one of those *Scream* masks and black robes, which completely obliterated any chance of identifying him. He looked out of place in a party where most of the guests were wearing suits and dresses. It was the reason I noticed him.

As I watched, he raised a hand and pointed a finger at me.

"Who's that?" Will asked.

"I don't know."

The masked man lowered his hand as a young girl approached. He turned to her and the eerie moment was broken.

"Uh-oh," Vicki said. At first, I thought she was talking about the man in the mask, but when I turned, she was looking the other way, toward the entrance. I followed her gaze and my stomach instantly dropped to the floor.

"Oh no."

Officer Paul Dalton was handing his umbrella to the waitress by the door. He was dressed in one of those old-style police uniforms you'd see in a Benny Hill skit, nightstick and all. He said something to the waitress and then held his arm out for the girl coming in behind him.

It was as if I'd been shot. Shannon, the waitress from J&E's Banyon Tree, was dressed in a gorgeous dress that looked handmade. Her hair was styled atop her head, so it left her neck bare, but still left strands trickling around her face. She was carrying one of those party masks that had straps around it so she wouldn't have to hold it all night. She put it on just before taking Paul's arm.

"Don't worry about it," Vicki said, keeping her voice low. "You've moved on."

If only, I thought. I'd once thought Paul and I could be an item, but after only one disastrous date, and a few arrests on my part, any relationship we might have had fizzled out.

Yet a part of me still really wanted to give it a shot, even though I was standing beside a good-looking, kind man, who was also a wealthy doctor to boot. I shouldn't be thinking of anyone else, yet I couldn't help myself.

Thankfully, I didn't have to explain anything to Will because just then, someone tapped a glass with a spoon. All eyes turned toward where the elder Mrs. Monroe, Margaret Yarborough, stood, head held high.

"I'd like to take a moment to thank everyone for coming," she said. Her voice rang out over the crowd as if she'd been holding a microphone. There were at least fifty people in the room now, and not one of them made a sound. "Howard would have been proud to see all of your faces, knowing what surprises he had in store for you this year."

She looked suitably sad a moment before breaking out in a wide smile. "And while I may not have the flair Howard did, I do hope you'll find your time here to be a most thrilling and terrifying one!" She waited for applause before continuing. "This house is open to you all. Explore. See the terrors waiting for you. And most of all, have fun."

Another smattering of applause. Margaret basked in it before tapping her glass again. "Now, before I let you go, there is one more piece of business to take care of." She turned toward a man who looked about ready to rocket from his shoes. "I give the floor to Quentin Pebbles." She stepped aside.

The applause this time wasn't nearly as enthusiastic. A few of the guests turned away and started talking amongst themselves as Quentin stepped up to where Margaret had stood. He was wearing a red bow tie and gray suit that made him look like Pee-wee Herman, though I don't think that was the look he'd been going for.

"I, um." He cleared his throat and adjusted his bow tie. "Jessica, if you would." He motioned to a spot in front of him.

Yet another Marilyn Monroe stepped forward, looking annoyed. She was probably about the same age as the first Monroe I'd seen, but her dress and jewelry looked to be the real thing. She looked absolutely stunning, and I could tell that her hair was naturally blond, not from a bottle.

"Popular costume," Vicki commented.

"Yeah." I glanced to the side to see the first Monroe looking down at herself, mortified.

"Jessica . . ." Quentin cleared his throat again. "I know we've had our ups and downs, and believe me, our downs can be pretty low."

There was a round of chuckling at that, and I noted not all of it was good-natured.

Jessica sniffed and looked away as she crossed her arms over her chest. Her eyes darted from face to face, as if looking for someone to save her.

"I . . ." Quentin was visibly sweating now. He tugged at his collar as if he were being strangled, and then so suddenly it caused a few people to gasp, he dropped to one knee. "Jessica Fairweather, will you marry me?"

The room fell silent. Jessica's head turned slowly until

she was facing Quentin. She didn't even try to disguise the look of horror on her face.

"Are you serious?" she asked, voice high-pitched and nasally. "You can't be serious." She huffed. "Get up, you idiot."

Someone barked out a harsh laugh as Quentin shot to his feet. He refused to raise his eyes past shin-level, and I got the distinct impression he had to do that often when he was around her.

"If you think I would ever marry you, you are delusional," Jessica went on, unrelenting. "I don't need your money, if that is what you think. And since you can barely perform in the best of conditions, I don't need that, either." Another round of laughter met that, further deepening the growing flush on Quentin's face.

"Jessica, please."

"Jessica, please," she mocked, voice going an octave higher. "God, what an idiot. To think I wasted so much time on you." She turned and stormed away, still muttering to herself. She nearly bumped into a man in a black suit and hat who was just entering as she left the room. The man looked startled, and then guilty, as he watched her go.

Quentin stood in the center of the room, unable to look at anyone for a long, horrible moment. When someone else started laughing—this time a woman—he bolted for the hall, calling out, "Jessica!" as he went.

"Wow," Vicki said under her breath. "That was rough."

"No kidding." If it had happened to me, I'd probably have died right then and there. I couldn't imagine ever being that cruel to someone, especially someone you were supposedly close to.

"Excuse me, Krissy."

I tensed and then plastered on a smile as I turned. "Paul. How good to see you."

A tense silence filled the air. Will took a step closer to me but didn't put a protective arm around me, which earned him a few points in my book. I didn't need someone claiming me like some sort of child's toy, though having him near made me feel a little better.

"I think we've met," Shannon said, giving me a friendly smile.

"We have," I said, doing my best to be pleasant. There was no reason for the claws to come out. Paul simply wasn't interested in me. I couldn't fault him for that. And from what little I'd seen of Shannon, she seemed nice enough.

And besides, I was here with Will.

Paul cleared his throat and turned to Will. "Paul Dalton," he said, holding out his hand.

"Will Foster." They shook.

Vicki and Mason had retreated a few steps but were keeping an eye on the festivities. Vicki was watching Paul like a hawk, as if waiting for him to do or say something she didn't approve of. I think Mason's hand on her wrist was the only thing keeping her from marching up to Paul and demanding to know why he'd turned his back on me.

We all looked at each other, unsure what to say next. As far as uncomfortable silences went, this one was a doozy. My eyes met Paul's for a heartbeat; then we both looked away as if just looking at one another would get us into trouble with our dates.

My eyes fell on someone I recognized, and I breathed a sigh of relief. I'd found a way out of this mess before it could get any worse.

"Oh! There's someone I'd like to talk to. I'll see you later, Paul."

I grabbed Will's hand and practically dragged him across the room to where Heidi Lawyer stood, looking as out of place and miserable as I felt. Her husband had been murdered a few months back, so I suppose she could be going by her maiden name, Harper, now, but she would forever be a Lawyer to me. She actually looked relieved when she saw me walking toward her.

"Ms. Hancock," she said with only a cursory glance at Will. "I'm surprised to see you here."

"Call me Krissy," I said, giving her a brief, uncertain hug. I hadn't been sure she'd want to talk to me. During the process of solving her husband's murder, I'd accused her of some pretty icky things. I wouldn't have blamed her if she never wanted to see me again, but so far, she seemed appreciative of my help. "I didn't think I'd see you here, either."

"Mom made me come," she said with a sigh. "She thinks I should be looking for a new husband and set me up with some creep old enough to be my dad." She nodded toward a fat man dressed as Alfred Hitchcock who was sixty if he was a day.

"Sorry about that," I said with a wince.

"Mom thinks I can put Brendon behind me like that." She snapped her fingers. "But I can't. He might not have been the best man out there, but I still loved him." She sighed. "When I pointed out she didn't start dating again until fifteen years after Dad's death, she only got mad. I think this date is punishment for that." Her eyes flickered to Will, who was standing a respectful distance behind me. "You here with Dr. Foster?" she asked me.

"I am." I beamed at her.

Heidi nodded in appreciation. "I wish I could be so lucky, but no, I get Chuck Butcher. What kind of name is that, anyway?" Her shoulders sagged. She looked nearly as defeated as when Brendon had been murdered.

"I'm sure it will work out for you," I said, patting her on the bare shoulder. Her dress was a little more revealing than she appeared comfortable with, and I somehow knew her mother had something to do with that. "Mason is here somewhere," I said, glancing back to where I'd left him with Vicki.

"Yeah, we've already spoken. He finds it hilarious I'm stuck here with that." She nodded toward her date.

I started to reply when a shriek silenced the entire ballroom as if it had been a gunshot. Everyone spun toward the hall as one, almost as if we'd rehearsed it. The scream came again as an older woman stumbled into the room, hand over her mouth, eyes bugging out of her head. She was as pale as a ghost.

"Someone help!" She gasped, pointing back the way she'd come. "There's . . . I . . ." She took a shaky step forward. "Someone has been murdered!"

And then she fainted dead away.

5

"Everyone, stay back!"

Paul knelt by the fainted woman and gently shook her. Her eyes fluttered open and she jerked away, as if she thought he might attack her.

"It's okay," he said. "I'm with the police."

"Oh, God!" She grabbed him by the arms hard enough that it had to hurt. "I found her. She's dead!"

"What's your name?" Paul asked, gently.

The woman looked surprised by the question, but when she answered she was somewhat calmer. "Isabella Ortega."

"Okay, Isabella, can you tell me who you found?"

The woman shook her head, unwilling or unable to answer.

"Can you show me where you found her?" he asked.

She bit her lip and then nodded.

Paul helped her to her feet and kept a hand on her elbow as they turned toward the doorway. "Everyone stay here," he said, before letting Isabella lead him down the hall.

There was a moment where no one moved and then

everyone in the ballroom started forward after Paul and Isabella. I glanced at Will, who shrugged, and we hurried after.

"There!" Isabella said, pointing. She'd stopped halfway down the hall and refused to go any farther. The room she indicated was two doors down.

"Okay," Paul said. "Remain here until I check it out. Can you do that for me?"

Isabella nodded.

He cast an annoyed glance over his shoulder before walking toward the door. The crowd who had gathered moved with him, and I don't think he could have said anything to keep them at bay. I went along with everyone else, curiosity winning out.

The door to the room was open. Pumpkins were laid out as if the room was meant to be a pumpkin patch straight out of someone's nightmares. Some of the pumpkins were carved so that they looked sinister. There were no friendly smiles on these jack-o'-lanterns. The walls of the room were painted in shades of dark orange and blue that were reminiscent of dusk. Guarding the pumpkins was a trio of scarecrows, their jack-o'-lantern faces grinning evilly down at where the body of Marilyn Monroe lay.

Gasps echoed through the crowd, and I heard Margaret Yarborough's name whispered more than once. I'd eased my way to the front with Will, so I could see that it wasn't the older woman's body, but rather one of the younger Monroes I'd seen earlier. Her head was turned at an unnatural angle and smashed through a pumpkin, so it was hard to tell which one without getting down on my knees to check—something I wasn't too keen on doing. I'd leave that job up to Paul.

"Is she really dead?" a man wearing a monocle asked.

"Move so I can see better!" a woman whined.

Will took my hand and squeezed. Our eyes met and I saw a deep sadness there.

"Did the scarecrows do it?" a man called. This was met with a round of nervous laughter.

"All right." Paul stood, clearly not amused. "Everyone get back into the ballroom. Now!"

Surprisingly, the crowd complied. I'd expected most of them to argue, maybe snap a few pictures, but they turned and started back the way they'd come. I took one more look at the dead woman, said a silent prayer for her, and then headed back to the ballroom.

The room was buzzing with excited conversation. No one seemed too broken up over the dead girl, which put a bad taste in my mouth. I knew many of these people thought themselves above everyone else, but someone had died! Money was no excuse for a lack of compassion.

Paul stopped just inside the ballroom. He had a look of deep concentration on his face as he removed his cell phone from a pocket, punched in a number, and held it up to his ear.

"Was that the girl who stormed out of here?" Vicki asked, coming up beside me.

"Jessica? I'm not sure." But now that I thought about it, I did remember catching a glimpse of an expensive-looking necklace around the neck of the victim. Unless there was a fourth Monroe running around the place, I was pretty sure our victim was indeed Jessica Fair-weather.

"I don't see the boyfriend," Will said, eyes scanning the crowd. "What was his name again?"

"Quentin," I supplied.

"You really don't think he would kill her just because she turned him down, do you?" Vicki asked, aghast.

Will shrugged. "You saw what happened. She didn't just turn him down, she humiliated him in front of all these people. People have killed for less."

"I don't see the hostess, either," Mason said with a frown.

I did a quick scan, though I couldn't see over anyone's head. Sometimes being short sucked. "None of the Marilyn Monroes are here." A surge of worry worked through me. Did we have a Marilyn murderer on our hands here? It didn't seem likely, not unless someone had some serious issues with the deceased star that was brought to the fore when he was surrounded by them.

Paul shoved his phone into his pocket and then raised his voice above the murmur of the crowd. "Okay, everyone, the police are on their way."

This was met with jeers and a few snotty remarks that caused his frown to deepen.

"No one is to go back into the pumpkin room for any reason. In fact, I want everyone to stay right here until we can get this thing sorted out." He looked around the room, almost as if doing a quick head count. "Do we have a list of guests?"

No one leapt forward to provide him with one, which wasn't much of a surprise. I was pretty sure many of the guests still thought this was some sort of sick joke. If it was, it was in pretty bad taste. I don't think this was what Margaret Yarborough meant when she said Howard had surprises waiting for us.

Paul heaved a sigh and caught my eye. He stood there staring at me long enough, I started to get nervous, before he motioned me over.

I glanced at Will, who released my hand and took a step back. "Go ahead," he said. "I'm going to go grab a drink." He looked pale and a little shaky. I was guessing he'd be hitting the alcoholic beverages rather than the punch.

"This should take only a minute," I told him, which earned me a strained smile before he walked away.

I took a deep breath and then headed over to where Paul waited. He looked as agitated as I'd ever seen him, which was saying something. The man was a police officer, so he'd seen his share of horrible things. When I neared, he stepped into the hallway a bit, presumably so we couldn't be overheard.

"Is that the girl, Jessica?" I asked.

He nodded. "I think so."

"Poor thing." She might have been cruel, but no one deserved to die like that.

"Buchannan is on the way," he said. "But I'm worried he might not make it up the driveway. It's raining pretty hard now, apparently, and some of the roads are washed out. The driveway here was pretty treacherous when I'd driven up it earlier, so it has to be a muddy soup by now." His frown deepened. "Until he makes it here, I'm all there is to keep order."

"You'll be fine." It felt good to be the one saying that for a change.

Paul rewarded me with a smile that revealed those dimples of his before his frown returned. "I wish I felt fine. This is a mess." He rubbed at his forehead and closed his eyes.

I gave him a moment before asking, "What do you need with me?"

Paul tugged at his ear and glanced past me, into the

ballroom where many of the guests were peering out at us. "I can't do this on my own." Another heavy sigh. "I can't control these people, either. I've already lost track of our hostess."

"Margaret Yarborough," I provided, in case he didn't know her name.

"And there are a few other faces I haven't seen since the body has been found."

"Like the boyfriend."

He nodded, distracted. "Until Buchannan gets here, I don't know how I am going to keep everyone in check."

I stood there and waited for him to go on, unsure why he wanted to tell me his doubts. It didn't make me feel any better that the only cop on hand was worried about keeping control. While it didn't look like anyone was panicking yet, that didn't mean it wouldn't eventually start. And once one person flipped out, it was only a matter of time before half the crowd started in.

Finally, Paul rubbed at his face and then leveled his gaze on me. "Did you notice anything out of the ordinary before . . . this?"

I gestured around me, indicating the Halloween decorations and costumes. "It's all out of the ordinary," I said.

That earned me a slight smile. "Well, if you notice anything especially out of place, let me know."

My eyes brightened. "Why, Paul Dalton, are you asking me to assist you on this?"

He looked annoyed, but nodded. "I'm going by the assumption that the boyfriend is our culprit, but I'm not going to rule anyone else out. There could be quite a lot of people who would want our victim dead."

"She didn't seem very nice, did she?" I hated saying it since she was dead and all, but it was true.

"No, she didn't," Paul agreed. "Did you see her talk with anyone else before the big scene?"

I shook my head. "I didn't even see her until that moment."

"What about after? I didn't pay close enough attention to see if anyone other than the boyfriend followed her out."

I thought back, but I hadn't really watched too closely, either. "I'm sorry," I said. "I don't think I saw anyone." And if I did, how was I to know at the time that it might be important? I would never in a million years have thought someone would have gotten murdered at a party.

Then again, this was my life we were talking about. Trouble followed me everywhere I went.

"All right. Okay." Paul ran his fingers through his hair. "I need to find something to block off the room so that no one goes poking around."

"Good idea."

"I . . ." He trailed off and frowned. It was obvious he was having a hard time asking me for help. He'd spent so much time warning me off his investigations, he didn't know how to handle it now that he wanted my assistance. "I need you to do something for me."

"Yes?" I asked, sweet as could be.

A flicker of annoyance passed over his features but cleared quickly. "Can you keep an eye on things for me while I'm gone? Until Buchannan gets here, I'm going to have my hands full. I need you to watch and see if the boyfriend—"

"Quentin," I said.

"Quentin," he agreed. "If you see him, don't try to detain him, but call me instead." He paused, uncertain. "Do you still have my number?"

I nodded. I might have given up on Paul and I ever dating, but that didn't mean I was going to excise him from my life entirely. We could work very well as friends, I was sure. I just needed to get over my crush and move on. Both of us deserved to be happy, even if it wasn't with each other.

"Okay. Good." He looked past me again, eyes roaming over the milling guests, who'd apparently lost interest in us. "If you see him, find me or call me. The same goes for Mrs. Yarborough."

I nodded, excited to be of some use, even if it wasn't a part of the actual investigation.

Paul's face grew serious. "I want you to be careful. We don't know for sure if the boyfriend did it or if the killer is planning to strike again. I don't want you wandering around, asking questions, okay?"

I winced, hating how well he knew me, but nodded anyway. "Is it okay to ask if anyone knows where Quentin and Margaret have gone?" Not to mention the other Marilyn Monroe.

Paul thought about it briefly. "That should be okay. If you find anything out, tell me immediately. Don't go looking for them yourself. Understood?"

I plastered on a smile. "Of course."

"Good."

"Can you tell me how she died?" I asked. I wasn't sure I was prepared to hear the answer, but thought it better to find out now, rather than later. If the killer was running around with a gun or knife, I wanted to know, just in case I bumped into him.

"I can't say for sure, but from the look of things, I'd say she was strangled." He looked sick to his stomach.

"That's horrible." Strangulation was the kind of death

often doled out by a jealous or angry lover, not a trained killer. It looked like we very well might be looking at the boyfriend, after all.

"Yeah, it is." Paul started to walk away, but then stopped. He turned back to me and gave me a smile that was somehow sad. "And, Krissy . . . you look good."

I floated back to the ballroom, feeling inordinately pleased, despite our main topic of conversation. Paul might not be my boyfriend, or even a suitor anymore, but his approval still felt darn good.

Will was waiting for me as I returned, putting a damper on my good mood; not because I didn't like him, but because I felt guilty. And I hadn't even done anything!

"Here," he said, handing me a cup filled with red punch. "I tested it to make sure it wasn't spiked." He looked almost disappointed.

"Thanks." I took a sip and winced. It might not be spiked, but it wasn't great, either. It tasted like one of those expensive health drinks made from acai berries and pomegranate, which were two of my least favorite flavors.

I took a moment to look over the crowd in the hope that I'd catch a glimpse of either Margaret or Quentin, but with all of the masks and costumes, I wasn't having much luck. There were more white dresses in the room than I'd first realized, and while most of them weren't the same as the Monroe dress, they did make the search more difficult. Quentin's gray suit would also blend in, just as long as I didn't see the silly red bow tie.

In a way, I felt bad for the guy. He might be our killer, yet he had been belittled in front of his peers by the girl he thought loved him. That had to be hard on anyone.

I didn't condone the murder, of course, but I could see where it might cause even the most rational of people to overreact.

"You still like him, don't you?" Will asked suddenly. When I looked at him, he smiled, though it was strained.

"Who?" I asked, playing dumb.

"The cop. Paul."

There was no use denying it. I was never a great liar, and since Paul had *just* complimented me, I knew my face would betray me if I tried. I'm an admitted chronic blusher.

"I suppose," I said. "But we're just friends now."

"And before?"

I shrugged, not really sure how to answer. What had we been? "We went on one date," I said. As they say, honesty is the best policy. "That's as far as it went."

A strange look came into Will's eyes then. I couldn't place whether it was anger or jealousy or simply mild curiosity. "Just one date?" he asked.

For some reason, the question ruffled my feathers. "Yeah, just the one." It came out harsher than I'd intended.

Will flinched, but his strained smile remained. "Okay." His gaze flickered over my shoulder. "Darrin's here. I'm going to run over and talk to him a few minutes." He walked away. He didn't ask if I wanted to come, which I suppose I deserved.

"Smooth, Krissy," I muttered, feeling like a dope. I was becoming a pro at ruining relationships before they ever got started. The guy had been curious, that's all, and I had to go and snap at him needlessly. The stress was really starting to get to me, I guess.

"It'll work out."

I jumped, startled, and turned to find Vicki standing behind me. I had a feeling she'd heard most, if not all, of our conversation.

"If you say so."

She winked. "Don't worry about it. He likes you. Guys are, well, guys. He'll get over it."

That brought a ghost of a smile to my lips. "I hope so. I really don't want to scare him off."

"You won't." Vicki put an arm around me and squeezed. "Just be you. That's all you can do. And if he doesn't appreciate you for it, well, then, he isn't the right man."

"And what if Mr. Right never comes along?"

She laughed, but didn't answer. "I'd better go find Mason. He's pretty upset after what happened."

"Go," I said, extracting myself from her grip. Just because I was terrible with men and on the verge of ruining my chance with Will, didn't mean Vicki needed to do the same with her man.

As she made her way to Mason, I turned back to the crowd and sighed. It was time to see if I could find one of our missing guests. If working on my relationship wasn't in the cards, I could at least start snooping around.

And sticking my nose where it didn't belong was the one thing I was actually good at.

6

Not surprisingly, no one seemed to know where the missing guests had gone, and it was quite obvious, no one even cared. When I wasn't met with indifference, I slammed up against an impenetrable wall of annoyance. These people didn't know me, and sure as heck didn't want to talk to me. They were far more interested in the lives of the people around them who they thought mattered.

"This is a disaster," I muttered as I walked away from a small group of women who'd only sniffed at me and turned away when I'd asked about Margaret Yarborough's whereabouts. While they had no intention of talking to me about it, I heard one of the women whisper Margaret's name the moment my back was turned. If nothing else, I was setting the gossip train rolling.

One of the waitresses who was working the party caught my eye. I hurried over to her. "Hi! Do you know where Mrs. Yarborough has gone?"

The waitress looked surprised, before shrugging. "I haven't seen her. I'm just serving drinks."

"Oh, thanks. If you see her, let me know."

She nodded, but I could see it in her eyes that she had no intention of seeking me out if Margaret were to show up.

I removed my deerstalker cap and wiped my brow with the back of my arm. It was getting hot in the large room, especially around the small clusters of guests. I noticed a good portion of them weren't heeding Paul's command and were wandering off to explore the house. Finding anyone in this mess was going to be next to impossible.

Will was huddled with Vicki and Mason, and I considered giving up and joining them, but only for a second. I wasn't one to back away from a challenge, no matter how annoying that challenge had become. I was going to find either Margaret or Quentin, and I wasn't about to let a few failed attempts stop me.

I headed for one of the hallways just to take a peek to see if maybe one of them was out there. Besides, I needed a little fresh air, and while the rainy outdoors would be better, Igor was letting no one out. At least someone was doing as Paul asked.

The hallway I'd chosen was empty but was cooler than the ballroom. I fanned myself off with my hat a moment and then shoved it back onto my head. Paul told me not to leave the ballroom, and I planned on keeping that promise. For now. If I kept striking out, I might have to do a little exploring, just to make sure one of the other Monroes wasn't lying dead in a room somewhere.

I turned to head back into the ballroom and found myself near face-to-face with the man in the *Scream* mask. He was walking straight for me, and by his gait I could tell he was moving with a purpose. I couldn't see his eyes, but I had a feeling they were zeroed in on me.

Panic flared through me. I was in a lonely hall with a man who was keeping his identity a secret. And what kind of person wouldn't want someone to recognize them? A killer, that's who.

I started to turn in order to hurry down the hall and find a bathroom to hide in. The masked man darted forward and grabbed me by the wrist, spinning me back around.

"Hey!" I shouted. "Let go of me!" I jerked my arm out of his grip and backed away.

"Krissy, wait."

The voice was muffled from the mask, but I'd recognize it anywhere. "Robert?" It came out as a confused question, before anger flooded in. "Robert!"

I could almost hear the smile in his voice when he spoke. "I can't believe I found you here."

"*You* can't believe it? What are *you* doing here, Robert? Shouldn't you be back home ruining someone else's life?"

Robert Dunhill was my ex-boyfriend, one I'd thought I'd put behind me when I'd left California. He'd cheated on me with some college girls—the number of which I didn't want to think about, let alone know. He never expected me to find out, thinking I wasn't bright enough to see what was right in front of me. When I did call him on it, he had the gall to think I would forgive him and continue on as we always had. When that didn't happen, he started stalking me, calling me on the phone, using secret accounts to contact me on Facebook.

And now he was here, in Pine Hills, at a party that was supposed to be by invite only.

"We really need to talk, Krissy," he said.

"No, we really don't." I tried to push past him, but he grabbed my arm again.

"Don't walk away from me."

I fought down the urge to kick him right between the legs. The man deserved it in more ways than one, but I managed to restrain myself. No sense making too big of a scene, at least not yet. If he put his hands on me again, then he'd be picking my shoelaces out of his teeth.

"What do you want, Robert?" I asked, putting as much venom in my voice as I could. "You shouldn't be here. *How* did you get here?"

He chuckled and let me go, allowing me to step back away from him. "I was invited."

I snorted. "Sure you were."

"Seriously! I was." I could hear the pride in his voice. If there was one thing Robert was full of, other than you-know-what, it was pride.

"Who would invite you here?" I asked. It was more likely he snuck his way in.

"Some girl I met at a bar in town."

I raised my eyebrows at him.

"When you blocked me on Facebook a few months back, I decided to see if I could figure out where you were hiding."

"I wasn't hiding, Robert. I moved on."

"Whatever." He adjusted his mask. "When I figured it out, I made plans to pay you a visit. It took me some time, but I managed." I figure it was money he needed. He'd never been one to save. "When I got here, I realized I still wasn't sure where to find you, so I went to a bar to think about it."

I rolled my eyes. The only thinking he ever did at a bar was whether or not he thought he could pick up any of the girls, and what it might cost him. It was more likely he'd seen it on the way in and stopped by for a little pick-me-up before heading in to make my life miserable.

"I met her there."

"Really?" I said, still not buying it. "If you met someone who invited you here, why aren't you with her?"

He shrugged. "She's busy. The chick is loaded. When she invited me to the party, I thought we'd go to some lame frat party and have a few drinks before heading back to her place, but instead . . ." He shook his head. "Wow. I never expected this."

I crossed my arms over my chest, unimpressed. It was likely the girl he'd met had just been dumped or was out to annoy Mom and Dad by bringing a loser to the biggest party of the year. I seriously doubted Robert of all people would be able to hook a girl with enough money to be invited to a place like this.

"You really should go hang out with your new girlfriend," I said. "I'm busy. Besides, she might get jealous if she sees you with me."

He laughed. "I doubt that. She's too hot to be jealous of you."

It says a lot about our relationship that I wasn't offended by the comment. It was the sort of thing that came out of Robert's mouth all of the time.

"Robert," I said calmly. "Would you please just leave me alone?"

"Not until we talk."

"There is nothing to talk about!" Some of my calm broke. How many times did I have to tell him I wanted nothing to do with him before he got the point? "You screwed up. I left. It's the end of the story."

"Nah," he said with a wave of his hand. "I know you. You still need me."

I sighed. "If you believe that, Robert, you are more delusional than I thought."

"Come on, Krissy. You're the one who needs me. Look at you. It's obvious."

My left eye twitched. He was about three seconds from me shoving his stupid mask somewhere where he wouldn't be able to reach it again.

"Robert. You need to leave me alone. I have no intention of ever seeing your lying face again. You make me sick!"

"You can't talk to me like that," he said. I heard anger in his voice. Maybe he was finally getting it.

"I can," I said. "And I will." This time, when I pushed past him, he let me go.

Of all the nerve. I almost wished Will would have been there to see that. I was pretty sure Robert would have received more than a bruised ego if he had been. Heck, even Paul would have put him in his place for talking to me like that. And if Vicki had been there . . . We might have had to deal with *two* bodies instead of one!

I returned to the ballroom with the intent of going over to my friends to dump on Robert a bit, when I saw an older, frantic-looking *Breakfast at Tiffany's* Audrey Hepburn enter from across the room. It took me a moment to realize who it was—her hair was a different color and she was wearing a new costume—but after a few seconds, I realized I was looking at Margaret Yarborough. She was looking wildly around the room for someone.

I hurried over before she could get lost in the crowd.

"Margaret?" I said. "I'm Kristina Hancock. Officer Paul Dalton sent me to find you."

She latched on to me like I was her saving grace. Perfectly manicured hands circled my wrists hard enough to hurt. "Where is he?" she asked. "I have a crime to report."

I thought she was a little late to the party but didn't call her on it. "We know about the body already."

A flash of annoyance passed over her face. "Not that." She waved a hand in front of her face as if brushing away a fly. "Someone has stolen my jewelry!" She started scanning the crowd again, presumably for Paul.

"He'll be back shortly." *I hope.* I didn't like the fact Margaret was so dismissive over Jessica's murder. I mean, a life is far more valuable than jewelry, no matter the price. "What makes you think it has been stolen?"

She gave me a flat look. "Really, dear? How else? I went in to change my costume and when I went to put on the jewelry I'd purchased to go with it, it was gone."

"I see." That still didn't quite tell me everything, though. "Why did you get changed?"

She huffed, letting her annoyance show. "Because there was a murder, dear, in case you've forgotten."

"I haven't." My own annoyance was starting to rear its ugly head.

Margaret sighed and rolled her eyes as if tired of explaining things to me. "I couldn't be caught dead wearing the same thing as someone who was murdered! It would be unseemly, and in dreadfully bad taste."

Or was it something more? *Did you get pumpkin guts on your once-white dress and couldn't wear it any longer?* I found it hard to believe that Margaret Yarborough would kill Jessica Fairweather, but then again, I didn't know either woman. As far as I knew, they had a deep, resentful relationship that stretched back for years.

"Do you know anyone who would have a reason to kill Ms. Fairweather?" I asked, figuring I'd go for broke while I had Margaret there. Paul would want to ask the same questions of her, but I thought I could save him some time.

"Maybe she saw the thief who stole my jewelry," she said. "He could have killed her so she wouldn't turn him in."

I supposed it was plausible, but it didn't quite fit. If Jessica caught the killer stealing jewelry out of what I presumed was Margaret's bedroom, wouldn't her body have been found there instead? I doubted she kept her expensive jewelry in the scarecrow and pumpkin room, not unless she thought no one would think to look there.

I didn't know the layout of the house, but based on general knowledge of most houses, the bedrooms were probably upstairs. If that was the case, the killer would have had to drag Jessica's body down the stairs, smash her head through a pumpkin, and then leave her there, all without being seen. Why not just shove her in a closet? It would have been easier, and far safer.

No, I didn't buy it. She could have tried to escape the killer and he chased her down, catching up with her outside the pumpkin room. That made more sense, but somehow, it still didn't quite fit. Someone would have heard or seen *something* if she'd run. She would have called for help at the bare minimum.

"Excuse me, dear," Margaret said, perking up. She pushed past me and sashayed across the room to where Paul had just entered.

I scurried after her, not wanting to miss anything. Besides, I *had* found Mrs. Yarborough and wanted credit for it. No matter what the status of our relationship was, I did want his approval.

Petty? Sure. But hey, we all have our needs.

"All of it!" Margaret was saying as I approached. "Taken straight out of its box."

"Where did this happen?"

"My bedroom, of course," she said with a wave of her hand. "Where else?"

"And are you sure you didn't misplace it?" Paul sounded as if he wanted to talk about anything other than her missing jewelry, which wasn't a surprise. He had a lot on his plate with the murder and all. He was just too nice to tell her she was wasting his time.

"I'm positive. I set it out earlier, just in case I needed a costume change. The door was closed, but wasn't locked, so anyone could have slipped in. I'm certain it was that poor girl's murderer who did it."

Like me, Paul didn't seem convinced. "I'll look into it," he said. "But first, I need to talk to you a few minutes about the victim."

"Me?" Margaret sounded aghast. She glanced behind her as if making sure no one was listening in before turning back to him. "I had nothing to do with this and have no idea who might have."

"I'm sure you didn't," Paul said. He glanced at me, and I smiled innocently at him, before he turned back to Mrs. Yarborough. "Is there somewhere we can talk privately? It will only take a few minutes."

Margaret huffed. "You should be worrying more about catching the maniac running around stealing and killing. You are wasting your time with me. Someone else might have seen something, though."

A little ping teased at the back of my mind. Someone *had* seen something; I had!

"The nervous man," I said. Why hadn't I thought of him before?

"Excuse me?" Paul asked, turning to me.

"When Jessica rushed out of the room after the failed proposal, she bumped into a man who looked nervous. I think he was wearing a black suit and hat. He was alone, and had just entered the room. He might have come from Margaret's bedroom."

It was pure speculation, but at least it was something.

"Can you describe him?" Paul asked, sounding excited.

I thought back. I hadn't really been looking hard, especially since my focus was on Jessica at the time. And then Paul had come up to talk to me, which made me forget about the whole thing until that very moment. I thought he might have had a mustache, but whether it was fake or real, I had no idea.

"Not really," I said. "He was wearing a costume like everyone else and I didn't get a really good look at him. All I know for sure was that he was wearing that black suit and hat, and looked guilty of something."

"He might have changed by now," Paul said with a frown. He peered past me, at the other guests milling around. "And he might not be guilty of anything more than sneaking off on his own."

"But we can't know that until we talk to him."

Paul's eyes narrowed at the "we" part, but nodded. "I'll talk to him." His frown deepened. "Are people leaving?"

I glanced back. There were definitely fewer people in the ballroom than there had been a few minutes ago. "They're wandering around," I told him. "Igor won't let anyone leave."

Margaret sniffed. "His name is Vince."

I shrugged. Vince? Igor? His name didn't matter just as long as he was keeping our killer from sneaking away.

Paul sighed and ran a hand over his face. He looked weary. "Okay." He turned to Margaret. "We'll need to talk at some point, but I'm going to put it off for now. Can you try to wrangle everyone back into the ballroom? We need to find the man in the black suit and hat."

She nodded. "I can."

"Good." He turned to me. "You'll have to come with me."

"Me? Why?" Instant worry shot through me. He couldn't possibly think I knew more than I was letting on.

"I need you to identify this guy when we find him," he said. "There are quite a lot of black hats and suits here tonight. I can't question them all." He paused. "Do you think you'll recognize him if you saw him again?"

"I think so."

"Good." He took a deep breath and let it out in a huff. "Are you ready for this?"

"As ready as I'll ever be."

"I'll go see if I can find everyone," Margaret said before heading down the hall.

Paul watched her go and then motioned for me to go ahead of him. "After you."

"Gee thanks." Just what I was looking forward to: hunting down a man who could very well be a murderer.

What could possibly go wrong with that?

7

"What about one of those men?" Paul sounded tired as we strode around the crowded room. No matter how many times he asked the guests to stay in one spot, they continued to mill about, making it hard to keep track of whom we had and hadn't already seen.

I followed his eyes and then shook my head. "I think we checked them already."

He heaved a sigh and we moved on.

I'd fully expected our search to be difficult, but it was starting to get a little silly. Both Paul and I were frustrated, and the longer we continued our search, the more convinced I became that the man was long gone. He could easily have slipped out before the body was discovered. Igor, as I continued to think of him, claims no one had left through the front door, but there were back exits as well. He might even have escaped through a window for all we knew.

"Maybe we should lock everyone up," I said. "If we section them off in groups of ten or so, we could check them over, and once we make sure our man isn't one of them, lock them in one of the rooms before moving on to the next group. It would keep us from checking the same people twice." Or three or four times as we'd already done in some cases.

"Tempting," Paul said. "But I don't want to start a riot. These people will rebel the moment we start locking people up. It would cause more problems than I'm prepared to deal with."

He was probably right, but I liked the idea, anyway. Once we locked everyone up, our murderer would be safely tucked away until Buchannan got here, and I could spend some quality time with Will. I'd already left him alone long enough.

We were moving along the wall near the drinks when I caught a glimpse of a black top hat just peeking over the edge of the table. I nudged Paul and pointed. The man was mostly hidden from view, which was why we'd overlooked him for so long.

Paul nodded and held up a finger to me to wait. As much as it pained me, I listened.

"Sir?" he said, approaching the slumped form. When the man didn't move, I became instantly worried we had another victim on our hands. "Sir, I need to talk to you."

Thankfully, the top hat moved as the man turned to face Paul. He didn't say anything, just sat there.

"Sir?" Paul said, wariness in his voice. "Could you please stand up?"

The man did as he was told. As he reached his feet, he paused to look around at those nearby, who were now watching with interest. As soon as I saw his face, I knew it was our guy. He did have a thin, dark mustache speckled with gray. Heavy bags rested under his eyes, making him look tired, though I had a feeling that was just how he naturally looked.

Top Hat's gaze moved from the onlookers to me. He stared at me for a long moment, ignoring Paul's "Sir, please step away from the table." His brow furrowed and his entire body tensed.

"Look out!"

My warning came too late. Top Hat took a step forward and shoved Paul in the chest, knocking him over in surprise. He bolted away from me, toward the nearest side hall. There was no one between him and the exit, meaning that if he got away, he was likely gone for good.

I gave chase, but after only a few strides, I knew I'd never catch up with him. I was never much of an athlete, and after walking around the party for as long as I had, my legs and feet were tired.

Top Hat reached the hall and glanced back. I was still too far away to reach him, and Paul was just regaining his feet. A relieved look came over Top Hat's face as he turned to run down the hall . . .

. . . And instead ran directly into a blond man in a red smoking jacket and sailor's cap.

"Lance!" I shouted. "Grab him."

Top Hat tried to dart past the muscular Hugh Hefner, but Lance lowered his shoulder and tackled him like a linebacker might. Top Hat grunted, his hat tumbling from his head, as he crashed against the wall and then sagged to the floor, gasping for breath.

"I take it I missed something?" Lance said, standing over the man in a way that was quite clearly a warning for him not to get up.

Paul rushed past me and pulled Top Hat to his feet. "Let's go," he said, sounding peeved before looking to Lance. "Thanks."

"Don't mention it."

Paul led our suspect over to where Margaret stood. She'd hurried over when she'd seen the scuffle, and looked absolutely horrified that something like this could have happened in her already doomed party. "Where can I take him?" he asked her.

She pointed to the exit across the hall. "Turn right from there, and the third door on the right will do."

Paul nodded and led Top Hat through the ballroom, and then down the indicated hall, and away from the party of onlookers who were talking in excited, loud voices.

I hesitated only a moment before giving Lance a quick, "Thanks. I'll fill you in in a minute." Then I hurried after Paul and our possible thief and murderer. There was no way I was going to miss this.

I caught up to them just as Paul reached the third door. He shoved it open and pushed Top Hat in before him, clearly still angry about being knocked over. He started to follow him in, but stopped when he saw me approaching.

"Krissy, you know you can't be in here."

"I deserve this," I said. "If it wasn't for me, you wouldn't have known to look for him."

"I need to ask him questions that pertain to the murder investigation. You can't be in the room for that."

"This isn't *really* an official investigation, is it?" I asked, almost pleading. "You aren't on duty. This isn't the police station."

"But . . ."

"Please, Paul." I wasn't above begging if I had to. "I saw him when no one else did. I found him for you. He might try to lie about what I'd seen. If I'm in the room, he won't be able to. He knows I saw him, I could see it in his eyes." I might not have seen much more than the man looking nervous, but that was beside the point. As long as he *thought* I knew more than I did, it would be enough.

Paul sighed and rubbed at his temples. "It's a bad idea."

"I promise I won't tell anyone," I said. "You *did* ask for my help, if you remember."

"And I'm starting to regret it." I was about to protest when he held up a hand, and said, "Fine. But if you come in, you don't speak unless I tell you to. You don't ask questions. You don't get involved in this in any way that might compromise my investigation. As far as we know, this guy is innocent of any wrongdoing. I won't have you making things worse. Understand?"

"But he ran!"

"Krissy . . ." He sounded close to changing his mind.

"Okay, I'll be good. I promise." I beamed at him.

Paul didn't look convinced, but stepped aside to allow me admittance. I entered the room, Paul right behind me, and took a quick look around.

The room looked to be a study or perhaps a conference room. There was a computer with a pair of large monitors attached to it against the wall under the window. Bookshelves stuffed with books were built into two of the three walls. I had to restrain myself from walking over and checking them out. More horror movie posters hung in the room here, though these were the old popular ones like *Frankenstein* and *Dracula*. A table in the middle of the room held a pair of skulls with candles glowing in their eyes. Wax dribbled down onto the table in what looked like bloody rivulets.

"Take a seat," Paul said, indicating a chair on the far side of the table.

"I didn't do it," the man said as he sat. "I didn't kill anyone."

"Then why did you run?" Paul gestured for me to sit in one of the chairs next to the one he sank down in.

"I . . ." The man frowned and looked down at his hands.

"Mrs. Yarborough claimed someone stole her jewelry. She is quite upset about it. Do you happen to know anything about that, Mr. . . . ?"

"Clements. Reggie Clements." The man sighed, looking somehow lost without his top hat. He continued to study his hands and didn't answer Paul's first question.

"Okay, Reggie. I'm Officer Paul Dalton of the Pine Hills Police Department. This is Kristina Hancock. She's currently assisting me in the investigation of Jessica Fairweather's murder."

"I didn't kill her."

"I'm not going to accuse you of anything without reason," Paul said. "But you did run from me. And refusing to answer questions only makes you look guilty. Do you understand the predicament you are in?"

Reggie nodded. "Yeah."

"So, I'll ask you again. Did you steal Margaret Yarborough's jewelry?"

Reggie's eyes flickered from his hands to me. I could see the urge to lie all over his face, so I raised my eyebrows at him. He scowled and looked back down at his hands.

"Yeah, fine," he said. With a sudden jerk, he shoved a hand into his pocket, causing both Paul and I to tense.

Instead of a gun, however, he withdrew a handful of jewelry. He tossed it onto the table in front of us before sagging, defeated, into his chair.

I think I stopped breathing for a few seconds as I eyed the small pile. Everything appeared to be made of nothing but diamonds—the necklace, the bracelet, and even the two rings. If there was metal in there some-where, it was well hidden beneath the shine. I couldn't imagine how much those few pieces of jewelry cost, and a part of me didn't want to know.

"I took the stuff, I admit it," Reggie said. "But I didn't kill that girl. I'd never seen her before in my life."

"She did almost run you over earlier," I said, pointedly ignoring the look Paul gave me. "If you'd just come from Mrs. Yarborough's bedroom, jewelry in hand, you might have panicked, thought she knew more than she really did."

"Come on," Reggie said. "I barely saw her. Even if I'd wanted to go looking for her, I wouldn't have known where to start. And besides, if you were watching me, you'd have seen that I didn't go back until a few minutes after the body was found. I was in the ballroom the whole time."

"Wait," Paul said, drawing Reggie's attention back to him. "You went back? To Mrs. Yarborough's room?"

"What else was I going to do?" Reggie shook his head as if we were the dumbest two people he'd ever spoken to. "I'd taken the jewelry and then the girl goes and gets herself killed. I couldn't stand around with stolen goods in my pocket. You'd eventually start searching people, and then what would you think? I doubt you'd simply look the other way. I didn't want to get arrested over some trinkets."

Trinkets? The diamonds in those pieces could probably buy my house.

"Go on," Paul said when Reggie stopped talking.

"Well, while everyone was busy freaking out, I snuck back upstairs, into the old lady's bedroom where she'd left the stuff out like she wanted someone to come along and steal it. I was about to put it all back when I heard some people arguing. They sounded like they were coming my way, so I hid in the closet, which was open at the time. I barely made it inside and closed the door before they entered the room to yell at each other."

"What were they arguing about?" Paul asked.

"How should I know? I was stuffed in a closet with dresses hanging all around me. The sound was muffled."

"But you said they were yelling."

"Not *yelling* yelling," Reggie said. "More like that hushed yelling you do when you don't want anyone else to overhear your argument. And besides, my blood was pumping pretty hard. I was scared they'd catch me and you'd show up and accuse me of murder." He crossed his arms over his chest. "I'm convenient."

Paul looked annoyed that his integrity had been slighted, so I asked the next question.

"Did you happen to see who it was then? You had to be curious."

"I was," Reggie admitted. "But by the sound of things, they were standing too close to the closet. I wasn't going to risk getting seen just so I could eavesdrop on a lovers' quarrel."

Lovers' quarrel? "Does that mean it was a man and woman arguing?" I asked.

"Yeah, a man and a woman."

"But you didn't recognize their voices," Paul asked.

He shrugged. "What can I tell you? Sound was muffled. And I really don't know a lot of the people here all that well. It wasn't anyone I knew, I don't think."

Paul studied Reggie for a long moment, using those stunning blue eyes of his to dissect the thief. It was a wonder Reggie didn't break down and confess to everything, including the assassination of President Kennedy, under his gaze. I could see why Paul had chosen to become a police officer, other than the fact his mom was the police chief.

"You still had the jewelry," he said, indicating the small pile of diamonds on the table. "If you went back into the bedroom to return them, why do you have them now?"

I thought it was a good question, but Reggie had an answer.

"I waited in the closet for a few minutes after the two finished their fight, then slipped out to replace my haul. But when I checked the dresser where I'd found it, the box they'd come in was gone. I panicked then, certain someone would be coming back at any moment, so I beat it out of there. If they were already looking for a thief, how long before they went to you and you used your tools to find my prints on the stuff?"

Paul's face remained passive. No sense telling Reggie that not only didn't we have police tools with us, but he was off duty and focused on a murder. Chances were good he would have gotten away with the theft if he hadn't panicked.

Reggie sighed. "I tried to leave the house, but by then, no one was getting out. The jerk at the door threatened to call you over if I tried."

"So, you have no idea who killed Jessica Fairweather, then?" Paul asked.

"None."

As unlikely as it all sounded, something about Reggie's story rang true. I wasn't about to declare him innocent of all crimes—he *had* stolen Mrs. Yarborough's jewelry—but I did think he had nothing to do with the murder.

Paul's pocket vibrated then. He jerked his phone out of his pocket, glanced at the screen, and then sighed. "I have to take this." He stood and started for the door. He paused halfway there and turned back to frown at me. "Krissy, let's go."

I wanted to stick around and ask Reggie a few more questions, but there wasn't much I *could* ask him. He hadn't seen anything as far as he was saying, and I doubted any amount of prying would get him to change his tune. He might have heard a man and woman arguing, but since he didn't know what was said, or who exactly had said it, there wasn't anything more to go on. It wouldn't surprise me to learn the argument had been Margaret Yarborough accusing one of her help of stealing her jewelry. It would explain why the box was missing.

"Thanks for your time," I said, standing. I followed Paul out of the room. He closed the door and clicked on his phone. He held up a finger to me and then walked down the hall a ways where I wouldn't be able to hear. I stayed put, dutifully guarding the door while he listened to whatever was being said. He replied a few times, his entire body tense, and then he sagged with a heavy sigh. He said something that looked like, "I understand," before clicking off and returning to where I waited.

"That was Buchannan," he said.

I knew without being told that it couldn't be good news. Anytime Officer John Buchannan was involved in anything, it was never good. "And?" I prodded.

"And he's stuck."

"What do you mean by stuck?"

Paul's frown turned into a genuine scowl. "The idiot tried to get up the driveway in his patrol car, rather than his truck, even though I specifically told him to. He got stuck in the mud."

I tried not to laugh, I really did, but couldn't help myself. The image of Buchannan, sitting in his car, wheels spinning uselessly in the mud, was simply too laughable. The man deserved it for all of the times he'd accused me of doing something I didn't do. I had a feeling that if and when he arrived here, it would be more of the same.

"It's not funny," Paul said. "He said he slid sideways about halfway up and his tires got stuck. He tried to drive out, but only made it worse. He's blocking access to the driveway, thanks to those trees. Until they get a tow truck, it looks like we're on our own."

That sobered me up pretty quickly. "So no one is coming to help?" And there was still a murderer on the loose. *That* was definitely *not* funny.

Paul shook his head. "Nope." He pushed his bobby hat back so he could rub his hands over his face as if he could scrub away his weariness. He looked horribly overworked, especially since he'd come to this thing thinking he was going to get a night off and spend time with a girl he obviously liked. Instead, here he was, searching for a murderer, in a house full of people who had little interest in making it easy on him, with a girl he'd once gone out on a date with.

It wasn't exactly the best way to relax, that was for sure.

"We need to find the boyfriend," I said, confident that once he was found, everything else would fall into place. He might not have killed his girlfriend, but since he'd chased after her and was currently missing, he might have seen who did. Hopefully, when we found him, he'd still be alive, and willing to talk.

"Maybe." Paul stopped rubbing at his face. He still looked dead tired. "Can you wait here a few minutes? I need to ask Mrs. Yarborough if there is somewhere I can keep this guy until I can sort this thing out. I don't believe he killed Miss Fairweather, but I can't be certain of it. I don't need him running around, trying to escape."

"Sure, I'll stand watch."

Paul nodded and then poked his head into the conference room where Reggie waited. "Wait here," he told him. "I'll come for you in a few minutes."

If Reggie replied, I didn't hear it. Paul closed the door and then gave me a weary smile before walking down the hall to go in search of Margaret. I tried not to admire how his costume fit him snuggly in all the right places, but failed miserably. Besides, there was nothing wrong with looking, even if I no longer had a chance with him and was at the party with someone else.

He vanished down the hall, leaving me alone to stand guard. Reggie was probably stuffing the jewelry he'd stolen into his shoe or something. Paul hadn't thought to take it with him, and I wasn't about to go inside to retrieve it, either. As long as he didn't try to run, everything would be okay. All I needed to do was stand outside the door and wait for Paul to return.

And miracles of miracles, I actually did what I was told.

8

Once Paul returned to take our jewelry thief somewhere secure, I went back to the ballroom in the hopes of talking to Will to explain what was going on. I felt bad for abandoning him, but what could I do? There'd been a murder, and apparently, to top it off, some good old-fashioned thievery. I couldn't sit back and do nothing.

Most of the guests were still milling around the ballroom, with the occasional groups leaving to explore. I don't think barbed wire or threat of prosecution was enough to keep many of the people within the room. Not many of them seemed the least bit distraught that Jessica Fairweather lay dead just down the hall. Either I was dealing with a whole lot of heartless people, or she'd really rubbed everyone the wrong way. I was guessing it was more of a combination of both.

It didn't take me long to spot Will. He was standing over by the punch bowls with Darrin, Carl, and two gorgeous women dressed in extravagant gowns with those small little masks on a stick. A flare of jealousy shot through me until one of the men put his arm around one of the women. *The mysterious wives then.*

The women were smiling and looking around like the conversation was an absolute bore. Darrin's, Carl's, and Will's faces were strained, as if they were trying to have a good time but just couldn't manage it. At least some-one seemed to be a little upset by what was going on.

I gave Will a moment to see if he'd look my way, and when he didn't, I decided to find the hero of the day, Lance, instead. I'd eventually want to officially meet Will's friends and their wives, but not yet, and maybe not tonight at all.

My blond Hugh Hefner stood near the wall, talking with an Asian version of the Hef. They both looked surprisingly comfortable in their jackets, as if they'd worn them before. When I started their way, Jules noticed me and waved me over.

"Where are the bunnies?" I asked.

"Lance wanted me to come as Pamela Anderson." Jules rolled his eyes. "He thought it was funny. I, on the other hand, would have felt like a fool running around in a red bikini." He lowered his voice and leaned toward me. "Besides, I need to work out a little more before I attempt anything like that."

"Think of the scandal," Lance said with a grin. "Can you imagine? I'd bet half of the men here would have a heart attack. If I thought I could find one in my size, I very well might have tried on one of those *Baywatch* outfits just to see the looks on their faces."

"Of course, then half of the women would be drooling all over themselves."

Both Lance and Jules laughed.

"Well, I think you both look great," I said, trying hard not to think about muscular Lance dressed up in a tight little swimsuit.

"Thank you," Jules said. He produced a pipe from his robe, stuck it in his mouth, and blew a bubble. "As nice as this place is, I don't think we really fit in."

"Don't worry," I said, watching as the bubble floated over to a tall, round woman, only to pop in her hair. She didn't notice. "I fit in even less than you two."

"Why do you say that?" Jules asked, sounding genuinely perplexed. "You look fantastic."

I touched my deerstalker hat and blushed. "Almost everyone here is dressed so nicely." My gaze flickered over to Darrin's and Carl's wives. "I look like a slob by comparison. I imagine half the women here feel better about themselves just by my mere presence."

"Don't worry about that," Lance said. "Even if you came dressed as Queen Elizabeth, you'd get sneered at. That's just how these people are. As long as you are happy, then who cares what anyone else thinks of you."

"I guess." I scuffed my tennis shoe on the hardwood floor.

Jules frowned at me, eyes filled with concern. "Are you okay?" he asked. "It sounds like there's more to it than you being worried by what a few snobs think of you."

"It's nothing." I glanced at Lance in the hopes of changing the subject. "Thanks, by the way. I thought that guy was going to get away back there."

"My pleasure." He beamed. "I played football in high school, and did a little wresting as well. I'm surprised I can still stick it to them after all these years."

I wasn't. Lance was built. I mean, really, really built. He was the sort of guy any woman in her right mind would fawn over if given the chance. Jules was a very lucky man.

"Did that man kill that girl?" he asked.

"I don't think so. He stole some of Mrs. Yarborough's jewelry and didn't want to get caught with it on him. When he saw Paul coming, he panicked, as anyone would, I guess. It wasn't smart, but I understand why he did it."

"And you're sure he couldn't have killed her?" Jules sounded worried, which was understandable. If he wasn't the killer, then that meant we still had a murderer on the loose.

"Pretty sure," I said, sounding as disappointed as I felt. "He doesn't have a great alibi, so Paul's locking him up just in case. We're going to keep looking."

A strange look came into Jules's eye then. "Is that why you look so upset?"

"Because he's locking the guy up?"

That earned me a flat look. "No, because your old flame is here with someone else."

"I don't know what you are talking about." I looked away as I said it.

"Uh-huh."

Lance put an arm around me and squeezed. "You can tell us, you know?" he said. "We aren't here to judge. You look like you need to get something off your chest and we are the perfect pair of listeners, aren't we, Jules?"

"We are," Jules confirmed. "And we won't go blabbing it all over town like some other people we know."

I wasn't sure if he was talking about Eleanor Winthrow or Rita Jablonski. I doubted it really mattered; both were fond of poking their noses into other people's business and then spreading it all over town.

"Well . . ." My eyes strayed to where Will was still

standing. Could I really talk about it? What if someone overheard and told both Paul and Will?

Don't be stupid, Krissy. No one in this place cared a whit about what I had to say.

"If you don't want to talk about it, that's okay, too," Jules said hurriedly, as if he was afraid their questions were too prying.

"It's just, I think I'm screwing things up with Will. I would have been okay, but then Paul showed up and then there was the murder, which made everything crazy. I've been helping Paul out with the investigation, which means I'm not hanging out with Will, which means he's off talking to his friends, and who knows who else. And as far as I know, he thinks I'm running off to the bedroom with Paul every time we leave the room. I'm not, of course, but with how my life is going, I just can't bear the thought of it all falling apart because I don't know how to handle . . ." I trailed off, out of breath, unsure how to go on.

"I'm sure Will thinks no such thing of you," Lance said. "In fact, from what I can tell, he seems pretty darn proud of you."

I snorted a laugh. "Not likely."

"Oh, no, Lance is right," Jules put in. "He might not like you running off and leaving him alone every few minutes, but you don't see how he smiles after you while you are gone."

"Or he's smiling because I *am* gone."

"Now, Krissy," Jules said. "Don't start putting yourself down because you're insecure. You're a far better person than you give yourself credit for, and these two men know it. We all do. I mean, in less than a year you've made all kinds of friends, helped put killers behind bars, and have significantly impacted the community with your service, and we're talking in a good way."

"If you say so. . . ."

"I do."

Lance was nodding right along. "Maybe Will Foster is jealous of the time Paul gets to spend with you," he said. "But that's okay. We all get jealous some of the time. And if he *is* jealous of what you and Paul still have, no matter what that might be, then that means he cares. Just as long as you tell him what he means to you, and he doesn't get obsessive to the point of violence, a little jealousy can be a good thing in a relationship."

I raised my eyebrows at that. I'd never been too appreciative of any sort of jealousy, even my own. I guess it has never turned out all that great on my end, though it did feel pretty good that Will cared enough to be jealous. Bright side, I suppose.

"Just talk to him," Jules said. "Put his mind at ease. I promise you it will all work out in the end."

They were right. Moping wasn't going to get me anywhere. In fact, if I kept it up, I would surely lose him. What guy wanted a girl who constantly talked about how unworthy she was? I'm not weak; I can handle myself. It was time I showed it.

"Thanks, guys," I said, feeling monumentally better than I had been. "I'll go talk to him now."

"You do that," Jules said.

"And remember to smile," Lance added.

I gave them both my best smile and then turned to go set not just Will's mind at ease, but my own as well.

He was standing where I last saw him, so I started that way, despite the fact his friends were still there. I'd spill my guts to him in front of them if I had to, though I was hoping he might take me aside so we could talk somewhere privately.

I was halfway across the room when my phone buzzed in my pocket. I almost ignored it, but then common sense took over. It very well might be an emergency, or Paul could be calling to ask for my help again. I pulled out the phone and answered it without checking the screen, eyes firmly planted on Will, who had just turned and was watching me approach.

"Oh, Lordy Lou!"

I groaned and almost hung up. I so didn't need this right now, but I wasn't willing to be rude to one of the few people who seemed to truly like me for some reason. "Hi, Rita," I said. "I'm at a party right now, so I can't talk long."

"I know!" She was shouting as if excited. "I heard there was a murder there!"

"How . . . ?" I trailed off, not bothering to finish the question. How else? Someone here was probably friends with her or one of her gossip buddies. Once word got to Rita, rumors of murder and mayhem would be all over town.

"I heard it through the grapevine that Jessica Fairweather was murdered at the party! Is it true?"

I really didn't want rumors flying around, especially with my name attached to them, so I answered with a noncommittal, "I can't talk about it right now."

Rita didn't seem put out by my refusal to answer. "Well, if it *is* true, I can't say it is much of a shame."

I held up a finger to the waiting Will and veered off into a hallway where it was quieter. "Why's that?" I asked, interested despite myself. If there was one thing

Rita was good for, it was rumors, many of which turned out to be true.

"She wasn't a very nice girl, now was she?" She huffed as if she'd met the sharp side of Miss Fairweather's tongue more than once. "I'm sure there were countless men who would want to kill her, so I'm not surprised her current boyfriend gave in to the impulse."

"No one said he killed her." I wanted to be clear on that so she didn't go around saying I told her he'd done it. "And by current boyfriend, I'm assuming that means she went through a lot of them?"

"Oh my, yes." I could almost feel Rita shake her head in disapproval. "That girl was a floozy of the first grade. I swear she kept more than one man on a leash at any given time. With her money and looks, these poor saps kept throwing themselves at her, like they thought she would suddenly change." Another huff. "As if."

I wasn't a big fan of dishing on the dead, but if it was true, then that meant Quentin Pebbles had a pretty good motive for killing her, not to mention the other guys she'd strung along. I wondered if Paul knew about Jessica's past, or if Rita was giving me unsubstantiated rumors? I'd have to find a way to ask around without seeming like I was prying.

"Do you know the names of any of these boyfriends?" I asked.

"Well, why would I?" Rita asked, sounding as if I'd just asked her if she knew the color of the deceased's underwear. "I'm not one to get involved in other people's personal lives."

I rolled my eyes and found myself looking at Will. He was standing a respectable distance away, mask turned in my direction. He was leaning against the wall, cane resting on one shoulder, looking absolutely dreamy.

"I, uh, got to go," I said, suddenly not quite as interested in Jessica Fairweather's love life as I was a moment ago.

"Oh, well, I—"

I clicked off, knowing that if I let her, Rita would continue talking. "Will," I said, stuffing the phone back into my pocket.

"You could have finished," he said with a smile. "I'm a patient man."

"You'd have to be with me," I said.

He strode down the hall to join me, still smiling. Our hallway was deserted, and all of the doors were closed, so there was no one around to watch us. My heart picked up speed as I thought about that, and it didn't help matters any that he was wearing that yummy suit. He looked like he'd come straight out of the movies.

"Krissy . . ." he started.

"Wait." I held up a hand. "Let me go first."

Will paused, opened his mouth as if he might speak anyway, and then, like a gentleman, he nodded for me to go ahead.

"I'm sorry for running off on you so much," I said. "I'm acting like a jerk. We came to the party together, so we should spend some actual time together. I really do like you, and before you ask, Paul is just a friend. We might have gone on a date once, but it didn't end all that great and we haven't been out together since. The only time I ever see him anymore is when someone gets killed." Which was happening far too regularly for my liking.

Will held his smile during my entire speech. "I don't blame you for what you're doing," he said. "I was going to tell you that I'm proud of you. I think you should keep doing it for as long as it takes to get to the bottom of this thing."

"Even if it means we don't get to spend any time together tonight?"

He shrugged. "I won't lie and say I'm okay with you putting yourself at risk, but it makes you happy. What you are doing is important. You don't have to worry about what I think. I have friends here; I can hang out with them until you're done." His smile widened. "I sometimes forget myself and act like a fool. I should be the one apologizing to you for acting as if I don't understand. I do."

I suddenly felt all warm and fuzzy. "I've been an idiot."

Will took a step forward and wrapped me in a big hug. He smelled good. Very good. It was all I could do to keep from melting into him.

"That makes two of us."

I started to smile, but just then, something thumped behind me.

I flew out of Will's arms like he'd burst into flames. Heart hammering, I spun and scoured the hallway, trying to determine where the sound had come from. Fake cobwebs hung from the ceiling, concealing fake spiders, and probably a few real ones to boot.

"Did you hear that?" I asked, voice shaking a little. The empty hallway that had been a blessing a moment ago suddenly felt oppressive and frightening. We were close enough to the ballroom that I doubted we were in any real danger, but then again, if the killer was here and had found a gun, we'd be on our own.

The thump came again, and I was able to pinpoint it as coming from the second door on the right. The door was made of heavy wood and a gargoyle face had been carved into it. Red rubies were inset as eyes. When the next thump came, the face shook.

"Let me," Will said, taking a step forward, cane clenched in his fist.

I really should have let him go first, but my stubborn streak kicked in then. I didn't need saving or protecting, darn it! I snatched the cane out of his hand and stepped up to the door. I didn't know if the person inside was the killer, a victim, or maybe not even a person at all. As far as I knew, Margaret Yarborough kept a pair of pit bulls locked away.

"We should wait for Paul," Will said from just behind me. "Just in case."

"You can go find him," I said at a whisper. "But I'm going to check this out." The murderer might have dragged someone into the room and could be killing them even now. I didn't want another Monroe's death to weigh on my conscience if I could have prevented it.

I pressed my face close to the door, listening for other sounds. I thought I heard what sounded like a heavy glass clunking up against the floor, but it was hard to tell since it was quickly followed by another thump.

"Hello?" I said, causing Will to hiss in a nervous breath. "Is everything okay in there?"

There was a snorted laugh, but otherwise, no answer.

I looked at Will, who looked back at me, eyes pleading with me to back away and let someone else handle it. It made me feel good that he was concerned about me, but not so much that I was going to give in.

My hand tightened on the cane as I reached for the doorknob. "Hello?" I asked again, this time louder. "Are you hurt?"

No answer.

"I'm coming in."

"Don't tell them that!" Will hissed.

I tried the door, fully expecting it to be locked. It clicked open halfway before smacking up against something and coming to an abrupt halt. I peered inside the room, terrified I'd find someone bleeding out, laughing madly as their life bled away onto the floor.

Instead, Quentin Pebbles sat on the bathroom floor, legs spread out in front of him, blocking the door. He held a mostly empty bottle of wine in his hands. His nose was red and his eyes were puffy from both crying and a little too much drink. His costume was open at the chest, exposing a sweaty white T-shirt beneath. His red bow tie lay on the floor next to him. He sniffed, wiped at his nose with the back of his hand, and said, "She doesn't love me."

And then he broke down into big, blubbery tears.

9

Quentin sat at the table in the room that was quickly becoming Paul's makeshift interrogation room, rubbing his head. Paul had managed to scrounge up a cup of coffee somewhere, though it was black and cookie free. Every few moments, Quentin would take a sip and grimace before going back to massaging his temples.

"I was stupid to think I could tame her." He spoke without any provocation. "I should have seen the signs."

Paul glanced at me and we both sat down. I didn't have to beg him to be allowed to sit in on the questioning this time. I think he would have even let Will come in if he'd wanted to. Instead, Will decided to go back to the ballroom, and had asked me to go.

I, of course, declined. There was no way I was going to miss this.

"What can you tell us about tonight?" Paul asked, keeping his voice low and soothing. No sense agitating a man who appeared willing to talk, especially if he was going to confess.

"We came to the party together," Quentin said without looking up. "I've been planning to propose to Jessica all week. I thought about doing it before we came, or perhaps when we were heading back home, but decided to do it here." He snorted a laugh. "What a plan that turned out to be, right?" He sighed and shook his head, slowly as not to jar his already throbbing skull. "I think she knew what I was planning from the start. She'd been acting funny lately."

"Funny how?" I asked, earning me a warning look from Paul. Apparently, the same rules applied here as they had when Reggie Clements had sat in Quentin's chair. I mimed zipping my lips closed.

He shrugged and then winced as if the gesture had hurt. "Secretive, I guess. Pushing me away. Stuff like that. I think she was preparing to move on from me and when she realized what I was going to do, accelerated the process." A faint smile lit his lips. "She does that a lot. When we first met, she was already dating a couple of other guys. She said she broke up with them, but I knew she didn't do it right away."

Paul and I shared another look. I couldn't imagine what it would be like to be dragged along like that. I guess Rita's rumor of Jessica having a lot of boyfriends was true. It didn't make things any easier, though it did help us with a possible motive.

Quentin looked a lot less like Pee-wee Herman now that he wasn't wearing the red bow tie. Now, he simply looked sad and defeated. He continued to rub his head, which was likely throbbing from all the wine he'd drunk. On the way to Paul, he'd told me the bottle had been full when he'd found it.

"Can you tell me why you were drinking in the bathroom?" Paul asked, calm as could be.

"To forget," Quentin said, sitting back and crossing

his arms. I did a quick once-over of him, but if he'd gotten pumpkin on him from killing his girlfriend, he'd cleaned it off. "To obliterate myself so I wouldn't have to think about Jessica Fairweather ever again."

"So, you wanted her out of your life?"

Quentin looked up and frowned. "Wait. What is this about?" He looked from Paul to me, and I thought I saw a hint of fear behind his eyes.

Paul laid both of his hands onto the table and leveled a stare at the man sitting across from him. Gone was the calm, friendly man, and in its place was the strong and in-charge policeman.

"Were you jealous of Jessica? What about the other men she was sleeping with?"

"What? No." Quentin's brow furrowed as he tried to think things through in his semi-drunk state. "She was rich, and she had other lovers, I'm sure, but I still loved her. She could be a downright bitch when she wanted to be, but aren't most women?" He paused and glanced at me. "No offense intended."

"Were you upset when she rejected you?" Paul asked, drawing Quentin's eye back to him.

"Sure," he said. I noted a slight panic to his voice. "She turned me down in front of everyone. I thought having people watching might keep her from blowing me off, but I guess she didn't really love me as much as I thought she did. Even though I knew what she was like, I thought a part of her might be willing to settle down if I were to ask. She couldn't go on like she had been forever, right?"

"And her turning you down, it made you angry?"

"Sure, yeah. It would upset anyone."

"Is that why you killed her?"

Quentin's hand froze halfway through the process of raising his coffee mug to his lips. It was like someone had doused him with ice-cold water. His eyes, red from his earlier sobbing and the start of his hangover, grew wide and aware. All signs of inebriation were gone.

"Killed her?" he asked at a whisper. "Jessica took off."

Paul held his gaze, blue eyes scouring the face of his suspect as if he could divine whether he was telling the truth or not. "Her body was found earlier this evening. She died just after you chased after her." He paused, seemed to consider whether he should go on or not, and then added, "She was strangled."

Each word seemed to stab Quentin like a knife. He winced and cringed back in his chair, as if he could escape the truth. He started to shake his head, stopped, and then carefully set down his mug. His face turned an ugly shade of white; then he was up out of his chair and over to the corner where a wastebasket sat. He fell to his knees and retched into it.

Paul didn't rise, didn't move to comfort him, so I stayed right where I was. I was mortified by how brutal the statements had been, especially if he hadn't killed her. I suppose he could have thrown it at him like that to gauge his reaction, but it was still cruel. I gave Paul a disapproving glare, but his gaze was firmly on Quentin.

After what felt like an endless couple of minutes, Quentin pushed himself to his feet and braced himself against the wall. "Are you sure it was her?" he asked, his voice breaking so much it made me want to walk over and hug him.

"We are." Paul was still all business. "Mr. Pebbles, if you would . . ." He indicated the vacated chair.

There was a long moment when Quentin just stood

there, staring at the chair like he couldn't comprehend what it was. I wasn't sure he even knew *where* he was anymore. He took a shaky step forward, wiped his mouth with the back of his hand, and then collapsed into the seat as if his strings had been cut.

"I can't believe it," he said.

"I'm sorry," I said, unable to hold back any longer. The poor guy looked about ready to break into more heaving sobs. Seeing it once was enough for me. "It has to be tough to hear after what happened."

"I . . . It is." He fisted his eyes so hard, I was afraid he might pop them out the back of his head. "She can't be dead."

And then the tears started again.

Both Paul and I could do nothing but watch him as he sobbed. If he'd killed Jessica, he was doing a pretty darn good acting job. I could feel myself getting choked up just watching him. I know there are heartless people who can fake misery, but looking at Quentin now, I was positive he could have had nothing to do with her murder. If he did, I'd eat my deerstalker hat.

"I'm sorry," Quentin said, snuffling back the tears. "I don't know what to do." He grabbed the mug from the table and downed the coffee like it was a fifth of Jack. He looked disappointed when it wasn't.

"Can you account for your whereabouts after you left the ballroom, up until you were found in the bathroom?" Paul asked. I noted his tone was back to being kinder, gentler.

"I, um . . ." Quentin's face screwed up in concentration as he wiped away his remaining tears. "I chased after Jessica after she . . ." He sighed. "After . . . you know."

Both Paul and I nodded in unison.

"She left the ballroom and was walking quickly down the hall. I called out to her and she screamed at me to leave her alone. I couldn't bring myself to walk away, so I kept following her, begging her to stop and talk to me. She found the nearest bathroom and then locked herself inside."

"Did you follow her in?"

"No, like I said, she locked the door."

"Was it the same bathroom Ms. Hancock found you in?"

"No, it was the one upstairs."

Paul and I shared yet another look. The pumpkin room was downstairs, so if she was killed there, she would have had to come back down at some point. Whether she did it on her own power or not was debatable. I couldn't imagine someone killing her upstairs and then dragging her all the way into the pumpkin room, so it was likely she'd come down on her own. If that was the case, then someone might have seen her, other than her murderer.

"Where did you go after she locked herself in the bathroom?" Paul asked. "Or did you wait outside it until she came out again?"

"I stood outside the room for a few minutes, asking her to come out and talk. We'd had fights before where she'd storm off and, after cooling down, would come out and we'd smooth things over. This time felt different, so when she refused to come out and see me, I left."

"Did you see anyone else upstairs in one of the rooms? Did anyone pass by while you waited?" I asked.

"No." Quentin shook his head and frowned as if he was having a hard time remembering things clearly. "The hallway was deserted at the time, though I do think I remember hearing a few voices down the hall somewhere.

I wasn't exactly in my right mind at the time, so I didn't pay any attention to them."

"So you don't know if the voices were male or female?" Paul asked. "Two or three people?"

"Sorry." Quentin's cheek hopped and I could tell he was on the verge of crying again. It had to be hard, knowing that if he would have stuck around, Jessica very well might still be alive.

"Where did you go after you left her in the bathroom?"

"Downstairs." He shrugged one shoulder. "I couldn't face everyone again, and I couldn't leave because Jessica's driver wasn't due to pick us up again for a few hours. I suppose I could have called someone to get me, but at the time, I wasn't thinking straight. I ended up going to the kitchen, hoping to find something to . . . well . . ." He gave me a sad, embarrassed smile.

"Did anyone see you there?"

Quentin nodded. "There were a few people there, talking. Some of the maids were there, too, dressed in those old-style dresses. I asked one of them for a bottle of wine and she gave it to me without question. I took it and wandered around for a little bit, avoiding everyone. When I started running out of places to go, I found that bathroom and decided to drink myself into oblivion."

It sounded like quite a lot of people had seen Quentin after he'd left Jessica in the bathroom, yet there was also a lot of time unaccounted for. He could very well have killed her and still had time to get the wine and drink away his misery. Or he might have left her, drank himself into a rage, and then found her again, this time in the pumpkin room, before going to the downstairs bathroom to finish off the bottle.

But I just couldn't make myself believe he was responsible for her death. There was too much pain in his eyes, too much confusion. He was the obvious suspect, of course, and until Paul or I could completely clear him, he would remain that way.

"Do you know who might have wanted to hurt Jessica?" Paul asked.

Quentin considered it a moment before shaking his head. "I'm not sure anyone would really want to hurt her. I suppose one of her old boyfriends could have done it, or maybe a new one, I guess."

"Do you know the names of these boyfriends?"

"No, I don't. I didn't want to know then, and I still don't." Quentin clenched his fists atop the table. "I just can't see anyone doing it. She might not have been the most pleasant person to be around sometimes, but when you were with her, she could make you feel like the king of the world." Fresh tears filled his eyes. "Why would someone do this?" He completely broke down again and buried his face in his arms.

Paul motioned for me to stand. "We'll give you a moment," he told the sobbing man, before guiding me to the door. We stepped out into the hall and he quietly closed the door behind us, leaving Quentin alone with his grief.

"I don't think he did it," I said immediately.

"My gut says you are right," Paul said. "But I can't go with my gut here. I'm going to have to put him somewhere safe until we either come up with the real killer, or can get out of here and perform a proper investigation."

"Have you heard from Buchannan yet?"

That earned me a brief frown before Paul tipped back

his bobby hat and rubbed at his face. "Not yet," he said, before sighing. "I'm going to have to find the people Mr. Pebbles claims to have talked to or seen, especially the maid who gave him the wine."

"That isn't going to be easy," I said. "Not unless he can give you a better description." I'd seen at least a dozen waitresses floating around, and I was sure there were a few more than that working in the kitchen.

"I know." His shoulders sagged. "But what else can I do?"

"I could look for her for you," I offered, anxious to be of more help, but Paul shook his head.

"You found my missing guests," he said. "Other than making sure no one tries to leave, I don't think you should involve yourself any further in this. I don't want you putting yourself at risk any more than you already have."

"I'll be fine," I grumbled. "I know how to take care of myself. And besides, there are a few other guests who I noticed were missing right around the time of the murder."

Paul gave me a disapproving frown. "And you're just now bringing this up?"

"Well, I wasn't sure it was important!" I lied.

Paul heaved a sigh and gave me a "give it to me" gesture.

"When you first got here, did you notice how many Marilyn Monroes there were?"

He shrugged. "I didn't pay that close of attention."

"There was Margaret Yarborough, who changed after she found out about the murder. She was one. Our victim was the second."

"Okay?" Paul prodded when I paused for dramatic effect.

"There was one other Monroe in the room, at least that

I saw. She was wearing the same dress but didn't have as many pieces of nice jewelry as the others. She looked a little out of place, like she didn't feel like she belonged."

Concern flashed in his eyes then. "She's missing?"

"I don't know that for sure," I hurriedly assured him. No sense starting a panic. "But I haven't seen her since. I suppose she could have left before the murder, but what if she's somehow connected?" I didn't want to say that I thought she might very well be another victim. "While you deal with Quentin and look for guests who can corroborate his story, I could look for her. She might still be in the ballroom and I've simply overlooked her, but I'd feel a whole lot better if I knew she was safe."

Paul scratched the back of his head as he regarded me. "You have to promise me you'll be careful," he said after a moment. "Just because we've found only one body, doesn't mean our killer is done."

"I know. I'll be careful."

"And don't go wandering off, either," he said, wagging a finger at me like I was a disobedient child. "I'm glad you found Mr. Pebbles, but I don't want you wandering through the halls anymore. If something were to happen to you . . ."

"I had Will with me when I found Quentin," I reminded him. "And if I get the urge to take a stroll, I won't go alone. If Will can't come with me, I'll take Vicki and Mason."

Paul didn't look convinced.

"I'll be fine," I said. "Trust me."

A smile played at the corners of his mouth, bringing out those dimples of his. Something smoldered in his eyes as he looked at me and I felt decidedly hot.

10

My first glance around the ballroom didn't reveal the third Monroe right away, so I decided I might best use my time by listening in on the various conversations going on around the room while I searched for her. Maybe someone knew where she'd gone, or perhaps, like Reggie Clements, she could be found sitting somewhere out of sight, but nearby.

Many of the guests were still standing in their little groups, talking amongst themselves, gossiping, if their amused expressions told me anything. There didn't seem to be the worry and panic that normally went with a murder. It was strange how unaffected everyone seemed. As far as they knew, they could be the next victim.

That is, unless the people here knew something I didn't.

"I don't see why we should be forced to sit around and wait for the police to do their work," the fat man with the monocle said as I approached. "I didn't come here to socialize."

The woman he was talking to snorted in a very unlady-like way. "You just came for the free booze, Bert." She waved a flippant hand toward the wineglass in his hand. "If you think I'm going to carry you back home, you are sorely mistaken." Her eyes flickered to me and narrowed. "Is there something you want?"

"No," I said with a smile. "Just looking for conversation."

She huffed and both her and the fat man turned their backs to me before moving off.

Nice work, Krissy. Still making friends like a champ.

I continued on. There had to be someone willing to talk to me, someone who knew something that might help me in locating Monroe three, or at least someone who might know why Jessica Fairweather was killed. I knew Paul didn't want me snooping around, but could he really be mad at me if I came up with information he could use? It wasn't like I was going to chase after the murderer myself.

I eased up close to a group of men, all dressed like they were rich aviators. They had on the brown leather jackets, the gloves, and the leather caps you see in old films. Their flight goggles sat perched atop their heads. It was quite obvious they'd dressed to match.

"She was always in it for the money," the oldest man of the group was saying as I approached. "I'm surprised she even bothered to hold this thing after his death."

"I don't think she even likes this party," another, younger man, said. "She'd probably be far more comfortable sipping martinis on a beach somewhere."

The three men laughed, with the third adding, "I won't be surprised if she is on the first flight out of town the moment this thing ends."

"Are you talking about Mrs. Yarborough," I asked with my best innocent smile.

All three men turned and looked at me as if I'd just crawled out of a trash heap.

"I'm just wondering," I added, not wanting them to stop talking just because I'd opened my mouth. "I barely know her. This is my first time here."

"Ah," the eldest said, as if that explained everything. "Margaret was never interested in the same things Howard was. I don't know what he saw in her, and quite frankly, she never did seem his type."

"I thought she enjoyed all of this." I gestured around the room, at the decorations and odd costumes.

One of the younger two men gave me a patronizing smile. "She went along with it simply because she wanted to make sure she wasn't left out of his will. She married him for his money."

I raised my eyebrows at that. "Are you sure?"

He gave an easy shrug. "It wouldn't surprise me in the slightest if she did."

"She probably killed the bastard, too," the eldest said.

"You don't really think that, do you?" I was appalled. Why would these men come to the party if they disliked and distrusted Margaret so much? It sounded to me like the rumor brigade was out in full force, yet I was intrigued.

"I do," he said. "His death was sudden. The Howard I knew wouldn't just up and die like that. I bet she poisoned him somehow, made him weak so she could work her magic on him. The woman is a witch, and in more ways than one if you ask me."

I frowned. "But if she was after his money and didn't care about these parties, why bother having this one?"

"Probably because her lawyer, Christian Tellitocci, put her up to it." The sneer he gave told me what he thought about Mr. Tellitocci. "Those two were always far too close for my liking."

"Is he here?" I asked, looking around as if I knew what he looked like.

One of the younger men laughed. "He never comes to these things," he said. "Thought it might be in bad form." He didn't expound on the comment, though I got the gist.

The aviator trio pointedly turned so they were no longer facing me, shutting me out of their conversation. That was okay; I was getting tired of their self-righteousness, anyway. Their disdain for Mrs. Yarborough left a bad taste in my mouth, but it did give me something to think about.

Margaret would have inherited quite a lot of money upon her husband's death, I would think. The house itself had to be worth close to a million, if not more. Could she have really killed her husband so she could inherit the money? Had she been cheating on her husband with her lawyer like the young aviator had insinuated? And if so, who all knew about it? And who would benefit if Mrs. Yarborough were to die next?

I hadn't seen or heard anything that indicated the Yarboroughs had any children. It was possible the kids were all grown up and had moved away, yet a part of me didn't think that was the case. Margaret didn't seem like the kind of woman who would want children, though I'd only spoken to her briefly. And I couldn't imagine trying to raise kids in a house like this.

But what if there was a son or daughter out there somewhere? Could they have gone after their mother, only to accidentally kill Jessica Fairweather instead?

It was a stretch, but at least it was something to go on.

Up until now, the only motive we'd found for Jessica's murder was the way she treated others, especially her boyfriends.

"You don't know what you are talking about!"

The bark of angry words came from a few feet away. I turned to find the man dressed as Clark Gable whom Will had pointed out earlier, Terry Blandino, glaring at the man in the horn-rimmed glasses and fedora I'd seen him argue with earlier. Apparently, whatever their trouble, they had yet to work it out because Terry was whispering something harsh at the man, finger pointing accusingly. I couldn't hear what he was saying, but the man in the glasses wasn't happy about it.

I started their way, hoping to catch what Terry was saying, but he was finished. He spun on his heel and stormed past me without a second glance, face red and angry. The other man's eyes fell on me and he grimaced.

"What do you want?" he asked.

"Was that Terry Blandino?" I knew for a fact it was, but I was curious to see how he'd answer.

He didn't disappoint. "What is it to you?"

I plastered on a smile. "He seems upset. I was just wanting to make sure everything is okay. My name's Krissy, by the way." I held out a hand.

He eyed it a moment before shoving both his hands into his coat pockets. "Terry thinks he knows something. He's a fool. There's nothing more to it than that."

"What does he think he knows?" I tried to make it sound like an innocent question, but it came out as prying, which it was.

His eyes narrowed at me behind his glasses. "Who are you again?"

"No one," I said. "I'm just trying to get to know everyone."

"Might want to be a little less nosy." He started to push past me.

Okay, I had to admit, their fight was really none of my business, but once I get started, it's hard for me to shut it off. Until proven otherwise, everyone was a suspect, and that included Mr. Horn-Rimmed Glasses and Terry Blandino. Could their fight be about Margaret Yarborough? About the dead girl? Or was it something else completely?

Either way, their argument wasn't the reason I was there. I still had a Marilyn Monroe to find.

"Hey," I said, stopping Horn-Rimmed. "Have you seen a girl in a white dress? She looks like Marilyn Monroe." I paused, remembering how the last girl dressed like Mrs. Monroe had looked. "Not the dead one."

He glanced back at me, frowned, and then walked away without comment.

"Gee, thanks," I muttered.

"Try over by the drinks." I turned to see a little old woman smiling at me. "I think I saw her there."

"Thank you," I told her. "You're a big help." And then I hurried over to where she'd indicated.

At first, I didn't see her. There were a few party guests by the drinks, talking, but no white Monroe dress. My heart sank, thinking the old woman had either been mistaken, or had led me astray for some unknown purpose, but then I saw her, standing against the wall as if she were trying to sink through it.

As I noted before, her dress wasn't as nice as the other Monroes', and she wasn't wearing nearly as much jewelry. That didn't mean she wasn't pretty, however. Even with her limited, less expensive necklace, and with a nose that was a little too long, a little too pointed, she still looked stunning.

"Hi," I said, approaching her carefully. She looked like she might startle easily. I wondered if I'd had that same deer-in-the-headlights look on my face when I'd first arrived. I'm guessing I did. "My name's Krissy Hancock. Mind if I talk to you for a moment or two?"

The girl shrugged. "I suppose." She hesitated, then added, "I'm Elaine, by the way."

"Hi, Elaine." I smiled reassuringly at her. "Did you come here alone?" I asked. On both occasions when I'd seen her, she hadn't talked to anyone. I wasn't sure many people came to a party like this without a date, but if she had one, she wasn't spending a lot of time with him.

Elaine nodded. "I was invited." She said it like she thought I might contradict her or accuse her of sneaking into the party. "But I don't know why." Her brow furrowed. "I'm not anyone."

"I'm sure that's not true."

A dainty shrug, followed by, "Sure."

Even though she clearly didn't want to talk, I plowed ahead with my questions anyway. "Did you know the girl who was killed?" I asked. "Jessica Fairweather was her name."

Elaine shook her head. "I didn't. She was wearing the same thing I am." She touched her dress as if wearing it somehow made her guilty of a crime. "What if the killer had found me first? He might have mistaken me for her." A hint of hysterics came into her voice then. "I could be dead right now."

I reached for her to put an arm around her shoulder, but she flinched away. "I don't think you're in any danger,"

I said, returning my arm back where it belonged. "Is there anyone here you could stick close to, just in case?"

She bit her lip before answering. "Yeah, I guess. My dad is here."

"Your dad?" I didn't know why that surprised me. Maybe it was how her clothing looked just as out of place as my own did. This didn't appear to be a girl with a lot of money, and since she hadn't come as some rich guy's plus one, I wasn't quite sure what I expected. Maybe her dad had gotten her an invite. Could he have cut her off for some reason, left her without a lot of money? She looked old enough to live on her own, early twenties maybe, so it could be he decided to let her see what it was like to live on her own, without having everything handed to her, for a little while.

"He doesn't talk to me," Elaine said. "He left me and my mom years ago, left us with nothing." She sighed and a profound sadness filled her eyes. "I thought he sent the invitation, which was why I came. But when I tried to talk to him when I first got here, he pretended like he didn't even know me."

I winced. That was pretty harsh, even from a father who was willing to leave his wife and child with nothing. "Who invited you then, if he didn't?"

"I don't know. I got a letter in the mail. I got a phone call a few days after that, asking if I was coming. They didn't say who it was, just said it was important that I made it."

"Did they give you a name?"

"No," she said. "I figured it was one of Dad's assistants. He usually has them do things like that for him." She glanced past me and practically whispered, "I'm going to go get something to drink."

I nodded absently, trying to put everything together. The poor girl looked so timid, so frightened, I felt bad for her. Could someone have been playing a cruel joke on her, inviting her to a party where she would stand out and be ostracized from everyone, including her dad? Or was something else going on? Had her invitation come from someone trying to get father and daughter back together?

And if so, could any of it have anything to do with Jessica Fairweather's murder? It was hard to see how, but like Terry Blandino and Horn-Rimmed's argument, I wasn't going to dismiss it out of hand.

"Krissy?"

I jumped, startled, and turned to find Will standing nearby. His friends—and their wives—were nowhere in sight.

"I'm sorry," I told him before he could say anything. "I'm not ignoring you on purpose."

He smiled. "It's okay." He glanced toward where Elaine was getting a drink of punch. "Do you know her?"

"No," I said. "Do you?"

He shook his head. "I haven't seen her before. She doesn't look like she wants to be here."

"No, she doesn't." I watched as she sipped her punch. She glanced my way and then retreated to a lonely corner where someone wouldn't ask her painful questions. "Do you have any idea who her father might be? She said he'd left her mom a few years ago, but I didn't get a chance to ask her who he is."

"I wish I did," Will said. "But in these circles it's no real surprise her parents are separated." His brow furrowed as he watched her. "Though looking at her, she does remind me of someone. I just can't place who."

"Huh." I tried to come up with a face that matched

hers, but came up blank. It wasn't surprising, really. I was a stranger here and knew practically no one.

"Anyway," Will said, drawing my eyes back to him. "I have something to ask you."

"Uh-oh." I played it off as light, but something in his voice scared me. He was suddenly nervous, fidgeting and looking everywhere but at me. It was making *me* nervous.

"It's not bad," he said. "Well, I don't think it is."

"Okay," I said. "What is it?"

"Well . . ." He cleared his throat and looked down at his hands. "My parents are here."

I stared at him. "Your parents?"

"Yeah, they didn't tell me they were coming. They dressed up and were wearing masks, so I didn't recognize them. They were going to approach me earlier, but then the girl died and, well, things got weird."

I was getting a sinking feeling in my stomach. "And?"

"And, well, they saw us together and know we came here as a couple." He looked up and gave me a sheepish look. "They want to meet you."

And there it went, right through the floor. "I . . ."

"It's not a meet-the-parents kind of thing!" he hurriedly said. "I mean, it is, but not in the way you're thinking. They know who you are, have heard about you from me and, well, from the news. They just want to say hi and whatnot. There's no pressure."

No pressure. Right. As if meeting a guy's parents for the first time was easy. What if they didn't like me? What if I said something so stupid, they forbade him from ever talking to me again?

Stop it, Krissy. He's a grown man. He can make his own decisions.

"Where are they?" I asked, plastering on a smile that shook just as much as my insides were shaking.

Will looked relieved that I wasn't running in the opposite direction. "Here," he said, holding out an arm. "I'll take you to them. They're going to love you."

11

"Mom. Dad. This is Krissy Hancock."

Will's parents turned at the sound of his voice and smiled. I was immediately struck by how different each of them was from one another. Will's dad stood at least six feet and looked lean and strong. His skin was a deep, midnight black, as were his eyes. When he smiled, his entire face lit up.

His wife—Will's mom—was shorter than me, putting her at five feet at the most. Her hair was a natural red, slowly fading to gray, and freckles specked her cheeks, making her look younger than she really was. Her eyes were a bright green that sparkled in the overhead lights.

"It's a pleasure to meet you both," I said, finding my voice. I was surprised it didn't shake.

"The pleasure is ours," Mr. Foster said. His voice held a heavy accent I couldn't place, but it made me think of Zimbabwe for some reason—TV more than likely.

"She is pretty," Will's mom said with a radiant smile. Like her husband, she had an accent, though hers was decidedly Irish.

"Krissy, these are my parents, Keneche and Maire Foster," Will said, pointedly ignoring his mother's comment.

"Call me Ken," his dad said. "Everyone does."

"We've heard quite a bit about you," Maire said, gently touching my forearm. "William is quite taken."

Will cleared his throat, a clear, albeit lighthearted, warning for her to stop.

Maire laughed and moved back to her husband's side. "William doesn't like it when I speak to his friends so bluntly. Says it embarrasses him."

"I'm not embarrassed," Will said, obviously lying.

"So, Krissy," Ken broke in, resting a hand on his wife's shoulder. I had a feeling if he let her, she'd talk my ear off. "Will has said you own a coffee shop in town?"

"I do," I said, thankful to be talking about something else. "Well, I co-own it with my best friend, Vicki. She's around here somewhere." I glanced around, hoping to spot her.

"I have yet to make it downtown," Ken said. "We've been on vacation, and then spent more hours at home than we probably should have." He gave his wife a loving smile. "But I promise to stop by soon. What is the name of your shop?"

"Death by Coffee," I said, wincing just a little. No matter how many times I said it, I kept thinking about my dad's book and the murder that had happened not long after we'd opened. I sometimes wish we'd change the name, but knew it would never happen. It was already a part of Pine Hills, and would stay that way until we were forced to close up shop—something I hoped wouldn't happen for a very long time.

"What a cute name," Maire said. "We'll definitely be stopping by soon." Her smile faded and she gave me a serious look. "I'm sorry we've met under such unfortunate circumstances." She glanced toward the hall that led to where Jessica's body lay. "It is quite dreadful."

"Have we seen you with the officer investigating the case?" Ken asked.

"Yeah." I glanced at Will, worried. Of what? I wasn't sure. That they'd ask if Paul and I had a history together? Of something more, something regarding Will himself? I think a part of me wanted him to speak up for me. To defend me? To say that it was okay I was spending most of the party running around with another guy?

Either way, he seemed to notice my worry and spoke up. "She's been helping him look into the murder," he said, pride in his voice. "Apparently, she's gained a reputation around town. This is what? Your third murder investigation?"

I felt myself flush. "I'm not really investigating. I'm just helping."

Both Ken and Maire were beaming at me as if I were the most precious thing they'd ever seen.

"I'm sure you're doing everything asked of you," Maire said.

"There's no need to be modest with us," Ken added. "I find it refreshing that you're willing to help. So many people stand aside and do nothing when a tragedy hits. It's impressive that you are willing to take the time to assist."

I lowered my head. I didn't feel worthy of the praise, but said, "Thank you," anyway.

"We should let them go," Maire said, suddenly. "I wanted to meet you, not interrupt your date."

Ken chuckled. "You're right. It was a pleasure to meet

you, Krissy. I hope we get a chance to sit down and have a longer conversation sometime very soon." He looked meaningfully at his son.

"I'd like that," I said, and I meant it. I liked both his parents. They seemed friendly and accepting of me, which was something I hadn't expected. Will had money. I didn't. Not every parent would approve of the pairing.

It's not like we're going to get married, I told myself, though a little part of me wasn't totally against the idea. I mean, Will was great. If things continued to work out between us, why not look toward the future.

Maire took Ken by the arm and with a farewell wave, they turned and blended in with the crowd.

"I'm sorry about that," Will said. "I really didn't know they were going to be here."

"It's okay," I said, smiling as I watched them walk away. "I like them."

"Good." He sounded relieved.

"They're an interesting couple," I said. "How did they meet?"

Will seemed to know exactly what I was asking, and why. "Dad moved to England from Africa when he was twenty. Mom was going to college there, having moved from Ireland. They met there, got married a year later, and had me a year after that. They moved to the U.S. shortly after I was born."

"And they kept both their accents." It was a statement, but he answered anyway.

"They did. When they go on vacation, they visit their respective homes, staying about two weeks in each place. They are often gone months at a time."

"And what about you? You don't have an accent."

I would have thought living in a house where everyone else spoke with one, Will would have picked up a thing or two.

"I used to," he said. "But I went to school here, and not many people speak like my parents. Every now and again I let it slip out, though I prefer not to."

"Huh." It appeared Will Foster was far more interesting than I'd first thought—and I'd always thought him special, so that was saying something.

"Now that that is out of the way, would you like to take a look around the house?" Will asked. "Everyone else is, and I figured that since I have you here, I should try to take advantage before you have to run off and help Officer Dalton again."

I wanted to accept, but couldn't. "I wish I could," I said, disappointed. "But I really need to find Mrs. Yarborough." I thought about the rumors I heard and realized I might get some answers from Will before I had to run off again. "Hey, weren't you Howard's doctor?"

He looked surprised by the question. "Me? No, Carl took care of Howard. I only subbed for him when Howard came in and he was working at the hospital. Why?"

"Well, I was talking to some of the guests, and a few of them claimed they believe Howard was killed by his wife."

Will's eyebrows shot up at that. "Murdered?"

I shrugged. "Murdered, or perhaps she did something that ended up killing him."

"I don't know about anything like that." He paused, eyes far away, as if considering something, before he took me by the arm. "Let's go ask."

I let Will lead me across the room, toward where Darrin and Carl were standing. Their wives weren't nearby, to which I was thankful. I hadn't met them, yet I was pretty sure neither one would approve of me asking questions, especially ones that might get their husbands in trouble. There was that whole doctor–patient confidentiality thing, and not to mention how nosy I was being.

Then again, maybe they were as gossipy as Rita and would love an opportunity to dish on someone.

"Hey, Carl," Will said as we drew near the pair. "You remember Krissy, right?"

"How could I forget?" He mimed throwing a bowling ball and then cringing as if he'd totally botched the shot. Carl was good looking. Not as good looking as Will, but it was a near thing. His smile was infectious, too. Even though I knew he was making fun of how poorly I'd done bowling, I found myself returning the smile.

"She was curious about something regarding Howard Yarborough and how he died."

Carl's smile slipped. "You know I can't really talk about it, right?" The question was directed at me.

"I know," I said. "But I heard a rumor that he might have been killed by his wife. I was just wondering if it was possible that his death wasn't from natural causes."

Carl glanced at Will, who gave him a short nod, as if telling him it was okay to talk to me. He rubbed at his chin before heaving a sigh.

"I suppose she could have slipped him something over a long period of time that might have weakened his heart; but if she did, she was really careful about it." He shook his head. "But I don't think so. Howard had a bad heart, something he told me he'd had since he was a kid. It simply gave out one day." He spread his hands. "That's really all I can tell you."

"What about kids?" I asked, remembering something else I'd thought about. "Do you know if Howard and Margaret had any?"

Both Carl and Will looked to Darrin. Like his coworkers and friends, he was good looking. The three of them together made me think of those TV medical shows where all of the doctors are young and hunky. It made me wonder what the other doctors and nurses at their small practice looked like.

"Don't look at me," Darrin said, holding up his hands. "If they had any kids, they'd have to be, what? My age? I wouldn't have treated them."

"And I have no idea," Carl said. "Howard never spoke of them if he did." He paused, brow furrowed. "Though I thought I remember someone saying Mrs. Yarborough was unable to have kids due to something that happened to her when she was younger." He shook his head. "But I might be thinking of someone else."

I looked to Will, who shrugged. "Margaret's doctor might know, but Paige isn't here. I could call her and ask, but these are pretty personal questions."

"No, that's okay." If nothing else, I could try to find a way to ask Margaret if she ever had kids but had a feeling she wouldn't take too kindly to the question, especially if she was infertile.

Darrin's phone chirped and he pulled it out and checked the screen. He grimaced. "We have been summoned," he said to Carl, who rolled his eyes.

"Go," Will said with a grin. "And thanks."

"Anytime." Carl sighed; then both he and Darrin headed for the nearest hallway.

"Their wives were exploring," Will said. "Probably got lost."

"Oh."

"Hey, do you have a doctor yet?"

The question came out of nowhere. I stared at him, mouth slightly agape, not quite sure how to answer.

Will suddenly flushed, and said, "I don't mean for *me* to be your doctor. I haven't seen you or heard your name around the office, and thought that since Paige is accepting new patients, you might want to come in and see her sometime."

"I'll do that," I said. "Things have been so crazy lately, I haven't even thought about getting a new doctor." The only doctors I'd seen lately were the ones who'd patched me up after my last couple of investigations, and I think they'd come from the hospital in Levington.

"I'll let her know to expect your call." Will smiled. "You'll like her. She can sometimes be overbearing, but she really is a nice person."

"I'm sure I'll like her."

Will cleared his throat. "I probably shouldn't keep you," he said. "You said something about looking for Mrs. Yarborough, and I'm assuming this has to do with the police investigation."

"It does." I winced inwardly. I didn't want to leave him, but if I wanted to help find Jessica's killer, I couldn't spend the evening with him either. "As soon as I find her and talk to Paul, I'll come find you. Then we can go exploring, okay?"

"Sounds like a plan." Will's smile was easy and understanding, which made leaving him even harder.

Without thinking about what I was doing, I stepped forward and gave him a quick hug. "Thank you," I said as I released him. It happened so fast, he didn't have time to hug me back.

Before he could say anything, I turned and hurried away, pulse racing. In that brief few moments of contact, I'd felt so safe and warm, I could have stayed there forever. If he would have had time to embrace me back, I don't think I would have been able to leave. I would have melted into a sappy puddle and let him hold me forever.

And if that thought wasn't scary enough, I was forced to turn my mind to the task at hand: finding Margaret Yarborough before the killer decided to strike again.

12

Despite hosting the party, Margaret Yarborough wasn't in the ballroom and no one seemed to know where she was. I roamed around, hoping to catch a glimpse of our elder Audrey Hepburn, so I could talk to her, report back to Paul, and then spend the rest of the party with Will. Meeting his parents had definitely solidified my feelings for him. I wanted to make sure he knew it, too, and running around the party alone wasn't the way to do it.

After about ten minutes of getting nowhere, I finally did what I should have done from the start and pulled aside one of the maids dressed in the old-style waitress outfits. She was middle aged and pretty, though the heavy bags under her eyes and the frown lines on her face told of how hard she'd been working. She frowned at me and said, "Can it wait? I'm busy," when I stopped her.

"This will take just a sec," I said, putting on my best smile. "I'm looking for Mrs. Yarborough but can't seem to find her." I glanced around the ballroom as if to prove my point.

The woman sighed and jerked a thumb toward one

of the exits in the back of the room. "She went to the kitchen to check on the status of the wine."

"Thank you."

The maid grunted and hurried across the room to where Igor stood, looking bored and tired. I turned away and headed for the indicated hallway. It was busy with help who were carrying food and drinks to and from the ballroom. Say one thing for the guests, a murder sure didn't dampen their appetites. Almost everyone I saw was dressed as a waitress; no males in evidence. I slipped past them with mumbled apologies and passed a large dining hall that was being used as a place where the help could take a few minutes to rest. A handful of them looked up wearily as I passed. I waved and smiled and continued on toward the kitchen.

Like the rest of the house, the kitchen was decorated with Halloween and horror firmly in mind. The knife block was in the shape of a human head. The butcher knife was slotted into the open mouth, which gave me the shivers. The curtains over the windows were of a cobweb design and were colored red and black. Severed fingers and ears lay forever beneath the surface of the clear counter, swimming in what appeared to be blood. It was enough to curdle my stomach and I wondered how anyone could be hungry after coming in here to get their food.

I made a quick scan of the room, doing my best to ignore the horrible imagery, and quickly deduced Margaret was nowhere in sight.

"Well, darn," I said. I hadn't passed her on the way in, and she definitely wasn't in the ballroom, so it looked like my search would continue.

"May I help you?" A man dressed as a chef approached. "You look lost."

"Maybe," I said with a sigh. "Krissy Hancock." I held out a hand, figuring it best to get introductions out of the way. If the chef could help me, I wanted to know his name so I could thank him later.

The man looked startled before shaking my hand. "Mitchel Riese."

"Are you . . . ?" I looked him up and down, not quite sure if I'd offend him by asking if he was part of the kitchen staff, or if he was one of the exploring guests.

He chuckled in understanding. "I am. I cook for Mrs. Yarborough; have for the last fifteen years." He sounded proud. His hair was graying at the temples and his eyes were pinched, but he looked happy. "I hope everything has been to your liking thus far?"

"It has," I said, painfully aware that I hadn't had anything to eat yet. My stomach grumbled in protest, drawing a smile from him. "Do you like working for Mrs. Yarborough?"

There was the slightest of hesitations before Mitchel answered. "It's good work. It took some getting used to." He gestured around the macabre kitchen. "But once you do, you hardly see it anymore."

I had a hard time believing that, but the other help working in the kitchen didn't seem bothered by the atmosphere. One man was cutting a carrot on a cutting board that looked like spilled blood.

"It's a shame about Mr. Yarborough," I said. "I heard he was eccentric and had come up with all of this himself. I would have loved to meet him. This is my first time here."

"He was definitely eccentric." A sad smile lit the

corners of Mitchel's mouth. His eyes glazed over for a second, as if remembering good times with the former head of the household before they firmed on me again. "He was a kind, generous man. We all miss him quite dearly."

There was something in his voice that drew my attention. I wasn't sure what it was exactly, but it made me feel that now that Mr. Yarborough was gone, Mitchel wasn't feeling the generosity he had before. Could Margaret be harder to work for than her husband? Was it simply the fact that Howard was such a good man, nothing else could compare?

Either way, it did remind me of the reason I'd come back here.

"I don't want to take up much of your time," I said. "I'm looking for Mrs. Yarborough. Someone told me she'd come back to the kitchen, but obviously, she isn't here. Do you happen to know where I can find her?"

"You just missed her by a few minutes," Mitchel said. "She'd come back to check on things, but someone drew her away."

"Do you know who it was?"

He shook his head. "I didn't pay attention. I try not to get involved with her guests. She doesn't approve."

Interesting. Was it because she didn't think the help was worthy of knowing her friends and colleagues, or was it because there were people she didn't want others to know about, people who were of a more seedy element?

"Can you tell me which way they went?" I asked. "I was sent to find her by the police officer in charge of the investigation," I added, so as not to appear too nosy.

Mitchel turned and pointed toward a side exit. "She

went down that hall," he said. "It was five minutes before you arrived at the most."

"Thank you."

Mitchel beamed at me. "It's my pleasure. It's terrible about what happened and I hope it gets figured out soon." He shuddered. "It's a shame it had to happen tonight of all nights." He sighed, shrugged, and then turned to talk to one of the female waitresses who was about to carry a tray of cheeses out of the room.

I left them to it and headed down the hall Mitchel had pointed me toward. Faces stared down at me from the ceiling, carved and lit to appear demonic. I quickened my pace, unsettled. With their inanimate eyes staring at me, I was seriously getting creeped out.

I'd gone only a short distance down the hall before I heard a raised voice, followed by a hushed murmur. I couldn't make out what was being said, but I recognized Margaret's whispered voice. The louder voice was male.

I inched closer to a door that was hanging open two inches. The argument was taking place inside, but I couldn't quite see who was inside yet.

"You owe it to me," the man said, voice lowered. "Don't you dare try to deny it."

I moved a little closer and caught a glimpse of Margaret Yarborough standing next to a zombie who was hunched over onto the floor with an ax embedded into its head. She was using its back to prop up her arm. She was holding a wineglass that was nearly empty. Her face was flushed red as she said something back to the man. I couldn't tell if it was from the wine, or if she was angry.

I couldn't see the man from my angle, though I did see his arms raise as if in exasperation before dropping back down to his side.

"How was I to know?" he asked.

Margaret huffed and rolled her eyes, as well as her head, turning it toward the doorway. I tried to jump back, but I was too slow. She tensed when she saw me, but it quickly faded and was replaced by a smile as she turned back to the man.

"I'll speak to you later, Philip." She spoke at a normal volume as she nodded toward the door and where I was hiding.

The man with the horn-rimmed glasses leaned forward and peered out at me. I waved at him and smiled, which earned me an annoyed frown. "We're not done talking about this," he told Margaret, before pushing open the door and storming out. He shouldered past me—bumping me intentionally if I wasn't mistaken—and strode angrily toward the kitchen.

"Is there something you needed, dear?" Margaret asked, taking a sip from her wineglass. She didn't seem the slightest bit perturbed I'd caught her arguing with the man she'd called Philip.

I hesitated just outside the room, not because I was worried about talking to Margaret—Paul *had* wanted me to find her—but because of the decorations. I don't know what the room was supposed to be, other than a zombie slaughterhouse. There were bodies everywhere, most of them in some form of frozen animation. The carpet was blood red in splotches, white in others, as if the massacre had only recently taken place.

"I didn't mean to eavesdrop," I said, easing into the room.

"Of course you did, dear. It's what people do when they hear people arguing."

"Okay." I cleared my throat. She was taking it pretty well, almost too well, if you asked me.

She sighed and once again rolled her eyes. "Philip is angry with me. It seems he always is lately."

My mind immediately went to Jessica Fairweather, who, at the time of her death, had been wearing the exact same costume as Margaret Yarborough. Could Philip have been so angry with Margaret that he'd gone to kill her, only to mistake the much younger girl for her?

"I know what you are thinking and you can stop right there," she said, holding up her free hand. "Philip wouldn't have tried to hurt me. He is angry, but he still loves me. We were together when she was murdered, if you must know."

Together how? I thought, before asking, "If you don't mind me asking, what was it you were arguing about?"

A coy smile quirked the corners of her mouth. "Inquisitive, aren't we?"

I went on the defensive. "I'm helping the police solve the murder. I'm asking just in case it is important to the investigation."

"Are you now?" Margaret took a sip from her wineglass. "I guess you have been helping." She glanced toward the window, which had fake blood splattered across it. "If you must know, Philip and I were lovers."

I coughed, startled by the declaration. "You were what?" I had to have heard her wrong.

"Now, don't get all flustered on me," Margaret said. "We all do it, you know?"

I was assuming she meant her circle of friends, because I, for one, didn't have a lover. With the way things were going, it was looking like it might be a very long time until I did. And here was Margaret, talking about sleeping with another man when her husband had just died. It seemed callous.

"Did Howard know?" I asked, unable to stop myself.

"Of course he did. Not only that, but he had his own fair share of lovers on the side. It wasn't a secret or anything."

I couldn't even imagine. I mean, they were married, and were sleeping with other people? I couldn't do something like that. I'd completely lost it when I'd found out Robert had been cheating on me, and we'd only been dating. If we'd been married, I probably would have killed the man.

Which, of course, made me think of the rumors of Margaret killing her husband. I wasn't sure how that played into Jessica Fairweather's demise, but if he'd been sleeping with her and Margaret hadn't approved, it would have given her a pretty good motive.

"You see, dear, we all need a release sometimes," Margaret explained, unperturbed by what she was saying. "Things can get tedious otherwise. Try being with the same person for years upon years, and you'll understand. These dalliances mean nothing, other than a way to try something different. Most of the men I've been with understand that."

"But some don't?"

Margaret shrugged. "Philip thought we were going to run off together. Now that Howard is gone, he sees no reason why I shouldn't sell this place and find somewhere more suitable for a woman of my stature. He wants to come with me, give me the life he thinks I deserve."

"But you don't want to do that?"

"No, I suppose not." She sighed, as if disappointed in

herself. "Philip has his benefits, but isn't my type. Not long term, anyway."

And he was young enough to be her grandson. I never did understand how people could look past such a large age difference. I didn't hold it against anyone who was happy in those situations; it just wasn't my thing.

"What about the girls your husband, uh . . ." I couldn't bring myself to say "slept with" or worse, "had sex with." It felt wrong on so many levels.

"What about them?"

"Were any of them too attached to him?"

Margaret looked into her wineglass and I thought I caught a glimmer of sadness in her eyes. Was it for her late husband? Was it regret surfacing now that he was gone and they both shared too much with so many other people? Or was it for herself, for her current situation? There was no way of knowing without asking, which I wasn't about to do.

"Some came asking for money when he passed," she said. "One of his favorites demanded it. She came right up to my front door and declared she was owed it."

"Is she here tonight?" Or perhaps lying dead in a room filled with pumpkins?

Margaret waved a hand as if shooing away a fly. "She wouldn't come near here after I turned her away and slapped her with a restraining order. If she thinks she is owed something, she should wait until we process the will. I doubt Howard would have included her in it, but if she is, I will give her what she is due. Otherwise, I don't care what happens to her, just as long as she stays away from me."

My mind was awhirl. I was trying to figure out if Jessica Fairweather's death could have been because the

Yarboroughs had slept around. If she'd been one of Howard's girls, could she have come asking for money? Or what if her boyfriend had been with Margaret? Could that have been why she rejected him?

Could it have led to her death?

"Was Jessica one of the girls who came along asking for money?" I asked, almost certain she had to be.

"I don't know." Margaret shrugged, disinterested. "She could have been, I suppose. If she did, she would have gone through my lawyer instead of coming to me directly."

"You mean Mr. Tellitocci?" I asked, remembering what someone at the party had said.

Margaret actually looked startled. "Well, well, well. It appears someone has done her homework."

I gave her a knowing smile, hoping she would think that she could slip nothing by me. I didn't know if it would help, or if she would clam up, but it made me feel good that I'd known something she didn't expect me to.

Maybe I'm not such a bad detective, after all.

"Do you know if Jessica was one of your husband's, um, girlfriends?" I asked. I couldn't bring myself to call her his mistress in front of his widow.

Margaret got a contemplative look on her face. "You know, I'm not sure. It's so hard to keep track of these things."

That made me wonder how many people they'd each slept with, something I quickly squashed. I really didn't want to know. Whatever the number, it was too many. I could keep track of all of the guys I'd kissed in my entire life on two hands. The way she was talking, it appeared she needed a Rolodex to keep everyone straight.

"I really should get back to my guests," Margaret said, draining the last of her wine. "Was there anything else you needed? I'll help you any way I can."

My head was so full of what she'd told me, I completely forgot the questions I originally was going to ask her. "I think that's it. Thanks."

Margaret gave me a simpering smile before striding out of the room, leaving me alone with my thoughts and the zombies. Could what she have told me have caused Jessica Fairweather's death? What about Howard's? A lot of people were dying around Margaret Yarborough, and I couldn't simply write it off as a coincidence.

I glanced down at the desiccated face of one of the zombies and decided this wasn't the place to contemplate it. I left the zombie room and went in search of Paul to tell him what I'd learned.

13

Finding time to talk to Paul wasn't as easy as I expected. I found him in his interrogation room, talking to a bored looking man in a top hat and suspenders. It didn't look like it was going well, which was confirmed when Paul tiredly told me he would have to talk to me later. He had a list of people to talk to and needed to get through it.

I considered telling him what I'd learned from Margaret anyway but decided it could wait. I wasn't sure how I was going to explain things without turning an unflattering shade of crimson and stumbling all over my words. Maybe a little time to sort things out in my head would help.

So, now free of burden—at least for a little while—I decided to go ahead and take Will up on his offer to explore the mansion. It wasn't the total freedom I'd been hoping for, but even twenty minutes where I didn't have to worry about killers and strange sex lives would be a blessing.

"Are you sure this is okay?" Will asked as I led him from the ballroom by the hand. He was smiling as he said it.

"I'm sure," I replied. It wasn't like everyone else

wasn't wandering around all over the place. Besides, if Paul needed to get hold of me, I had my cell phone with me. It wasn't like I was going to drop off the map.

"Good." Will's grin warmed my insides to the point I felt light-headed.

We turned down one of the unexplored hallways. A few feet ahead, another hallway intersected the one we were in. Train tracks filled the hall, and when I peered down to the far end, two bright lights flashed on and a horn blared. I jerked back with a startled yelp, only to realize the "train" that had surprised me was really only a pair of lights and a speaker attached to the far wall.

"This place is crazy," I muttered, stepping over the tracks. While I knew the train wasn't real, I peeked both ways, just in case something came hurtling down the hall at us.

"Wait until you see some of the rooms." Will paused and pushed open a door. Something scurried inside, and before I could see what it might be, he slammed the door closed. "You don't want to know," he said when he turned back to me.

I decided to take his word for it.

We continued on, down dark hallways, past spiders and mummies, and peered into rooms that were all variants of the same theme. There was a bathroom that looked like a mad scientist's lab. The toilet was covered in green slime that actually looked radioactive, though it was probably colored plastic.

"How could anyone live like this?" I asked, closing the door with a shudder. I'd much rather let my teeth float away than use a bathroom like that.

"It does take a certain personality type to be around this every day and not go a little crazy." Will gave a shudder of his own as he eyed one of the myriad of large spider webs throughout the house.

"I'm worried all of this stuff has gotten to Margaret over the years. She seems a little . . . off." I thought back to the conversation in the zombie room, though I'd told myself I wouldn't. Would she have been so free with her information about how she spent her spare time if she hadn't been surrounded by the walking dead? It was enough to unsettle anyone.

"She's not all that bad," Will said. "Yeah, she's a little weird, but aren't we all in some way? She has her quirks, as do you and I."

"I didn't mean to . . ." To what? Offend him? To talk down about someone he knew?

"It's fine," Will assured me with a smile. "I'm not defending her or anything. I don't know her well enough to say for sure whether or not she's a little crazy. You'd have to ask Paige about that."

We reached the end of a hallway where a set of stairs led up into the next level. A couple was coming down. The woman looked concerned, her hand firmly planted on the man's elbow as she helped him down. He appeared pale and shaky, as if something had scared the life right out of him. He gave me a wild-eyed look before staggering past.

Something in me quailed at walking up those stairs at the sight of the couple. There *was* a murderer on the loose. As far as I knew, one of the bodies lying around the house wasn't made of plastic or rubber. It could very well be another of Margaret's guests, murdered by a madman who was stalking those dumb enough to wander the halls alone.

"You okay?" Will asked. We were standing halfway up the stairs and had stopped moving some time ago. "You look a little sick."

"I'm fine," I said, not quite sure that was true. "I was thinking about Jessica."

Will reached out and gently touched my hand. He didn't quite take it, but his touch was enough to galvanize me. I started up the stairs, determined not to let my trepidation ruin our time together.

"Kim isn't too thrilled about all of this," Will said as we reached the top of the stairs. "She's near ready to drag Darrin out into the mud, just so she doesn't have to deal with any of this any longer."

"Kim his wife?" I guessed.

I was rewarded with a nod. "I forgot you haven't met her yet." He sounded as if it was his fault, rather than mine for not being around when I should have. "You really do need to meet Kim and Diana. They're . . . special."

I laughed. "I'm sure they are."

"They're not fans of dressing up for Halloween." He touched his white mask as if reminding himself it was there. "They only came because it was the 'in' thing to do."

"Darrin and Carl don't seem that bad."

"They aren't. But when it comes to their taste in women, they have a lot to learn. Looks aren't the only thing that matters." He glanced at me out of the corner of his eye before quickly looking away.

We peeked into a roomful of porcelain dolls, some hanging by their necks from the ceiling. I turned away quickly, before one of them blinked and sent me screaming out a window.

"Your friend seems nice," Will said as we walked away.

"Who? Vicki?" He nodded. "She's great. All the guys drool all over her. Always have. And she really doesn't seem to notice, which is what I love about her. She's the prettiest girl in the room almost all of the time, and while she doesn't hide it, she doesn't flaunt it on purpose, either. It all comes so naturally to her. I'm just lucky whenever anyone notices me when I'm around her." It came out sounding more pathetic than I wanted.

"Why's that?" Will asked, sounding genuinely perplexed.

I stopped in front of a life-sized poster of Boris Karloff as Frankenstein and gestured between it and myself as if saying, "See! Twins!"

Will sighed and put a hand on my shoulder. He looked me dead in the eye, and for a moment, I was completely lost in their chocolate depth. No man should have eyes like that. A girl could get sucked in and never find her way out again.

"You are fine the way you are," he said, voice serious, no hint of sarcasm in his tone at all. "You shouldn't put yourself down so much."

"Yeah, but . . ."

"No," he said firmly. "Vicki is pretty; I'll give her that. But so are you."

I warmed from my feet to my head. "You're just being nice." I suddenly felt as if I were fourteen again, talking to a boy who didn't immediately scream "Cooties!" the moment he saw me coming.

"No, I'm not." Will looked around, but we were

alone. When he turned back to me, I could see his intent in his eyes.

My entire body went from hot to cold and back again. Every muscle tensed so that I felt as rigid as a plank. Will's hand was still on my shoulder, so I was sure he felt it. My mouth, which was usually running nonstop, went completely dry, as did the words that usually fell from my lips in an endless, idiotic stream. I could feel my eyes widen as he leaned forward.

Let me tell you, I could have lived in that moment forever. He didn't have to kiss me, or even touch me, and I would have been content. His words were enough. When his lips actually did press against mine, it was like fireworks going off in my brain. Everything short-circuited. Angels didn't quite sing, but it was a near thing.

The kiss was all too brief, just enough to whet my appetite for more. His lips, soft and dark, had my heart hammering hard enough, I thought I might choke on it. A sound like the squeak of a mouse escaped my lips, bringing a smile to his own.

"I'll take that as a compliment," he said with a laugh.

My mind went blank and I flushed again. God, I was a mess, and I saw no way out of the situation. I needed to say something.

Nothing came to mind right away, so I did the dumb thing and let my mouth work without thinking about what I was about to say.

"Did you know Jessica Fairweather well?"

Both Will and I winced at near the exact same moment. He clearly hadn't been expecting me to say that, and I sure as heck didn't anticipate asking such a moronic question after what we'd just done. If I could rewind time and do it all over again, I would have.

"Pretend I didn't just ask that," I said, turning away. "In fact, let me go find that room with all the chains and axes hanging from the ceiling so I can go hang myself now." I started back the way we'd come, feeling as stupid as I'd ever felt in my life.

"No, it's fine," Will said, catching up to me. "You caught me off guard, is all. I wasn't expecting the question."

"That makes two of us," I muttered. At least I'd stuck to my usual foot-in-mouth way of doing things. There had to be someone out there who would find it endearing.

"Jessica and I . . ." Will trailed off with a contemplative frown. I paid him a sideways glance but didn't slow my pace. A part of me thought that if we moved far enough from where I'd asked the question, maybe we'd escape it. "We knew each other," he finished.

I stopped and turned to face him. "I'm so sorry," I said, feeling like a fool. Well, a bigger fool than I already had. "I didn't know you were friends. You should have said something."

Of course, if I'd been paying closer attention, I might have realized sooner that he had. I remembered how his eyes had turned sad when he'd found out about Jessica's death, how he'd acted afterward. The signs were all there, I just hadn't seen them. I was far too wrapped up in my own business to notice.

It wasn't exactly my best moment.

"It's okay," he said for what felt like the thousandth time. "We weren't really friends anymore. We hadn't talked for a few years now." Something in his voice added, "And now we never will."

"I should have been there for you," I said. It might have been cheesy, but there was nothing wrong with that. Friends were supposed to be there for each other, and I'd been off running after a killer while Will was hurting. What kind of person did that make me?

Will looked down at his hands. "We dated." He said it almost shyly, as if afraid to admit it. "Very briefly. I'm not even sure the word *date* really applies. We went out a few times and then drifted apart." He shrugged.

My mind immediately went back to everything I'd learned about Jessica from Quentin, and what Margaret had just told me. If she was sleeping around, moving from man to man, had Will been sucked in? I'd like to think that their two dates had been nothing more than dinner and a movie, but I wasn't going to count on it.

"Did you, uh . . ." I cleared my throat. "Did you tell Paul about your relationship?"

Will looked relieved that I hadn't asked him something else, something more personal. "No," he said. "Should I?"

I didn't want him to, didn't even want to think about it myself. It shouldn't matter that he'd been with Jessica before me. Almost all guys my age would have had previous girlfriends, possibly even serious ones, but it didn't make it any easier. The poor girl was dead. Somehow, that made it worse.

"I'm not sure," I admitted, doing my best to sound as if none of it bothered me. I was afraid Paul would begin to suspect Will of killing her. Ex-boyfriends were always questioned and looked at with suspicion. I knew deep down he was safe—he had been with me when Jessica was killed—but I didn't want him to have to go through the questions, the uncertain, doubting looks. I knew from personal experience how miserable it was.

Something akin to panic rose in his eyes then. "You don't think he could suspect me of killing her because I knew her, do you?" It was as if he'd read my thoughts.

"You're safe," I assured him. "You were with me the entire time. Paul will remember that. He was right there."

Will visibly relaxed, though there was still tension running through his shoulders and worry in his eyes.

"But it might be an important enough piece of information that Paul should know," I added, not quite sure how it would matter. "The more he can learn about Jessica, who she was, the more likely he'll be able to figure out who killed her. If he suspects you are keeping secrets, he might think you have something more to hide."

Will's face fell, but he nodded. "I suppose you're right."

I hated being right. I didn't think Paul would consider Will a suspect for a second, but it was better to be safe now than sorry later, especially if Buchannan showed up. If someone were to come forward and tell one of them that Will and Jessica had been together once, it would be far too easy to jump to conclusions.

But it did make me wonder how many people here had been with the victim, whether it was just on a few dates or something more. How many had been with Mr. Yarborough before his death, and could it be somehow connected?

It was starting to look like it could very well be a real possibility. And the more dirty laundry that got aired, the worse I felt about it.

"We'd better go," Will said, looking like a man about to head to the hangman. "I want to get this over with."

I took his hand and we started back toward the ballroom. No matter what happened, I wasn't going to let him do this alone.

14

Paul was waiting for me when we got back. He strode over to where Will and I stopped, just inside the ballroom. Will's hand had gone clammy with sweat. Our eyes met and I saw a nervousness there that made *me* start to feel sick to my stomach. Paul, thankfully, didn't notice. He had his hat off and was running his fingers through his hair in a frustrated way.

"Have you learned something new?" I asked, worried he'd somehow already heard about Will and Jessica's relationship and was going to grill him about it.

"Nothing that will help," he said with a sigh. He nodded to Will and then replaced his hat. "It seems like everyone here knew our vic, and very few of them had a positive view of her. It doesn't make my job any easier when it seems as if half of my possible suspects act as if they are happy she's dead."

Will's hand tightened on my own.

"Hey, there's Darrin," I said, noticing the other man near the drinks. "Why don't you go ahead and visit with him while I talk to Paul?"

"You sure?"

I could tell he really wanted me to say yes. He didn't want to tell Paul about his past any more than I did.

"I'm sure," I said, plastering on a smile. "Go have fun."

He gave me a relieved smile. "I'll find you later," he said, before hesitating and then leaning down and giving me a quick kiss on the cheek. He gave Paul a nod and then walked briskly away.

We both watched him go, Paul with a bemused expression on his face. When he turned back to me, it sobered pretty quickly. "Okay," he said. "I take it there is something you wanted to talk to me about?"

"I talked to Margaret Yarborough," I said.

Paul didn't look impressed. "And?"

"And I learned a few interesting things about her and Howard's relationship."

A skinny man with a liver-spotted scalp turned to face us, interest in his eyes. He didn't bother to hide the fact he was eavesdropping on our conversation. I wondered if you could even call it eavesdropping with how open he was being about it.

Paul noticed, grimaced, and then took me by the elbow. He led me out of the ballroom, giving the man a glare as he went, and took me down the hall, into his makeshift interrogation room. He closed the door behind us before he turned to face me.

"I figure we should do this privately." He leaned on the edge of the table. "These people don't seem to know the meaning of decorum. For as much as they try to act as they are better than everyone else, I'm finding it hard to like anyone." He sighed. "So, what did you learn?"

I took a deep breath to prepare myself. This wasn't something I was going to enjoy.

"Turns out, both Margaret and Howard Yarborough had their share of extramarital lovers."

"Were they open about it?"

"Margaret says they were." And I still couldn't wrap my mind around it. "She claims everyone does it, though I assume she means her friends and acquaintances, because I sure don't." And I had no intention of ever taking part in something like that.

Paul chewed over the information for a moment. I saw when he came to the same conclusion as I had because his eyes widened slightly and his shoulders tensed. "Did Mr. Yarborough sleep with our victim?"

"I'm not sure," I said. "Margaret didn't seem to know either, or at least, she said she didn't." I wouldn't put it past anyone to lie if they thought it would serve them better than telling the truth, especially since Jessica had been murdered.

"Someone has to know," Paul said, clearly speaking to himself.

I answered anyway.

"I think I know someone who might."

"Really?" He rose from his seat at the table and slid into full-on policeman mode. He was ready to march right out of here and snatch whomever I named right out of the ballroom and drag them down here by their ear if he had to.

Fortunately, he wouldn't have to go that far.

"Quentin Pebbles," I said. "He might know." I bit my lip, worried about how he might take what I was about to say next. "I want to talk to him."

Paul's face went carefully blank. "Why?"

"If anyone would know about Jessica's love life, it would be her boyfriend," I said. "He might have learned about the affair and proposed to her to make it seem like he still loved her, but was planning to kill her the entire time."

"Which means you are back to suspecting him of murder," Paul said.

"Not really," I admitted. "But he might know someone else who might want to kill her for similar reasons. If Quentin doesn't know about Jessica's past lovers, whether they include Mr. Yarborough or not, maybe one of her girlfriends might. She could have confided in one of them at some point. You know, girl talk."

Paul frowned. "I have yet to meet anyone who liked her enough to be her confidant."

"Which is why I should talk to Quentin!"

Paul crossed his arms and gave me a skeptical look. "And he will talk to you about it because . . . ?"

"Because he might be willing to talk to a kind face, rather than a policeman who suspects him of murder?" It came out as a question when I was really shooting for confidence.

Paul actually smiled. "You do have a friendly look about you."

"Flatterer." I looked away so he wouldn't see the blush that colored my cheeks.

Paul sighed and closed his eyes as he rubbed at them. I was afraid he would turn me down and insist on talking to Quentin on his own. I had no doubt he would be able to get the information he needed out of the other man, but I really wanted to be involved in the questioning. At this point, it felt like it was just as much my case as it was Paul's.

"I have to be in the room," he said, opening his eyes. "If you're right and he knew about an affair with

Mr. Yarborough, he might react poorly about being questioned about it. Even if he didn't know, he might not like being confronted with it. And I'd rather not leave you in the room alone with what could very well be a murderer."

"I'll be okay," I said, but then hurriedly added, "but I'd like you to be with me, just in case he's stubborn."

"I shouldn't be doing this," Paul muttered. "Wait here. I'll go get him." He stepped out into the hall and closed the door behind him.

Alone, in the room with the skull and movie posters, my nerves started jumping. I went for the bookshelves, hoping to find something to get my mind off what I was about to do. I felt bad questioning Quentin, especially if he had nothing to do with Jessica's murder. I might be asking about things he didn't know about her, which, in turn, would make him even more miserable than he already was.

As expected, the books were mostly about scary stuff: horror movies, Halloween decorations, and the like. I pulled one of the books, *The Art of Blood*, from the shelf and flipped through the pages. Who knew there were so many ways to create and display fake blood? I was pretty sure Howard had employed them all somewhere within the house.

I put the book back on the shelf with a shudder. I couldn't imagine spending my life dedicated to the macabre. I didn't hold it against him. In fact, I was sort of intrigued by it. I would have loved to meet the man face-to-face, but it was far too late for that.

The door opened behind me and I moved to stand beside the table. Quentin walked in, Paul behind him as if to make sure he wouldn't try to run. His eyes were red and puffy, and his hair was a tangled mess on his head. He looked as if he'd just been dragged from bed.

His gaze fell on me and the faintest flash of annoyance passed over his face before he sat down at the table. He looked from me to Paul, then heaved a sigh. "What now?" he asked, sounding as put out as he looked.

"My associate would like to ask you a few questions," Paul said. He nodded to me and stepped back against the wall, which put him out of Quentin's line of sight.

I didn't want to hover over the poor man, so I took a seat across from him. I folded my hands and rested them on the table in front of me. I felt stupid in my deerstalker hat and considered taking it off. I'd had enough of the costume party and was in no mood to continue with the charade. I might be dressed like Sherlock Holmes, but I was about as far from the master detective as you could get.

"Once again, I'm so sorry for your loss," I said, not sure I'd actually expressed it earlier. I doubted he would remember either way.

Quentin nodded and looked down at his hands. I noted absently that his fingernails weren't nearly as manicured as Will's.

Focus, I warned myself. Getting distracted and thinking of Will, no matter how innocently, wouldn't help me get Quentin to talk. I'd be more likely to drool all over myself.

"I've had a chance to talk to a few people around the party," I said. "I was hoping that I could ask you a few questions about what I've heard?"

Quentin shrugged, not looking at me. "Sure. Fine."

I considered multiple ways to say it, from blurting it out, to talking around the issue, but nothing seemed

right. How do you ask a man if his murdered girlfriend
had climbed into bed with a man three times her age? I
was beginning to regret not letting Paul deal with the
questions, especially since he was a real police officer
and, well, I wasn't.

Finally, I decided just to start talking and hope something I said would get to the point.

"Mrs. Yarborough was telling me about the way . . ." I
almost said, "you people," but that sounded off-putting
and rude. "She says her husband had many mistresses."

Quentin didn't even so much as blink or glance up at
me. "Yeah? So? What does that have to do with me?"

A new tactic sprang to mind and I ran with it. "She
admits that she has done the same." I paused, hoping I
wasn't overstepping my bounds. "But with men."

Quentin glanced up at me then, clearly confused. "So?"

"Were you one of them?"

He didn't explode at me or make a disgusted face like
I expected he would. Instead, he shook his head. "I was
with Jessica."

"And she was faithful to you?"

Now I had his attention. Quentin's gaze rose to meet
mine. "She was with me."

"You said earlier you wanted to tame her, that you
thought she might have had other boyfriends, including
while she was with you."

His eyes narrowed slightly and his jaw bunched as he
clenched his teeth. "I did."

"Do you think Mr. Yarborough could have been one of
them?"

Silence. Cold, stony silence.

Paul shifted by the door as if he expected Quentin to
leap across the table at me. With the look he was giving

me, I wasn't so sure he wasn't thinking about it. There was an anger to his eyes, though I wasn't sure whether it was targeted at me or at some residual hate for Jessica and what she'd done to him, real or perceived.

But Quentin didn't budge from his seat. He forced himself to stop clenching his jaw and spoke slowly. "Jessica . . . did things." He took a slow breath. "I don't know any of the men, never cared to. I'm not naïve. She wouldn't suddenly change just because we were dating."

"So you think it could be a possibility that she'd slept with Howard?"

His left eyelid twitched as he answered. "If she thought she could get something out of it, I suppose." It looked as if it hurt him to admit it.

I glanced at Paul, who made a "go on" gesture.

"What do you mean by that?"

Quentin closed his eyes and rubbed at his temples. He kept rubbing as he spoke. "Money. Gifts. She viewed sex as a means to an end. If the guy was young and good looking, then she might do it for fun. If he was older, or ugly, she would look for other ways to benefit."

I was aghast, but couldn't say I didn't suspect it, not after the rumors I'd heard about her. "And you were okay with this?"

He snorted for an answer.

"Do you think she could have slept with Howard Yarborough in the hopes of making some money from it?"

Quentin's hands dropped into his lap as he leaned back in his chair. "I don't know. I blinded myself to how she really was, okay? I wanted her to love me, but I was a fool. Still am, I guess. I knew she went out with me the first time because she thought she could get something from me, but we somehow connected. It might not have been a strong connection, but it was there. I know she felt it, too, or else she would have dropped me long ago."

He looked like he was about to break down and cry, but I couldn't stop, not until I was sure I had everything I could from him about this. I didn't want to have to ask him about any of this ever again. He was already hurting enough, and I was making it worse. If he turned out to be the killer, I wouldn't feel as bad, but for now, I felt like garbage prodding at the wound so much.

"Do you know if she had this 'connection' with anyone else?"

The hurt in Quentin's eye was nearly enough to get me to back off, but one look at Paul told me I was getting somewhere. It might not prove who killed Jessica Fairweather, but it would go a long way in giving him a firmer suspect.

"She might have," he said after a tortured moment. "In fact, after what she did to me, I'm almost sure of it."

"Do you know who?"

He shook his head. His entire body sagged as if defeated. "I was blind."

I hated to do it, but I had to ask, just to be sure. "Did you kill Jessica because you found out she was sleeping around behind your back?"

Quentin didn't get angry. I think he'd already spent it, and all that was left was misery. He looked up at me, eyes filled with sadness, and said, "I didn't hurt her."

"Do you know anyone who might have? Were there any guys hanging around her lately she didn't seem to approve of? Any strange calls or visits? Anything at all you can remember might help."

"When you get involved with Jessica Fairweather, you

know what you are in for," Quentin said. I wasn't sure he actually heard my questions. "No one who had any interest in her would hurt her. She didn't put on airs. She didn't pretend to be something she wasn't." He looked up at me then. "What happened to her had to have been a mistake."

I had nothing further for him. He didn't know who Jessica had been with, and I wasn't going to push the issue any more than I had. Paul seemed satisfied with my questions. He stepped forward and gently led Quentin out of the room, out to wherever he was storing him. I remained seated, feeling like crap for asking such horrible questions. How could anyone do this on a regular basis?

Jessica had been murdered after a failed proposal. It would be easy to simply assume the boyfriend had done it, or one of his friends, or even a jaded ex. It would also be easy to assume she'd been killed because of all of the people she'd been with. Someone had to be unhappy about it.

But we weren't dealing with normal society here. Many of these people here tonight had slept around, if Margaret Yarborough could be believed. Until now, no one had died because of it as far as I was aware. Sure, there was always a first time, but I had a feeling it went deeper. There was something I was missing, some small piece of information that would break the entire case wide open.

But what?

Paul returned a minute later. He stopped just inside the door and crossed his arms over his chest. "What do you think?" he asked.

15

Paul let me return to the ballroom without pressing me on why I thought what I did about Jessica's murder. Either he agreed with me, or he didn't think my assumption had any merit. I was okay with both, really. We would know the answer eventually.

Will was with his friends, and I decided to let him have some time with them. I was afraid he'd want to go talk to Paul about his former relationship with the victim. I know I'd told him he should do it, but I was second-guessing myself. From what I gathered, they'd dated a really long time ago. It shouldn't be pertinent now.

I scanned the rest of the crowd, hoping to spot some of my friends. Jules and Lance were nowhere in sight, and when I saw Vicki, she was standing with Mason, talking to his dad, Raymond, and his latest flame, Regina Harper. No one looked happy in that conversation, and I for one wasn't about to join in on the less-than-pleasant gathering.

I wandered over to the snack table as my stomach gave a loud protest about being ignored for so long. I picked up a cookie and carried it over to the punch, where I grabbed a cup and filled it from the nearest punch bowl. One sniff told me that both my cookie and my drink were pumpkin. I started salivating.

And then I remembered Jessica Fairweather and the pumpkin her body was found sprawled in.

That did it. I set aside the cookie, no longer hungry, and the drink went right back down onto the table. I hoped I wasn't put off pumpkin forever, but for right now, I'd take a pass on it.

"Krissy."

I closed my eyes, counted to three, and then turned, not bothering to even attempt a smile. "What do you want, Robert?"

"I just want to talk," he said, holding out his hands as if to show me they were empty. He wasn't wearing his mask, which was something of a relief. It meant I could tell him off, and look right into his eyes while I was doing it.

"I'm not in the mood to talk," I said with a weary sigh. "There's been a murder if you haven't noticed."

"I have." Robert ran his fingers through his sweaty hair, making it stick up comically. The mask must have come off recently because he looked as if he'd just stepped out of a sauna. A trickle of sweat ran down his forehead, right between his eyes. "And I've been watching you."

"Robert," I said in warning. If he was stalking me again, I was so going to kick his butt into next week.

"It's not like that." His smile appeared genuine, but I knew from experience not to buy it. He could very well be smiling because he was thinking about how he was going to annoy me into dating him again. "You've been running all over the place, talking to everyone. From what I can tell, you've made something of a name for yourself here, solving murders."

"Only two," I said, doing my best to keep my annoyed tone, though I couldn't help but feel flattered. Were people actually talking about me? And here of all places? I would have thought I was as invisible as the help to most of these people, but I guess some of them *were* paying attention to something other than their own personal interests.

"You've changed," Robert said. "You are important in this town. I like that."

"Good for you." I was back to being annoyed with him. He was my ex for a reason and I knew all too well where this conversation was going. "I really have some things to take care of now. Have a nice life." I started to push past him.

Robert grabbed my arm, just above the elbow, and held me firm. "We're not done talking."

"Robert." The warning was much stronger in my voice this time. I had a feeling he was tone-deaf when it came to women telling him they weren't interested. He didn't understand the concept. "Let me go."

Instead of releasing me, he tightened his grip and walked me backward, past the snack table, and into the hall where we were mostly out of sight.

"We need to talk," he said. "I don't think we should keep going like this. We both know that it isn't healthy to harbor so much resentment for each other. We mean far too much to each other for a little mistake to come between us."

I wrenched my arm out of his grip, but stayed where I was, too angry to just walk away. Even if I tried, I knew he would simply grab me again. "You meant something to me once," I said. "But it's over. Can't you get it through your thick skull? I want nothing to do with you."

"You don't mean that."

My eyes widened in disbelief. Did he really not get it? I wasn't sure how I could be any clearer. "Robert," I said as levelly as I could manage. "You cheated on me. You did it more than once. That was more than a little mistake. I *moved* to get away from you." That wasn't quite true, but it was close enough to the truth, I let it slide.

"You ran," he said. "I get that. You needed time to clear your head. I gave you that time."

"No, you didn't. You called me, you invaded Facebook to harass me. And now you're here. That's not giving someone time or space."

He gave me a patronizing look that made me want to hit him. *Keep it cool, Krissy. No need to make a scene.* I breathed in and out slowly and forced my fingers to unclench. I hadn't even realized I'd balled them into fists until that very moment.

"Give me another chance," Robert said. "I could move here; you don't need to come back home." He looked around as if he was thinking of moving into this very house. "I like it here."

"And what about your date?" I asked, snidely. "Will what's her name be happy that you're hitting on your ex? I should go find her right now and have a little talk with her about you."

Robert laughed as if the thought was ridiculous. "Her name is Tiffany, and she doesn't need to know about this." He grinned. "I figure we could get together a few nights and if it doesn't work out, I can go back to her. I'm sure she'll wait for me. There are a few things I could show her."

"Oh. My. God." If anything, or anyone, was about to get shown anything, it was Robert meeting my fist. "You're disgusting."

"You don't mean that." And I could tell he really thought so. It was plastered all over his face in the form of a smug grin.

"I do, Robert. I'm through with you." I took a deep, steadying breath. "You'd better turn around and march your bony butt right out of here or I'm going to break something." His nose was looking like a likely target.

He laughed again, as if he thought I was joking. "Come on, Krissy. What do you have to lose? We had a lot of fun once." He took a step toward me and I took a similar one back. His eyes flashed with annoyance. "Stop being like that."

"Robert, let me spell it out for you." I glanced past him, but as far as I could tell, no help was on the way. I had to admit, I was getting a little scared having him so close, and us being so isolated. "You screwed up. I moved on. I don't want to date you. I don't even want to see you again. Go back to your latest conquest and stay out of my life!"

He blinked at me, slowly, as if trying to process what I'd just said. For a moment, I thought he finally got it, that he would walk away and go bother someone else.

And then he made his move.

He moved so fast, I didn't have time to react. He took two quick strides forward and grabbed both of my arms, jerking me toward him. As I opened my mouth to yell at him to leave me alone, he leaned forward and kissed me, tongue immediately darting into my mouth, choking off any words I might have said.

I reacted instinctively. I didn't think about what I was doing, or what damage I might cause. My teeth clamped shut just as my knee shot straight up with all of the force I could put behind it. It struck Robert right in the crown jewels and I swear I felt something give.

He grunted and then made a high-pitched keening sound as my teeth released his tongue. His hands lost all strength as he staggered back and hit the wall. He slid down it with a moan.

"I warned you," I said, wiping my mouth. He hadn't bled, thankfully, but I desperately wanted the taste of him off my lips. "Leave. Me. Alone."

"Is everything okay back here?"

I looked up to find Will entering the hallway. The girl I'd seen Robert with earlier—Tiffany, I assumed—was right behind him.

"It's fine now," I said. "Isn't that right, Robert?"

He whimpered as he nodded slowly, as if even the movement of his head hurt. Good. I hoped I broke something down there.

"What happened, Robbie?" Tiffany said, hand going to her too-thin waist. When he'd said she was pretty, he hadn't been kidding. From a distance, she'd looked good. Up close, she was a knockout. Her makeup was done in a way to make her look young—like thirteen young—but I could tell she was older. She couldn't have been any more than five feet, and I was pretty sure that was stretching it. Her fingers, like the rest of her body, looked like tiny twigs.

Will looked me up and down as Robert tried to choke

out something. If it wasn't for the wall, he would have been flat on the floor, more than likely in the fetal position, clutching at whatever remained of his manhood.

Since Robert was incapable of answering for himself, I did it for him. "*Robbie* here thought he could try his luck with me again, while stringing you along." I grinned at him. "It didn't work out."

Tiffany gave me a look as if she couldn't fathom his hitting on another girl while she was around. Chances were good it didn't happen often, if ever.

"Robbie, is that true?" she asked him, other hand finding her hip.

He sneered at me as best as he could and shook his head. "Was all her." I think it was all he could manage through the pain, and thanks to his swollen tongue, came out muffled.

Tiffany looked from me, to Robert, and then huffed as she spun on her heel and walked away, leaving Robert on the floor to writhe in pain alone.

"Looks like you've lost another one, champ," I said, stepping past him. A slight pang of guilt swept through me, but I ignored it. He deserved it after everything he'd done. Maybe now he'd get the point.

Will took my arm as we left the hallway and returned to the ballroom. "Are you sure you're okay?" he asked. "I thought I saw you duck into the hall, but I thought you were just talking. When you didn't come out again right away, I started your way. I met her halfway there, heading in the same direction." He nodded toward where Tiffany was already flirting with an older man. "Looks like she saw the same thing I did and got worried."

"I was okay," I said. "Robert pushed a little too hard,

so I was forced to deal with him." And I was darn proud of it, too. I'd wanted to cut Robert down to size for a very long time now, and it felt great to finally have done it. Maybe he'd been right when he'd said I'd changed. And from the looks of it, I was thinking it was for the better.

"I saw that, too," Will said with a grin. "I hope I never get on your bad side. You have a lot of oomph in that knee lift of yours."

I grinned back. "I was motivated." I happened to see Vicki standing alone with Mason, and nodded toward her. "Let's go over and talk to them for a minute." I was anxious to talk to her, especially if we could discuss anything but Robert.

Will nodded his agreement and we headed over to where Vicki and Mason were laughing.

"That was absolutely awful," Mason said. "Did you see how they looked at each other?" He shuddered.

"I bet they don't wait until they get home," Vicki said with a laugh. She saw us approaching. "Mason's dad is in *love*. They snap at each other like they still hate one another, and glare at anyone who even thinks about coming near them, and yet, you can see how much they enjoy it. There's a fire between them, one I hope to never, ever see again."

"They probably spend each and every night insulting each other," Mason added.

"It's just pillow talk," Vicki said with a grin.

Mason faked a heave and then put his arm around Vicki before growing serious. "How are things coming along with the investigation?" he asked me. "You aren't going to point your finger at me again, are you?"

I could tell he was joking, so I stuck my tongue out at

him before answering. "I'm not sure how much progress we're making. The boyfriend is the obvious answer, but I don't think he did it."

"What about that other man?" Vicki asked. "The one who tried to run?"

"Same thing. He admitted to stealing from Mrs. Yarborough, but swears he had nothing to do with Jessica's murder. I believe him, as does Paul."

"Officer Dalton is running himself into the ground on this," Mason said with a nod toward the man in question. He was leaning against the doorframe, scanning the ballroom as if he could pick out the culprit by sight alone. "I hope he comes up with some answers soon. I don't like the idea that there is a killer on the loose, especially since we are trapped in here with him."

"Or her," Vicki added.

"Or her," Mason agreed.

"Has the rain let up yet?" I asked, knowing the answer already. I could hear it pounding the roof of the house over the sound of all the voices.

"No, and I don't think it's going to for a while," Mason said with a glance toward where Igor stood by the doorway.

"Beware the flood," Vicki said, just as the front door flew open and slammed hard against the wall.

Everyone jumped, including Igor, who just about fell over himself to help whoever had entered. It was pitch-black outside and the wind gusted into the room, bringing with it the smell of rain and mud.

"Who could that be?" Will asked, craning his neck.

"I don't know." No one in their right mind would be

out in such a downpour. I stood on my tiptoes to get a better view.

I really wish I hadn't.

Striding into the ballroom, looking like a dirty drowned rat, was Officer John Buchannan. He shook water off his hat, glared at the room in general, as if the rain was all our fault, and then his eyes landed on me. With a grimace, he started my way.

Great. It looked like my already-bad night was about to get a whole lot worse.

16

"It's not stopping anytime soon," Buchannan said. His voice was muffled by a towel as he swept it over his face and hair. "We're stuck in here until it's done."

We were sitting in the makeshift interrogation room. Paul had intercepted Buchannan on his way to me and they'd headed off to talk, alone presumably. I wasn't about to let the investigation go on without me, especially now that Buchannan was here. If I wasn't there to defend myself, I knew he would try to find a way to pin the murder on me. He always had it in for me, and I didn't know why. I didn't do anything to him, yet John Buchannan thought I was the devil incarnate.

Or, if Rita Jablonski was to be believed, he had a deep-rooted love for me. If he did, I had yet to see it.

"Is anyone else coming?" Paul asked. He hadn't wanted me to join them, but since I *had* been helping, he couldn't bring himself to leave me out. After giving him my best puppy-dog eyes, he'd grudgingly stepped aside to let me in.

"Not that I know." Buchannan sighed and threw the towel onto the table, next to the skull. He grimaced at the decorations before going on. "They were still working to get my car out of the way when I decided it best that I come up here to see how I could help."

"We were handling it just fine," I said.

He snorted and paid me only the briefest of glances before turning his attention back to Paul. "Fill me in. All I know so far is that some girl got herself killed. What was her name again?"

"Jessica Fairweather." Paul then related everything we knew about the case to Buchannan. Admittedly, it wasn't much, especially since none of the facts seemed to directly tie to the dead girl as far as we could tell. No one could confirm or deny whether or not she'd slept with Howard Yarborough, let alone whether she was more than an acquaintance to him, or his wife, Margaret.

As Paul talked, I listened, hoping he'd let something slip that I hadn't already known. I couldn't be the only one sticking my nose where it didn't belong, yet the longer he spoke, the more certain I became that I already knew all of the facts, at least all of the ones immediately evident.

We had to be missing something. I couldn't see Quentin as the killer. I suppose if Jessica had slept with Mr. Yarborough and had come looking for money, Margaret could have gotten angry enough to kill her. But I just couldn't see the older woman strangling the much younger, much fitter, Jessica. If it was the other way around, then maybe.

And what about my theory that her death was an accident? I didn't have any facts that pointed to that being the case, but I didn't have any that said otherwise, either. Could she have been in the wrong place at the wrong time? I hated the idea that she'd died for nothing, so it was best I abandon that line of thought until I was certain it could be nothing else.

So where did that leave us? With a mystery killer? Were we both wrong about the boyfriend? As much as I wanted to pin everything on Jessica's less-than-monogamous love life, I couldn't make myself believe it. It was almost *too* obvious, like she was chosen because of her reputation, just to throw us off.

To throw us off of what?

I noticed then that the room had fallen silent and both John and Paul were looking at me.

"What?" I asked.

Before either could say anything, there was a knock at the door. Paul shared a quick look with Buchannan before getting up and crossing the room. He opened the door to find Margaret Yarborough standing with a pile of folded clothes in her arms.

"I thought the officer might want to change out of his wet clothes," she said with a nod to Buchannan. "I didn't know his size, but he looks pretty close to what Howard was before he died."

Buchannan made a face like he didn't like the idea of wearing a dead man's clothes. I didn't blame him; I wouldn't like it, either.

The expression vanished as he stood and smiled. "Thank you," he said, as friendly as could be. He was still dripping mud and water. It was pooling at his feet and on the chair he'd been sitting on. The towel on the table was so filthy, I thought it might be wise for Mrs. Yarborough to save her cleaning lady the trouble and throw the thing out instead of trying to wash it.

But despite the mess he was making, Margaret gave Buchannan a smile and a wink before handing the clothes to Paul. Her gaze passed over me, and I thought I saw the smile grow a tad bit strained, before she turned and closed the door.

Paul set the bundle onto the table, well away from where Buchannan had dripped. A pair of running shoes sat atop a pair of silk boxers. I looked away, unable to keep from snickering. Wearing a dead man's clothing was bad enough; putting on his underwear was just the icing on the cake.

Buchannan grimaced and nudged the pile. "I'll be fine without," he said. "I need a little time to dry out."

"Change, John." Paul was grinning as he said it. "We can't have you running around looking like a drowned cat. This *is* a prestigious party."

Buchannan's grimace turned into a scowl as he set aside the underwear and shoes so he could pick up the shirt. It was a tan button-up shirt, the kind you might see someone's grandpa wear while sitting on the porch, reflecting on the good old days.

"It's too big," he said. He eyed the rest of the outfit— a pair of tan slacks, the silk boxers, white kneesocks, and the running shoes—and shook his head. "I'm not wearing this."

"Just wear the shirt and pants, John. Leave the rest. I don't care if you go commando, just as long as you look more presentable than you do now."

I snickered, which earned me a glare from Buchannan and a brief smile from Paul, who was desperately trying to keep a straight face.

"We'll leave you to it." Paul held out an arm for me.

I took it, savoring the moment. Buchannan looked ready to spit rocks, and I was enjoying every last second of it. He'd tormented me so much in the past, I felt pretty darn good that the shoe was on the other foot now. I really wanted to rub it in, to make fun of him until his head exploded, but decided I was better than that. No need to stoop to his level.

Paul led me out of the room and closed the door behind him, giving Buchannan some privacy. "He's going to hate every moment of this," he said, keeping his voice low so Buchannan couldn't hear.

"Good." The smile that spread across my face measured a mile. "He deserves it."

"Only sometimes," Paul allowed. "He *is* a good cop, and a good man if you let him. He tends to get a bit overzealous at times, but don't we all?" He smiled. "But I do enjoy making him miserable every now and again. Keeps up morale."

A curse came from inside, causing us both to laugh. Our eyes met, and for an instant, it felt like nothing had ever come between us. Those blue eyes of his were like deep pits of clear water sparkling in the afternoon sun. And those dimples . . . I wanted to reach out and trace them with my fingertips so badly, my hands actually moved a fraction of an inch before I caught myself.

We both looked away at the same time. My heart was pounding and my palms were sweaty. I felt like a cheating jerk, though I hadn't actually done anything. I was at the party with Will, and Paul was here with Shannon. We both had dates, and that meant we shouldn't be making eyes at each other, no matter how innocent they might be.

Paul cleared his throat and took a step back. "We should get back to the ballroom. I'll have Buchannan meet us there when he is done and can bring himself to come out." The smile flickered back to life before slipping away.

I nodded, still cursing myself over my moment of perceived weakness. I suppose it was good that I hadn't gone crazy and kissed him, let alone reached out to touch him. If I'd given in, I would be no better than that jerk Robert. Maybe it served me right that he was here on a night when I felt pulled between two men. Maybe I should go back to California with him and let him sleep around on me and party like he was eighteen again. It was what I deserved.

Stop it, Krissy. You didn't do anything. And really, I didn't plan on doing anything that would hurt my chances with Will.

Paul knocked on the door with the back of his hand. "John, meet us in the ballroom when you are done. We're going to have a look around."

His only answer was a string of curses. This time, however, neither Paul nor I could manage a smile.

He led the way back toward the ballroom, walking a good five feet ahead of me, as if he thought the separation would keep anyone from realizing what had happened in the hallway.

But what *did* happen? Nothing, that's what. It wasn't like we'd torn at each other's clothing or anything. In fact, we'd just looked at each other, something people do all of the time. What made it any different for us? Just because we'd once almost dated, doesn't mean we couldn't be

friends. We hadn't touched each other, which was what
would have pushed the moment too far.

The little voice in the back of my head refused to
relent, no matter how much I rationalized it. I kept wondering if Paul had felt something in that moment, too, if
he'd wanted to reach out and touch my cheek. I mean, he
would have had to, right? He'd looked as embarrassed as
I'd felt, so something had to have passed between us.

We entered the ballroom a moment later. Paul stopped
just inside the room and glanced around. Most of the
guests looked annoyed, more than likely because they
felt trapped in the house, which indeed, they were. Even
though they hadn't stopped enjoying the snacks, or visit-
ing the various rooms, they acted as if they were locked
away in a cell at the police station, rather than at a party.

"I should wait here for Buchannan," Paul said.
"Thank you for, uh . . ." He shrugged helplessly. Turns
out, my presence while filling in for Buchannan hadn't
been necessary.

"You're welcome," I said, not really sure what I'd
done, and not caring. It wasn't often I was thanked for
my help. Most of the time, I got told to keep my nose out
of the dangerous investigation. And even after I helped
solve the cases, I was warned not to do it again.

So, this, I would take.

I wasn't sure where to go from there. I glanced around
the room, hoping to spot Will, but I didn't see him anywhere. He was probably exploring with Darrin or Carl,
or off with his parents. Vicki was with Mason, talking to
a couple I didn't know. Both Jules and Lance were
back, picking over the snacks and talking with their
heads nearly touching. Both were smiling, as if they

were sharing some deep, dark secret about someone or something in the house.

I decided I'd head over and see if they'd include me in on the joke. Lord knows I needed something to lift my spirits just then. Even the thought of seeing Buchannan dressed like an old man wasn't as appealing as it was only a few minutes ago.

I made it only a step when Igor came running over to where Paul stood. I did a complete three sixty and turned to face them, not wanting to miss whatever he had to say.

"Officer," he said. He was out of breath as if he'd run this entire way. "I tried to stop him."

"Stop who?" Paul was all business, alert and ready for action. His back straightened and those blue eyes of his sharpened like razors.

"I don't know his name." Igor glanced over his shoulder before turning back to Paul. "He pushed past me when I tried to stop him. He went out the front door."

Paul and I shared a look. We were both thinking the exact same thing.

Someone was trying to escape.

"Stay here," Paul commanded, loud enough that most of the people around us heard. He bolted for the door, hand going to his bobby hat to keep it from flying off his head.

I looked at Igor, who looked back, eyes wide and scared, like he just now realized there really *was* a killer on the loose, and that he might very well have had contact with him.

"Keep everyone inside," I told him. "If the other policeman comes looking for us, tell him where we've gone." I didn't like the idea of Buchannan looking for

me, but if it *was* the murderer out there, I'd appreciate
the backup.

And then, pointedly ignoring Paul's orders, I took off
after him.

The rain was still coming down pretty hard, making it
hard to see as I stepped outside. I squinted into the downpour and, at first, didn't see anyone. Then, I caught a
glimpse of Paul, dressed in that silly old police uniform.
He was heading toward the parking lot, shoulders
hunched against the rain.

I took a step forward, wincing as the icy cold rain
slammed into me like it was intent on driving me into the
ground. I pulled my hat down over my ears, for the first
time thankful I had it, and started for Paul. I'd only taken
a couple of steps when I saw movement out of the corner
of my eye.

This man wasn't near the cars where Paul was investigating. In fact, he was moving away from them, heading
toward the side of the property where the trees would
give him cover.

And Paul didn't see him.

"Paul!" I shouted, waving my arms above my head.
"Over there!"

He didn't so much as glance my way. The rain hitting
the hoods of the cars was probably as loud as a drum.
Even if I'd been standing next to him, he would have had
a hard time hearing me.

The shape stumbled and fell in the mud before he
pushed back to his feet. He staggered forward a few more
steps and then vanished into the deluge.

I had a split second to make up my mind. I could run
over to Paul and tell him what I saw so he could give chase.

But that would take too much time. The man was already out of sight. By the time I reached Paul, told him which way to go, our suspect would be gone.

There was really only one option.

With one last futile glance toward where Paul was leaning down to peer between the cars, I hiked up my pants and started running.

17

My foot sank a good three inches into the soft, rain-drenched soil as I attempted to run toward where I'd last seen the retreating figure. For someone with so much money, Margaret Yarborough did a pretty poor job of taking care of her property. I knew it was raining, but there were muddy holes filled with water in the yard, as if she had a big dog that had decided to go on a buried bone hunt. It was making progress difficult, to say the least.

A curse broke through the downpour and I altered my course toward it. I was closer than I thought because after only a few soggy steps, I saw my target rising from the ground where he'd apparently fallen. The man was fat, and while I couldn't see his face, I was pretty sure I recognized the shape of his body from the party. If I wasn't mistaken, he'd been wearing a monocle and doing a lot of complaining.

"Hey!" I shouted. "Stop!"

The man glanced back once and then started slogging through the muck again. He wasn't wearing a monocle now, but that one glimpse of his rain-slicked face was enough to assure me it was the same man.

It was like running through a swamp as I gave chase. I was making better progress than the fatter man, thanks to our weight difference. He seemed to sink down to mid-calf with every step.

Still, it felt like I'd run three miles, even though we were only a dozen yards from the house or so. I sucked in a deep breath, nearly choked on a mouthful of rain, and then rushed forward with everything I had. There was no way I was going to get outrun by a man twice my size!

The property had started to slope gently downward, toward the smattering of pine trees that lined the property. The man was making for them, huffing and puffing with every step. I had a feeling that if he made it to the safety of the trees, I would lose him for good.

"Halt!" I shouted, putting as much command into my voice as I could.

"Leave me alone!" the man shouted back, pausing in his escape long enough to look back at me. "I just want to go home."

Right, I thought. *And I'm the queen of England.* I had no doubt he would make a quick stop at home, long enough to pack his things so he could flee the country. Why else would he be running away, in the rain, after a murder, if he wasn't the one who had committed it?

"Careful, Krissy. He might have a weapon." It was Paul's voice in my head, yet I ignored it like I would ignore my own. If the big man pulled a gun on me, I'd just have to hope the rain would foul up his aim enough that I could get inside his reach and disarm him. Never mind the fact I'd learned how to go hand to hand. I was hoping my adversary was just as ignorant as I was.

My quarry gave an exasperated sigh and turned to face me. "You really shouldn't have followed me out here. I have nothing you want." He reached into his inside coat pocket.

My mind flared a bright scarlet. *Holy crap!* He really did have a gun! I was only a handful of slippery strides away, so if I let him pull the weapon, he'd have to be blind to miss me. I sucked in a deep breath, and not wanting to give him the chance to shoot me, I threw myself at him, just as his hand came from inside his coat, holding a large, cylindrical object.

I roared in defiance. It might not be a gun, but he could bludgeon me with it all the same. He opened his mouth as I barreled into him, using my arm to knock the item from his hand. We both went down into the mud, me on top, and him on his back. He grunted in pain as we hit the ground. I grabbed for his wrists, but he slapped my hands away.

"What are you doing?" he shouted. His face was splotchy red, as if he was having a hard time breathing. I doubted a man his size could sleep on his back comfortably. "Get off of me!"

"You're not going to hurt anyone else," I said. "I'm putting you under citizen's arrest until Officer Dalton gets here." I wasn't sure that was an actual thing, but it sounded official enough in the heat of the moment.

"Arrest?" the man sputtered. Water pounded into his face, causing him to have to squint at me. "I didn't do anything."

"Tell that to the cops," I said, feeling more and more empowered by the second. This was the first time I'd taken down a suspect on my own, without breaking something in the process. "Stand up slowly and don't try anything, or else I'll have to knock you down again."

"You'll have to get off of me first."

I scrambled off the man and stepped back, just in case he made a lunge for me. He rolled over onto his stomach and pushed himself to his feet, grunting and cursing all the way. He gave me an annoyed look before scouring the ground for the item he'd pulled out of his coat.

"Leave it," I warned him, tensing. If he made a grab for it, I wouldn't hesitate. I refused to let anyone get the jump on me ever again.

The man ignored me. He took two steps to the left and I prepared to tackle him again. He looked down at something between his feet for a long moment before spinning to face me.

"You broke it!" he shouted in obvious rage. "Do you realize how expensive that bottle was?"

"Bottle?" My face crinkled up in confusion. "What bottle?"

"The bottle of wine you broke, you nincompoop!" His voice rose in pitch. "It's ruined." He sounded ready to cry.

I looked past him to the spot behind him, and sure enough, shattered glass lay around a quickly thinning pool of deep crimson.

My first instinct was to apologize, but I squashed it immediately. He'd pulled the bottle out of his coat after fleeing the scene of a crime. How was I to know he wasn't planning on hitting me with it? If he didn't want the thing broken, he shouldn't have run in the first place.

"Let's go," I told him, sounding far less sure of myself than I had a moment ago.

The man huffed and began trudging his way back to

the house. After one last quick look at the shattered bottle of wine, I followed after him.

Igor was standing at the door when we returned. He looked anxious until he spotted us. His face brightened, and he looked so relieved, I thought he might faint, before he stepped aside, and said, "This way, madam. He's waiting for you."

I put a hand on the fat man's elbow and led him after Igor, who was leading the way. I was dripping wet, covered in mud, yet as we passed through the ballroom, I felt like a hero. People stood at the doorway, watching, muttering to each other as they pointed at us. I straightened my back and raised my chin, happy I'd finally done something right and was going to be recognized for it.

"In here," Igor said, motioning toward the bathroom I'd found Quentin in earlier that night.

"Thank you," I told him. "Inside." That to my prisoner.

He muttered something under his breath, but entered. I followed after, a grin splitting my face.

Paul was standing at the sink, a towel draped over his shoulder. He was drenched, but still in the same old-style police uniform I'd last seen him in. His scowl turned to concern when he saw us enter.

"Are you all right?" he asked, looking right past the big man, to me.

"Peachy," I said, and I meant it. I might be dirty and out of breath, but I'd caught my man. "I found our killer."

"Killer?" the fat man said, sounding surprised. "I didn't kill anyone." He turned to Paul and jabbed a finger at me. "You should be arresting *her*!"

Paul looked back and forth between us before shaking his head. "Not here." He grabbed two towels off a stack on the counter, tossing one to each of us. "Follow me."

We headed down the hall, Paul in the lead, me bringing up the rear, and into the makeshift interrogation room. I glanced back once and winced at the trail of mud and water in our wake, but figured Margaret could afford to have it cleaned. As soon as we were all inside, Paul closed the door and turned to face our latest suspect.

"Tell me why you ran, Mr. . . ."

"Berry. Bertrand Berry." The fat man looked down at himself and grimaced. "These clothes are ruined." He held the towel in one hand, not using it.

"I think you have a little more to worry about than how much your dry cleaning will cost you," Paul said, motioning toward the chairs.

Bertrand heaved a sigh but didn't sit. "I didn't do anything," he said. "Well, nothing that anyone else here wouldn't do." He leveled a finger at me. The ring there was coated in mud. "She destroyed a very expensive bottle of wine."

Paul glanced at me.

"He pulled it out of his coat," I said. "I thought it might be a weapon."

Bertrand snorted. "I never would have hit you with it, you moron. I was going to show it to you so you would leave me alone."

"Maybe you should have *told* me that first!"

"Maybe you should have paid more attention to what was going on, rather than assault me." He turned to Paul. "I want to press charges!"

"You! You're the one who was running away and threatening me!"

"I never threatened you."

"You did!"

Paul raised both of his hands, and his voice. "Both of you, stop. Tell me what happened, like reasonable adults."

Before either of us could speak, there was a knock at the door. Paul jammed his fingers into his eyes and rubbed as he called out a weary, "What?"

"Mrs. Yarborough wishes to speak to you," Buchannan said from the other side of the door. "It has something to do with the man you're currently talking to."

Paul continued to rub at his eyes a moment longer before sighing, and said, "Okay, fine. Bring her in."

The door opened and Margaret strode in, looking aghast. I wasn't sure if it was because of our suspect, or if it had to do with all of the mud and water we'd tracked in. I held up my towel, as if proving that I wasn't doing it on purpose and was in the process of trying to sop up most of the mess.

She didn't look impressed. "My heavens," she said. "What happened?"

"That's what I'm trying to figure out," Paul said. He nodded once to Buchannan, who stepped back out of the room and closed the door.

"He was trying to flee the premises," I said, trying to sound official. "I stopped him before he could escape."

"As I told you before, I was trying to get home." Bertrand said it like he was talking to a stubborn child. "And this woman knocked me over and shattered my bottle of Pétrus."

Margaret's hand fluttered to her chest. "The Pétrus? It was the last one!"

"Hold up," Paul said. "Start from the beginning and tell me exactly what happened."

Bertrand patted at his pockets as if looking for something, before frowning. "I was . . . borrowing a bottle of wine from Mrs. Yarborough. I wanted to take it home before something happened to it, when this woman came out of nowhere and attacked me."

"You weren't supposed to leave," I said. "Police orders!"

Paul's jaw clenched as he looked to Margaret. "Is what he said true?"

"I don't know anything about him getting attacked, but I am sure Bertrand had the bottle. He takes something every year."

A suspicious look glinted in Paul's eye. "Takes?"

Margaret waved a dismissive hand in front of her face. "It's nothing. Every year, things come up missing. Wine. Art. Silverware. It happens."

"So, he was stealing it?" Paul asked.

"I suppose you could call it that."

I looked dumbly from Margaret to Paul, then back again. "He was stealing from you, and you're okay with it?"

"It's just wine."

"But the jewelry. You were upset that someone had taken it."

"That's different, dear." Margaret gave me a simpering smile. "They are far more personal and dear to me than some old bottle of wine, no matter the vintage."

"It's ruined," Bertrand lamented. He looked like he was going to cry. "And I didn't even get to taste it! The bottle was still unopened."

"How much are we talking about here?" Paul asked.

Margaret shrugged. "It was a good vintage," she said. "I believe Howard had paid just over two thousand for it."

The whole room seemed to tip sideways. I took a

hasty step back and braced myself against the wall. *Did she just say two thousand?*

Paul looked as flabbergasted as I did, but managed to keep his cool. "Why were you running, then?" he asked.

"I wasn't running anywhere," Bertrand said. "With the police all over the place, I thought it would be prudent to get the wine out of sight before you started searching people. I didn't want to have to explain myself."

Too late for that. His excuse was sounding all too familiar. It was almost identical to the story Reggie Clements had told us, just replacing jewelry with wine.

"Do you really think we would have been suspicious of you?" Paul asked, his patience clearly at an end. No one was listening to his commands, and it was making his job harder. "Running only makes you look guilty."

"It *was* an expensive bottle." Bertrand said it as if it made everything okay.

Paul took a deep breath and let it out slowly. "Okay." He glanced at me and I could see a hint of irritation there. I wasn't sure if it was directed at me or at the situation in general. Under the circumstances, I let it slide without getting offended. He was having a rough time of it and didn't need me telling him it wasn't my fault.

"I'm going to need you to come with me," he told Bertrand, turning to the big man. "Once you're secure, I'll get you something else to dry off with." One towel was obviously not going to be enough.

"There are more towels in the hall closet upstairs," Margaret put in.

"Thank you." Paul took Bertrand by the arm. "Once you're dry, we'll have a nice little chat." He glanced at me again. "Alone." And then he led him out the door, and away.

Margaret clucked her tongue at me the moment they were gone. "You are quite the mess, aren't you, dear?" She looked me up and down as if appraising me. "I think I have something that will fit you."

"Thank you," I said, stepping away from the wall. A smear of mud remained behind.

"Come with me." She crooked her finger at me. "We'll go somewhere private where you can change. I think you might want to take a shower." Her eyes went to my hair where my hat was somehow still in place. "You look absolutely dreadful."

We started for the door, but she stopped just before we reached the hall. "Would you mind taking off your shoes?" she asked. "I can't have you tracking mud all over my carpet upstairs and ruining it. Now *that* would be a shame!"

18

Margaret led me upstairs, into her private bathroom where, in her words, "No man will accidentally walk in on you." She set a pair of white towels on the sink for me to use.

"Thank you," I told her, marveling at the size of the bathroom. It was as big as my living room and, thankfully, missing all of the horror furnishings of the rest of the house.

"It's nothing, dear," she said. She started for the door and then paused, turning back to me. "I hope you settle this mess soon. It's putting everyone through a tremendous amount of stress."

For the first time since Jessica's murder, Margaret Yarborough *looked* like it was wearing on her. She'd been so composed and restrained before, yet now, I could see the stress lines at the corners of her eyes, the way those eyes were pinched with worry. Her hands were clutched at her waist, bones showing through the skin. She was no longer the demure Audrey Hepburn, but instead, an overly stressed widow, trying to hold it together.

"I'm going to try my best," I said.

Her smile was shaky as she stepped outside the bathroom. "I'll find you something to wear." She closed the door behind her.

The bathroom smelled like lilies in bloom. A garden tub teeming with jets rested beneath a skylight. A stand-up shower was in the corner. I eyed the shower for a long moment and nearly eschewed it for a nice, long bath in the tub. If it wasn't for the fact I was in someone else's house with a murder to solve, I very well might have done it.

With a sigh, I stripped out of my filthy clothes and left them in a pile by the sink. The floor would need to be cleaned afterward, but I didn't know where else to put them. With a quick check to make sure the door was locked—it wasn't—I stepped into the shower.

There was enough room behind the frosted doors to fit six or seven people. I couldn't help but wonder if it had ever held that many. After what I'd learned about the Yarboroughs, I felt it likely. The showerhead was as large as a dinner plate and had so many dials and knobs, I wasn't quite sure what to do.

Thankfully, turning the shower on was easy enough. The spray was a bit soft for my tastes, but I wasn't about to start fiddling with all of the knobs, knowing I'd probably break the thing before I found a setting I liked. I hurriedly soaped up, shampooed my hair, and rinsed off. I smelled like expensive perfume as I stepped out of the shower and reached for the towels. Like most everything in the bathroom, they smelled of flowers in bloom, and I felt like I was wrapping myself in a very large, very soft kitten.

"I need to find better towels," I grumbled as I dried

off. My hair wasn't going to dry anytime soon, not unless I wanted to search for a hairdryer, so I did the best I could with the towel. I stepped into my still-damp underwear, strapped on my bra, and then wrapped the other towel around me, tucking it in so it would stay in place. I headed for the door, which led into Margaret's bedroom, hopeful I would be left alone to change.

No one was in immediate evidence as I peeked out the door. Margaret's bedroom looked like something straight out of a *Dracula* movie. There were red silks hanging from the walls, which were designed to look like castle walls. A chill worked through me as I stepped into the room, as if I could feel a cold breeze seeping through the faux stone. A fireplace sat against one wall, and the charred logs inside told me it was a real one.

A bundle sat on the gigantic gothic bed, right beside two large white Persians who were watching me with interest. Both had eyes that were pale blue, and I was instantly in love.

"Hi, kitties," I said as I walked over to them. "You really are beautiful." And they were. I loved cats, though they often weren't nearly as fond of me as I was of them. These two sat on the red bedspread, looking all the world like show cats waiting to be judged.

Carefully, as not to startle them, I reached out and pet one. Its purr was deep, and rewarding blue eyes closed ever so slightly. "That's a good kitty." If I could have taken them home, I would have. Misfit might not have approved, but he'd get over it. He might be a terror sometimes, but really, he's a giant softy, and I was sure he wouldn't mind a few play friends.

After petting the other cat—neither had moved, other than to lean into my hand—I turned my attention to the pile of clothes Margaret had left for me. The shirt was plain white and a little too large for my frame. The pants were just a pair of gray sweatpants that were likewise too large and baggy. Neither were Margaret's, of that I was sure. She wouldn't have been caught dead in something like these. At least the sweatpants had a pair of pockets in the front where I could shove my cell phone and keys.

I dropped the towel on the floor, beside a pair of sneakers I assumed were for me. My shoes were currently sitting inside a trash bag sitting beside the sneakers. I put on the borrowed clothes, grabbed the trash bag, and went into the bathroom to deposit my Sherlock Holmes outfit into the bag with my shoes. I went back to the bedroom and slipped on the off-white sneakers, which smelled oddly of olives.

I started to head back for the trash bag, as ready to return to the party as I was going to get in my unflattering garb, when a devious thought entered my head.

No one else was in the room with me, and Margaret had no way of knowing if I was done with the shower or not. She was probably back downstairs, entertaining guests, which meant I might not be disturbed for a good long while.

My eyes fell on the closet where Reggie Clements had hid when he'd attempted to return the stolen jewelry. Could a clue be inside? I doubted Jessica had been in here, and as far as I knew, the killer hadn't been in the room, either.

But I couldn't pass up the opportunity. I checked the bedroom door to make sure no one was standing outside and then closed it again before heading over to the closet. It was one of those large walk-in types that I always wanted, but never had. Fancy clothes hung on hangers, many of them in dry-cleaning bags. There was a rack for Margaret's shoes that seemed to go on forever. How could any one woman own so many shoes? I had a half dozen at best.

There wasn't much else of interest at first glance. I pushed aside some of the clothes, and there it was, hanging from a hanger, looking rumpled, as if hastily shoved inside and forgotten.

I restrained myself from touching the white Monroe dress, just in case it was needed for evidence later. I carefully lifted the hanger and pulled it from the closet where I had better light. Other than its rumpled state, the dress looked pristine. There were no telltale pumpkin stains or smudges on it as far as I could tell. It looked like Margaret had been telling the truth and she'd simply changed because she didn't want to wear the same costume as a murdered woman.

But if that was the case, why did she have a spare costume at the ready?

I looked back into the closet and checked the other articles inside, including peeking into some of the dry-cleaning bags. I couldn't find any other costumes, though there were some dresses extravagant enough for a queen. I supposed it was possible she'd bought two costumes just in case she spilled something on the first, or perhaps had a planned costume change during the evening. It was something I'd have to ask her the next time I saw her.

I shoved the Monroe dress back where I found it and then did my best to push the other clothes back where they'd been. I doubted Margaret would realize I'd been snooping, but figured it would be best not to take any chances.

My next stop was at the long dresser where the jewelry box had been. Had Margaret removed it once she realized the jewelry was missing? Had someone else? I opened a few drawers and peeked inside, feeling like a thief, even though I wasn't planning on stealing anything. There were boxes inside, but all of them were full. I was pretty sure Paul still had the set Reggie had attempted to steal, so where was the box? And did it even matter?

I turned and glanced around the room. There were other drawers and dressers, including the bedside nightstand. And I hadn't bothered looking under the bed, though it was often a place people hid things they didn't want people to stumble across.

I felt guilty about my snooping and didn't think I could bring myself to go through more of Margaret's life. There was nothing in here that pointed to a reason for Jessica Fairweather's murder, so why keep poking around? It wasn't like I'd read Margaret's diary if I were to find it.

I started to walk away when I noted a framed photograph lying facedown atop the dresser. A box of tissues sat on it, mostly obscuring it from view. I removed the tissue box, set it aside, and then picked up the photograph.

It was of Margaret and Howard Yarborough, dressed as if they'd just come from a party. She was wearing a tight black dress and diamonds that sparkled in the light. He was wearing a tux, white hair parted at the side. They were both smiling, and I had the impression that the smiles were genuine. These weren't unhappy people. They stood close together, her arm tangled in his own. I couldn't imagine the rumors were true and she'd killed him for his money.

Of course, jealousy and greed often made people do strange things. This photograph could be a few years old, and had been lying facedown with something sitting atop it. You didn't treat treasured memories that way. Could someone else have done it? Or were things between Margaret and her husband tenser than it appeared.

I started to set the photo back down, but paused. Something bothered me about it, something I couldn't put my finger on. Margaret looked much the same as she did now, though the stress wasn't as evident on her features. Howard, with his white hair, his pointed, beak-like nose, was the one who was causing the pinging in my mind. I stared into his dark blue eyes and tried to figure out what it was.

Had I seen him somewhere before? He very well might have come into Death by Coffee a few times. But if he had, I sure didn't remember him. I tried to make out what was in the background of the photo, but the lights were too bright, and with how the focus had been on the couple, it was too blurry to make out, anyway.

I placed the photograph back where I'd found it, replaced the tissue box, and stood staring at it, head buzzing. There was definitely something about the photo of Howard that had my brain running triple time.

I peered around the room one more time, hoping something there would jog my memory. There were no photographs or portraits on the wall, nothing that hinted that Howard ever lived here—other than the horror movie decorations.

"I'm going to hate myself for this," I muttered to myself as I started for the bed. I pet each of the Persians and then got down on my knees. I might not have wanted to keep snooping around, but the photograph was pointing me somewhere, and I needed to figure out where and why.

I lifted the comforter and leaned down to look. Other than a toy mouse, there was nothing beneath the bed.

A gentle cough brought me flying to my feet in a flurry of damp hair. A middle-aged woman dressed in the waitress outfits that all the female help was wearing stood just inside the doorway, a disapproving frown on her face.

"Sorry," I said meekly. "I was looking for my shoes."

Her eyes traveled down to my borrowed sneakers before returning to my face, skepticism heavy.

"These aren't mine," I said. "Margaret gave them to me to wear since mine are soaked."

The woman sighed. "I don't care." She stepped aside, a clear indication I was to leave. "Mrs. Yarborough wished for me to make sure you were okay, and to invite you back to the party."

"Thank you," I said, knowing I'd been caught but hoping the woman wouldn't tell. She looked bored, and really, not the type to tattle. It wasn't like she'd caught me with an armload of jewelry.

"Uh-huh." The woman tapped her foot as she waited for me to go.

I took a moment to grab my phone and keys from the bathroom counter and then hurried out of the room, leaving my dirty clothes behind. I made my way back to the ballroom, hoping that, once there, I'd figure out what had bothered me so much about the photograph, and whether or not it had anything to do with Jessica Fairweather's murder.

19

"Here we go again." Buchannan leveled a glare my way. "Is there something I can help you with, Ms. Hancock?"

I almost turned and walked away, not wanting to deal with Buchannan while I asked Mrs. Yarborough a few questions. For whatever reason, the man despised me, and the feeling was mutual. He thought of me as an annoyance, someone who couldn't keep her nose out of other people's business. He'd accused me more than once of inserting myself into an investigation and mucking things up.

And I guess he had something of a point, but come on! How am I *not* supposed to get involved when the murders are happening around me, sometimes in my very own store? And while he might think I'm screwing things up with all of my nosy questions, I've actually helped out. Two murderers were behind bars because of me. Without my interference, they very well might have gotten away with it.

Of course, Buchannan thought otherwise. If he could

get away with locking me into a cell and throwing away the key, I was pretty sure he'd do it.

"I have a few questions for Mrs. Yarborough," I told him, doing my best to sound as if I had every right to be interrupting whatever he'd been saying to her.

Buchannan scowled at me. "Does this have anything to do with the murder investigation? Because if it does . . ."

"It doesn't." I paused, not quite able to follow through with lying to the police, even if it *was* John Buchannan. "Well, not really."

His eyes narrowed at me. "Ms. Hancock . . ."

"It will only take a minute," I said, hurriedly. "I'm not trying to butt in. Mrs. Yarborough was kind enough to let me use her bathroom to clean up, and I want to thank her." Along with asking her a few choice questions, of course.

Buchannan eyed me up and down and a grin inverted his scowl. "I'm not sure the new outfit does what you were hoping for."

"Ha, ha," I deadpanned, but blushed anyway. I wish I could have forgotten about the horrible outfit Margaret had left for me, but it was kind of hard considering I was wearing it. "Just a minute," I said. The next came out with some difficulty. "You can listen in if you want."

"It's okay, John," Margaret said, resting a hand on his wrist. "If it will help, I'll answer anything. This whole mess has put a damper on my party, as well as my husband's memory. I want to put it all behind me as fast as I can."

John? I thought, watching as his eyes softened and his entire posture relaxed when he turned his attention back to her. I don't know what it was, but it seemed like older women always erased some of his harsher edges.

Buchannan glanced at me and then sighed. "All right," he said. "But if you go too far, I'm going to step in."

"Works for me."

He snorted and crossed his arms.

I did my best to ignore him as I turned to Margaret. "First of all, thank you for letting me use your facilities. I feel much better." Despite my still-damp hair and ugly clothing.

"It was no problem, dear."

I gave Buchannan a sideways glance. "You told me earlier that you and your husband . . ." I trailed off, uncertain I wanted to air her dirty laundry in front of my arch nemesis, but it couldn't be helped. I told him he could stay. "That you slept around."

She nodded, not a bit perturbed. "We did. It was a mutual agreement, let me assure you." She smiled at Buchannan. "Many young men have crossed my bed." And then she winked at him, causing his face to turn a deep crimson.

"How many of these people are here tonight?" I asked, pressing on. I wasn't convinced their sex life was the reason Jessica Fairweather was murdered, but right then, it was really all I had to go on. Maybe a name would jump out at me, or somehow tell me why Howard's photograph had pinged something in my mind.

"Quite a few, actually." Margaret glanced into the ballroom, as if looking for them.

"Would you mind writing the names down?" I asked.

Buchannan's embarrassment had passed. Instead, he

looked interested in the conversation. "Does Officer Dalton know about this?"

Both Margaret and I nodded, though she was the one to answer. "It is common knowledge, really. Most everyone here has spent time with a few people in the room." She shrugged dismissively. "It's natural to seek out the influential for companionship, even if it is for only a few hours."

I wasn't so sure about that, but hey, whatever floated their boats, right? "The list would really help," I said. "Maybe someone on it could tell us more about Jessica, and whether or not she was involved with Howard in any way."

Margaret gave me a smile that was just this side of condescending. "I'm sure it will be a waste of time, dear. None of the men I've been with would know anything about that, let alone hurt the poor girl."

"But the woman your husband was with might have a reason," I said. "And perhaps someone saw something one late night that would lead to catching the killer. You know, like boats passing in the night?"

She rolled her eyes. "If you say so," she said. "But I find it highly unlikely. And as I said before, I don't know all of their names, just the ones who have come asking for handouts since his death."

"Any would help."

She sighed, clearly put out. "Let me get it for you. I'll be right back." She turned and strode down the hall.

"You should let me handle this," Buchannan said as soon as she was gone. "You shouldn't be the one asking these questions."

"Paul sent me." It was a lie, sure, but he had asked me

to help earlier, so I was just extending my assistance. "I'll take him the list as soon as I have it." And had a chance to peruse it for a name I might recognize.

Buchannan looked skeptical but didn't press. He appeared contemplative. I think it was the first time I ever did or said anything he didn't immediately dislike. If he kept it up, he might actually start to like me a little.

Margaret returned a few minutes later, a piece of paper in hand. She handed it to me. "As I said before, I don't know how this will help. Everyone on here is here tonight. I left off anyone who isn't present, or with us anymore." She looked past me, as if remembering a long-lost love, before sighing. "I should mingle." She started away.

"Mrs. Yarborough, wait," I said. She turned to face me slowly, as if she'd considered pretending not to have heard and walking away. "I have a few more questions."

"I really am busy, dear."

Buchannan's eyes narrowed at that, as if he found the reaction suspect. I took it more like she was annoyed at being asked so many questions. It was a common reaction most people had when I was around. Go figure.

"It will only take a sec."

Margaret's sigh was more of a huff this time. "Fine," she said, waving a dismissive hand at me. "Ask your questions."

My feathers ruffled a bit at that. *Let it go, Krissy.* Some people were just like that. And I *was* asking her some pretty personal questions.

"You said earlier that you changed your costume because you didn't want to be seen wearing the same thing as the victim."

Margaret nodded. "That's right."

"It's totally understandable. I know I wouldn't have wanted to be seen in the same outfit."

She frowned. "Is there a point to this?"

"I was just wondering; why did you have a spare costume on hand?"

She seemed surprised by the question. "What do you mean?"

"Well, I only had the one outfit," I said, lamenting the condition of the Holmes costume. I might have felt uncomfortable in it before, but it had been far better than what I was wearing now. "Yet, you had a second on hand. Why?"

Margaret didn't answer right away. She eyed me, as if determining whether or not I was accusing her of something. To be honest, I wasn't sure if I was. I was curious, and maybe just a little suspicious. Chances were good I was reading too much into it.

"It was a spare," she said after a moment. "Howard had asked me to wear it to this year's event. He was going to wear something to go with it. It was decided on last year and I bought the dress then, certain I was going to wear it." She looked down at her Audrey Hepburn dress. "When Howard passed, I no longer wished to wear it. Then I saw the Marilyn Monroe outfit and decided to make the switch. I kept the other outfit because it was far too late to take it back, and it could serve as a spare in case something like this happened."

"A murder?"

"No, dear," she said with a wry smile. "Someone else wearing same thing. It happens more than I would like, so I thought it would be a perfect backup. I only wish that officer would give me back my jewelry so I could complete the outfit."

I considered asking her about the whereabouts of the box the jewelry had been in, but decided that would give my snooping away. It wasn't important, anyway. She could have put it somewhere else, or perhaps Reggie had taken it and dropped it in the trash at some point. Just because I believed most of this story, didn't mean he'd been entirely honest with us.

Besides, after hearing her reason for having two costumes, I felt bad. It had to be hard, even now, to wear the Hepburn dress. It had to remind her of her husband, as did everything else in the house. Was it any wonder she'd turned the photograph facedown? It probably hurt too much to look at it.

"If there isn't anything else . . . ?" She motioned toward the ballroom, eyebrows raised in question.

"That will be all," Buchannan answered for me. "Thank you for your time and cooperation."

"It was no trouble." She glanced at me and then gave Buchannan a curt nod, before sashaying into the ballroom.

"What was that all about?" he asked when she was gone.

"I'm trying to get all of the facts," I said. "Officer Dalton asked for my help and I'm giving it."

"I'm pretty sure he doesn't want you grilling the guests. What does her dress have to do with anything?"

I shrugged. "I don't know. Maybe nothing." At least now I understood her reasoning better.

Buchannan chewed on his lower lip and then held out his hand. "Let me see that."

I considered hurrying away without giving him the list but decided that while he was being civil with me, I should do the same. I handed it to him and waited while he read through the names.

"Does any of it mean anything to you?"

His eyes flickered up toward me, before going back to the list. "There are a lot of names here."

"Any of them familiar?" I had yet to peek at the list and was curious.

"Some." He frowned, as if coming across a name he didn't suspect. Then he surprised me by handing the list back to me. "Take it to Officer Dalton. Get his take on it."

I nearly fainted. Was Buchannan actually accepting my help? I glanced upward to make sure the sky wasn't about to come crashing down on my head before taking the list.

I walked away, almost certain Buchannan's usual nature would kick in and he'd yell at me to get back there and hand over the evidence. Yet I made it all the way to the ballroom without him calling out to me. When I glanced back, he was gone, presumably to continue his own investigation.

Maybe he's not so bad, after all. It was a thought I never imagined having.

I looked down at the paper in my hand. The list was indeed extensive, so much so, it was mind-boggling. I couldn't imagine sleeping with this many people, not in an entire lifetime. I didn't recognize most of the names, thankfully. There were a few that made my skin crawl, like Raymond Lawyer, and some that didn't surprise me at all. Nothing immediately jumped out at me, but I never truly thought it would. I didn't see Jessica Fairweather's name on the list, but I expected that, since Margaret already told me she didn't know if the girl had been with her husband or not.

Once through the list, I carried it over to Paul, who was standing only a few yards away, talking with Shannon, who didn't appear to be happy. Her arms were crossed as she listened to him, not meeting his eye. She looked hurt, perhaps even sad. I actually felt bad, as if it was somehow my fault, though I knew it probably had more to do with the investigation than anything.

I gave them a moment before approaching. "Paul," I said. "I don't mean to interrupt, but I have something for you."

He glanced at me before turning back to Shannon, as if to say something. She waved him off, and said, "Go. Do what you have to do."

"I'll make it up to you," he said. "I promise." He turned to me with some reluctance and led me a few paces away. "What do you have?"

I handed him the list. "They're names of people Margaret Yarborough, uh, slept with." My ears felt suddenly hot.

He eyed the page. "There are women's names here."

"Those are Howard's." Pause. "Before he died." As if he wouldn't know that.

Paul read the list a couple of times before glancing up at me. "Do you think anyone here could have had anything to do with the murder?" He sounded as skeptical as I felt about the possibility.

"I don't know, but figured it would be a good place to start. We're getting nowhere otherwise."

"No, I'm not," he muttered, before sighing. "I should

talk to Mrs. Yarborough." He glanced around the room, spotting her almost immediately. "Thank you," he told me.

"No problem." He started to walk away, but I stopped him as another thought hit me. "Ask her about what Reggie said about hearing people arguing in her bedroom, if you haven't already. If it was her, maybe she can shed some light on what it was about. If not . . ." I left the rest for him to fill in.

Paul nodded absently and then went off to talk to Margaret. I watched him go before turning, only to find Shannon a few paces away, looking at me.

"I don't hold it against you," she said.

"Hold what?" I asked, honestly confused.

"This." She gestured around the room. "That." She motioned toward Paul.

"Shannon, I . . ."

"It's okay." She smiled at me and then walked away.

What in the world could that have been about? I watched her vanish into the crowd, completely at a loss. If she thought there was still something between me and Paul, she was mistaken. Sure, some of the old flame was still there, but not enough that either of us would act on it. I'd moved on. *So you think.*

I stood alone in the middle of the ballroom and realized that my part in the investigation was done. The police could handle the rest. Paul had the list. Buchannan had heard what Margaret Yarborough had to say. I had no other leads and didn't think I was going to come across any more. Even the rain sounded as if it had started to let up. We might actually get to leave before the night was out.

My eyes scanned the crowd until I found Will. A smile spread across my face. We were finally going to get to spend some real time together now that I wasn't chasing after a murderer.

With one last glance at Paul, and a slight pang of jealousy that he was still on the case, I headed for Will, hoping I could still salvage something positive from the night.

20

"Someone said we might be able to leave soon. Do you know anything about that, Karen?" Diana twirled her finger in her hair.

"I haven't heard," I said through gritted teeth. "And it's Krissy."

Diana gave me a simpering smile.

I was trying to like Darrin's and Carl's wives, I really was, but it was like making friends with a ravenous tiger. Actually, I think I'd be better off with the tiger. At least it would want to eat me. Diana and Kim refused to learn my name, no matter how many times I told them.

"This party is a total bust," Kim said, smoothing down the front of her extravagant gown. She looked as if she were ready for a high school prom, though I knew the youth was painted on. When you got close to her, the caked-on makeup became evident.

When I'd come over to talk to Will, I hadn't anticipated getting dragged into a conversation with the wives of his friends. Will, Darrin, and Carl had all gone off together, leaving me stuck with women who clearly had nothing in common with me. I caught a couple of grins from the men as they slunk off to hide.

Jerks.

Diana sighed for about the twentieth time since I'd gotten there. "You've been running around with that policeman, right, Carrie? Can't you make him let us go? Everyone knows *we* could have had nothing to do with the killing."

"Sorry," I said, not bothering to correct her this time. "Even if the case was solved, we'd be stuck here until the driveway is clear."

Diana huffed and Kim rolled her eyes. "This is the last time I ever come to one of these," the latter said.

"Totally," Diana agreed.

I ground my teeth together and tried not to blow up at them. No wonder Darrin and Carl had beat a hasty retreat the moment I was introduced. If I had to listen to these two women complain all night, I'd go insane. Now I knew what Will had meant when he'd talked about his friend's wives. I guess sometimes looks aren't the only thing that matters in a person; personality goes a long way.

"So, what do you do for a living?" I asked the women, hoping to have some sort of decent conversation where I wouldn't want to throttle them.

Diana looked at me as if I'd just asked her what color her undergarments were. Kim looked confused.

"Never mind," I muttered, knowing they probably spent their days lounging by the pool, going to parties, and acting as if they were better than everyone else.

"I hear you work at a coffee shop," Kim said, appalled. "You don't actually touch the food, do you?"

"I own the place," I said. "And, yes, I touch the food."

I wiggled my fingers as if I personally stuck my thumb in every cup of coffee.

Diana's nose crinkled. "I can't imagine."

"Can we please go now?" Kim asked. I think she was more concerned about getting away from me than leaving the party.

I tuned them out and scanned the crowd for an escape. There had to be something better to do. The two women didn't want me there, and I surely didn't want to stand around, listening to them complain and put me down. Vicki and Mason were talking with Lance and Jules. That was more my crowd; not these two rich bimbos who cared about nothing other than themselves.

I mentally chided myself for thinking of Diana and Kim so poorly, but it was hard not to. I might have to eventually spend more time with them if Will and I became serious. There would be dinner parties, triple dates. Maybe they aren't so bad. Could I really judge them based on one little conversation?

Glancing over, I decided, yeah, I could. Diana was twirling her hair around her index finger, looking as bored as could be. Kim kept huffing and sighing as if she thought someone would eventually take notice and call in a helicopter to airlift her out of here.

"I'll talk to you two later," I said. "I see some friends I'd like to say hi to."

Diana looked surprised when I spoke, as if she'd forgotten I was there. "Oh. Okay. Have fun, Missy."

She was closer this time. Maybe someday she'd get it.

"Bye." Kim gave me a finger wave before looking away.

I started for where my friends were chatting when I saw Terry Blandino striding purposefully across the room.

I altered my course, thinking that this *had* to be more interesting than anything else going on at the moment. I followed him across the room, until I saw exactly where he was heading.

The man in the fedora, Philip, was glowering at Terry as he approached. He was alone, standing apart from the rest of the guests, almost as if he'd been ostracized, and it looked as if he wanted to keep it that way. The last time I saw him and Terry together, they'd been fighting, and this looked like another outburst in the making.

I worked my way as close as I could get without standing out. I'd been caught eavesdropping once already; I wasn't looking forward to having it happen again. Unfortunately, there weren't many people standing near Philip, which meant I couldn't get within hearing range without him noticing me. I moved to the snack table, which was as close as I could safely get, and pretended to pick over the various cheeses while watching their lips, hoping I could make something out.

Terry didn't give Philip much of a chance to speak. He leaned in close and said a few harsh words I couldn't make out. He leveled his finger at the other man, nearly shoving it up his nose. Philip took the tongue-lashing stoically before removing his horn-rimmed glasses. For a moment, I thought he was going to slip them into his pocket and then punch Terry in the face. Instead, he wiped them clean, seemingly disinterested in whatever Terry had to say, before shoving his glasses back onto his face. He muttered something that sounded like, "So?" before shrugging and walking away. Terry stood there, fuming after him for a long moment, before turning and storming the other way.

Well, that was quick.

I was pretty sure I saw Philip's name as Philip Carlisle on the list Margaret had given me. I didn't recall seeing Terry's, but that didn't mean they hadn't been together. She might have forgotten, or kept it off the list for some reason. Could that mean the friction between the two men was because they were both smitten with Mrs. Yarborough?

I thought back to what Margaret had told me about how Philip thought that since Howard Yarborough was dead, he and Margaret would run off together. Was Terry Blandino somehow connected with the Yarboroughs, more than a simple party guest? If he was in love with Margaret, I could see how Philip's plan would rub him the wrong way.

So, what if Philip was in love with Margaret, had wanted their affair to mean more than it really did, but when she told him she wasn't interested, he decided to kill her? He might have mistaken Jessica Fairweather for her since they were both wearing the same costume, killing the younger girl by accident.

But I found it hard to believe. If he'd slept with Mrs. Yarborough, it would be hard to mix the two up. Jessica had been strangled. In order to do that, the killer had to get up close and personal with the victim. Even if he'd snuck up behind her, he would have realized his mistake as soon as he laid his hands on her. I supposed he could have killed her to keep her quiet, even after realizing his mistake. But if that was the case, why not go after Margaret when I'd caught them alone together?

I needed to know more.

And I thought I knew exactly where to go for the information I needed.

I snatched up a couple of cheese cubes and stuffed

them into my mouth before heading for the hall. My stomach grumbled at the limited sustenance and I promised it I'd treat myself to a pot of coffee and an entire cake when this was all over.

There were people in the hallway, so I continued on past them until I found an unoccupied room. I stepped inside and closed the door behind me. There was no lock on the door, so I could only hope no one walked in on me. It wasn't that I was doing anything bad, but I didn't want the wrong person to overhear the questions I was about to ask and tattle on me.

Turning, I grimaced at the decorations. Chains hung from the ceiling with dull hooks on the ends of them. On the table in the middle of the room was a recognizable puzzle box. On the wall opposite the door was a movie poster for *Hellraiser*. Next to that was a mannequin of the villain himself, nails sticking out of his head as he glowered at me.

I shuddered and turned my back on the straight-out-of-a-horror-movie tableau. If I'd been married to Howard, I either would have made him take everything down, or would have moved out. There was no way I could live with this stuff in nearly every room.

I pulled my cell phone out of my baggy sweatpants and went to recent calls. I clicked on the first number there and waited as it rang.

"Hello?"

"Hi, Rita. It's Krissy."

"Oh, Krissy!" Rita shouted into the phone. "I'm so glad you called. You *must* tell me everything that is happening. You're involved in this, aren't you? From what I hear, you and Officer Dalton are close to catching the killer. Is it true? Of course it is! You two do such good work together. I don't know how you two aren't dating anymore. You're such a match!"

I waited for her to take a breath before cutting in. "We're working on it," I said. "But we've run into a few snags." I wasn't quite sure I was talking about the murder investigation or our relationship.

"Snags?" Rita asked. "That's terrible! Do you remember the James Hancock novel, *Partied until Death*? The whole thing took place at a party just like the one you are at, and the killer was picking everyone off one by one."

"I remember it," I said with a sigh. "Only one person has died here." And the party in the book wasn't a costume party. Really, other than the word *party* there weren't any similarities between the book and what was happening here.

"But maybe the result will be the same!" Rita sounded beside herself with excitement. "Remember how the butler had an affair with the cook and they conspired against the host, killing his friends and family to drive him insane and steal his fortune? Absolute brilliance!"

I rolled my eyes. Dad was never happy with his "the butler did it" solution, but at the time, didn't know what else to do. He felt it was too cliché, and I had to agree. Nothing I'd seen here pointed to the butler, or any of the help, killing Jessica, however.

"This isn't a novel," I said, feeling it had to be said, but knowing Rita wouldn't care.

"Of course not." I could almost see her waving a hand at me. "But perhaps you can use it as a guide to solve the case."

I pinched the bridge of my nose. Why was it that nearly every time I talked to Rita, she had to bring up one of my dad's books? I knew she was a fan, and I was sure he appreciated her fandom, but come on! This was real life. Things didn't happen nice and orderly like they did in a book. She had to understand that.

"I have a few questions about some of the guests," I said, changing the subject to the reason for my call. "I don't know anyone here and instead of interrogating them, I thought that you might know a few things about them."

"Oh!" She sounded excited by the prospect. "Are they all suspects?"

I knew she was hoping I'd tell her the names of all of the people Paul and I suspected of committing the crime, but I knew if I did, it would be all over town in seconds, with my name attached. I had to be careful here. I wanted to get information, not start rumors.

"No," I said, eyeing Pinhead over my shoulder. "I'm looking for background information, so I know a little more about the guests. I'm hoping it will help me narrow the suspect list down."

"Oh, well, okay then." I could hear the disappointment in her voice. "What do you want to know?"

"Terry Blandino," I said. "What is his relationship with the Yarboroughs?"

"Blandino . . ." There was a clicking sound I assumed came from her tapping the phone with her fingernail. "Blandino . . ."

I waited, suddenly afraid my source of gossip had come up blank. What if she didn't know Terry or Philip, or any of the guests here well enough to know anything juicy about them? These people ran in entirely different circles than Rita. There was no way one person could know everyone in town, even one the size of Pine Hills where everyone *seemed* to know each other.

"Oh, yes, Terry!" she exclaimed, as if suddenly remembering him. "I'm not sure, but I thought either Terry or his ex-wife might have had an affair with one of the Yarboroughs. Or was it their daughter?"

"He has a daughter?"

"Oh yes," Rita said. "Her name is Ellen." There was a pause. "No, wait. Elaine. Her name is Elaine."

I gaped into the phone. "Monroe three is Terry Blandino's daughter?"

"Monroe?" Rita asked, confused. "No, I think she goes by Harmon; her mother's maiden name. The separation wasn't a happy one, but what breakup is?"

My mind was churning as I tried to figure out how Terry having a daughter, one who was at the party tonight, wearing the same dress as the murder victim, could have led to Jessica's death. As far as I was aware, Elaine didn't know anyone other than her father at the party. Could he have killed his own daughter?

It didn't fit. I couldn't imagine anyone hurting their own child, even if they hadn't had contact in a while. And as with anyone mistaking Jessica for Elaine, I seriously doubted her own father would mistake Jessica for her.

I needed to think about it some more before coming to any sort of conclusion, so I moved on and asked about the other person I'd called her about.

"What about Philip Carlisle?" I asked.

There was a moment of silence before Rita answered, sounding as if she had a personal hatred for the man. "I don't care much for him."

"How so?" I asked.

"I'm not one to spread rumors, but that man is not to be trusted. I've heard some dark things about him. Stay away from him if you know what's good for you."

My heart was pounding now. *Could he really be the killer?* Maybe my speculation about a relationship gone sour wasn't too far off the mark. "What sort of dark things?"

"I'm sure you know, but he was connected with Margaret Yarborough before her husband's death. An affair, if you can believe it."

Oh, I believed it all right. His name was on the list, and Margaret had told me as much to my face.

"Well, when Howard died, some believed Margaret had killed him," she said.

"You don't believe that." I could hear it in her voice.

"I don't think she did it on her own." Rita sounded grave for what was probably the first time in her life. "That Carlisle man was around at the time. There were always rumors that he was a hitman for some mafia before he moved here."

While Philip looked the part, I had a hard time believing it. He was thirty at most. I suppose it was possible he'd gotten involved with the wrong people at a young age, but even if he did, why move to a place like Pine Hills where there wasn't much need for a hitman?

"If he's there, you obviously have your killer," Rita said. "There is absolutely no doubt in my mind; that man is up to no good."

My heart wasn't just pounding now; it was trying to blow out my eardrums from the inside. *Could Philip Carlisle have killed Jessica Fairweather?* If so, why?

Hadn't Margaret said she was with Philip during the

murder? Had she lied? Or was I jumping to conclusions that had no basis in fact? If Margaret *did* care for Philip more than she'd let on, she might have claimed they were together to protect him.

But that didn't seem like her. Could she have been mistaken on the timing? Had he killed Jessica mere moments before heading to Margaret's bedroom?

Of course, that didn't matter now. Philip was roaming the party at this very moment. The rain had all but stopped, and the tow truck would have Buchannan's car out of the way before long, if it wasn't already out. Once the guests started leaving, the chances of figuring out who killed Jessica would diminish. And even if we did, he might be long gone by the time we found him again.

"Krissy, dear? Are you still there?"

"Thank you, Rita," I said. "I've got to go."

"You just have to—"

I hung up before she could finish.

My first instinct was to run into the ballroom, hunt down Mr. Carlisle, and accuse him of Jessica's murder in front of everyone. With all of those witnesses, he surely wouldn't try anything. Then again, I'd seen firsthand what a desperate person could do when cornered. Maybe it wasn't such a great idea, after all.

No, this was better handled by the police. I'd done my part. I'd learned my lesson from the last couple of times I tried to do things on my own. I didn't want someone else to get hurt, especially if that someone was me.

And now that I thought about it, I was pretty sure I wasn't the only one who suspected Philip was responsible for Jessica's death. Why else would Terry have confronted him on a night like this? I only hoped that he had solid evidence of Philip's involvement, because right now, I was working on pure speculation. It wouldn't be enough to convict him, even if Paul were to arrest him.

But for now, I needed to let Paul know what was happening, whether Philip was the real killer or not. I shoved my phone back into my sweatpants, straightened my back, and went in search of Paul before the police started to let people leave.

21

"Have you seen Officer Dalton?" I asked Buchannan, who was talking to a group of people, notebook in hand. The page was empty, telling me he wasn't getting anywhere, so I didn't mind butting in.

"What is this in regard to?" he asked, turning to me. He was in full-on professional mode, more than likely for the benefit of the men he'd been interviewing.

I hesitated before answering. How much should I tell him? Buchannan was a police officer, just like Paul, but he was also the man who was constantly hounding me, accusing me of getting involved in things I'd be better off leaving alone. He was right, I suppose, but it didn't mean I had to like him any more than I did, or trust him to do the right thing.

"I think I might have found a break in the case," I said, figuring that lying would only make my life worse. Besides, the last time we'd parted, it hadn't been on entirely horrible terms.

Buchannan glanced back at the group of men, and said, "Thank you for your time," before taking me by the elbow and leading me toward a more private corner of the room. There were still people nearby, but not close enough to listen in if we didn't start shouting at one another.

"What do you know?" he asked.

I pulled my arm free and made a show of rubbing my elbow as if he'd hurt me, which he hadn't; he'd made me feel like a child.

"I'd like to speak to Officer Dalton," I said. "He's more informed about the case and suspects than you at the moment."

Buchannan's eyes went hard. "Ms. Hancock, you best not be withholding information from me."

"I'm not," I said, though I guess I was. "It's just that what I have to say will mean little to you." Of course, that wasn't quite accurate, but after he'd escorted me to the corner like I was a troublesome toddler, I didn't want to tell him anything. "Paul knows the suspect, has spoken to him." I hoped. "He'll be able to tell me whether or not my information is important."

Buchannan ground his teeth together. He looked like he was debating on whether or not to lock me up somewhere. Really, I didn't blame him. I was being difficult, and I knew it. Maybe if I cut him a little slack sometime, he might not be so mean to me.

"Please," I said as sweetly as I could. "Tell me where he is. I'm sure he'll fill you in afterward. If I thought you could help, I'd tell you."

He continued to grind his teeth for another few seconds, eyeing me as if he suspected some sort of trick, before he sighed. "Fine," he said. "He's talking to a suspect at the moment."

I didn't have to ask him where. "Thank you."

Buchannan grunted in response.

I hurried for the hall that led to the makeshift interrogation room, eyes scanning the faces around me in search of Philip and his fedora. Had he slipped out while I'd been on the phone? Was he roaming the halls, searching for another victim? Or could fortune be with me and Paul was already interrogating him, getting the man to admit his role in the murder.

If, indeed, he was our killer.

I was running by the time I reached the door to the interrogation room. I forced my way inside without knocking, out of breath and excited.

Paul was seated at the table. Isabella, the woman who'd discovered the body, sat across from him. She looked just as frazzled as before, as if she had yet to recover from her ordeal. They both looked up at me in surprise at the exact same moment.

"I need to talk to you," I told Paul, paying Isabella only a cursory glance.

"I'm in the middle of something," he said, but stood anyway.

"It's important." I tried to give him a meaningful look that wouldn't tell Isabella anything. I think I only managed to look half-crazed.

"Could you excuse us a moment?" Paul said to the other woman before walking over to where I stood. "In the hall," he told me.

As soon as we were outside and the door was closed, I launched in. "I think I know who killed Jessica."

Paul, who had been about to speak before I cut him off, went suddenly alert. "How?"

"I was talking to some people," I said carefully. I

didn't want to tell him I'd gotten my information from Rita, nor did I want him thinking I was roaming the ballroom, questioning everyone I saw. "I learned a few interesting tidbits about some of our guests."

"Such as?" The impatience was clear in his voice.

"One of the men here is rumored to be a hitman, or at least, was when he was younger."

"Krissy . . ." He sounded disappointed with not just the information, but with me. "You can't believe every rumor you hear."

I kept my flare of anger in check. He was only being reasonable. How often were rumors completely blown out of proportion, to the point of being flat-out lies?

But I knew there was more to it than simple rumor. There was definitely something off about Philip Carlisle, something that I'd felt the moment I'd laid eyes on him. If anyone could be a natural-born killer, it was him.

"There's more to it than just rumor," I said, managing to sound only mildly defensive. "I saw this man arguing with more than one person tonight. Heated arguments."

A frown crept over Paul's features. "Who did he argue with?"

"I overheard him arguing with Mrs. Yarborough about where their relationship was heading. He believes they should run away together. She doesn't."

"That doesn't seem relevant."

"Later, I saw him arguing with another man, Terry Blandino. Twice. I think Terry was accusing him of the murder."

"Did you hear him come out and say it?" Paul asked. "Did this man admit to killing Mrs. Fairweather?"

"Well, not exactly," I said. "But I'm sure that's what I saw."

Paul didn't look convinced, so I began ticking points off on my fingers.

"This man has been seen arguing with multiple people. He seems out of place and keeps to himself. I don't think I've seen him mingle once. He is antagonistic and didn't take too well to me talking to him earlier. Currently, he is nowhere to be seen. And he is rumored to be a hitman, possibly in connection to Howard Yarborough's death."

Paul frowned. "He wasn't murdered as far as I am aware."

"No, and I have no proof of it. But this man was on the list Margaret gave me. She'd slept with him, which meant they'd have time to plan Howard's murder together. Some people believe Margaret had a hand in her husband's death. What if she didn't do it on her own? What if this man did? They had ample opportunity and time to discuss it. And then after the deed was done, I catch them arguing here of all places. What if he killed Jessica to get at Margaret some way, to show how far he would go for her?"

Paul was silent a long moment before he spoke. "I suppose it wouldn't hurt to talk to this man. What is his name?"

"Philip Carlisle. He's wearing—"

"A fedora, long coat, and glasses," Paul finished for me. "I talked to him a little while ago. He claims he was with Mrs. Yarborough at the time of Jessica's death."

Which was the same story Margaret had given me. "He could have lied." Which meant Mrs. Yarborough had done the same.

"There was something peculiar about him," Paul went on. His eyes met mine and all uncertainty seemed to have fled. "I felt he was lying to me the entire time we talked."

My excitement grew. "He has to be the one. I don't know why he killed Jessica Fairweather—it's all speculation on my part so far—but I'm positive he had a hand in it. It fits too much for him not to be involved."

"The boyfriend maybe," Paul said. I could see his mind working a million miles a minute. "If he knew about Mr. Carlisle's supposed past, he might have gone to him after his girlfriend rejected him." He started striding forward, still talking. Isabella was apparently forgotten. I followed after him, not wanting to be left behind. "We'll need to talk to them both again, see if we can get one of them to break and give the other up."

We entered the ballroom, stopping just inside. Paul scanned the crowed, face serious. I joined him, though I had to stand on my tiptoes to see over most of the heads. Being short sucked sometimes.

"He's not here," I said, having already looked for him. "He might be on the run!" Igor was still standing by the door, but I was pretty sure that wasn't the only exit in the mansion.

"Buchannan!" Paul barked, drawing nearly every eye. "Over here."

Buchannan flipped his notebook closed and strode across the room. He stopped in front of us. "Yes, *Officer* Dalton." It was clear he didn't appreciate being called over so rudely.

"Have you seen a man in a hat and glasses, wearing a long coat? He goes by the name Philip Carlisle."

Buchannan glanced at me. I could read the question in his eye: *Is this what you wanted me for?* I held his gaze for a long couple of seconds before he answered.

"I think I saw someone of that description leave a few minutes ago with Mar . . . Mrs. Yarborough." He nodded toward the opposite exit, flushing as if embarrassed by nearly saying her name. "She didn't seem too happy about it, but went along willingly enough."

Instant panic. Could Philip be plotting his next murder? Could he have accidentally killed Jessica when he'd meant to kill Margaret all along? Or could it have indeed been a warning shot, meant to make her realize he was serious about running away together and he wouldn't take no for an answer? Perhaps she lied for him because he'd threatened her. But what if that wasn't enough for him?

Could he be killing her even now?

Paul and I glanced at one another. I could see the same questions running through his mind.

"Buchannan," he said, all business. "Secure the room. Keep an eye out for both Margaret Yarborough and Philip Carlisle. The moment you see him, take him into custody."

Buchannan gave a sharp nod and strode into the room. For the first time since I'd met the man, I felt as if he was a *real* cop. His entire demeanor had changed, telling me that when he wasn't blaming me for something I didn't do, he could actually perform his job exceptionally well. Huh. Go figure.

Paul turned to me. I straightened, ready to receive my orders. I was excited. Another killer might end up behind bars thanks to me.

"Stay here," he said, before turning and loping off toward the hall where Margaret was last seen.

I gaped after him. I'd just solved the case, or at least, thought I did. Without me, he wouldn't have gotten this lead, at least not before we'd left for the night. I looked toward where Buchannan had gone, but he was no help.

Even if I begged him for something to do, he'd simply shoo me away.

Paul vanished down the hall. I had a decision to make.

I snorted. This was me we were talking about. There was only one decision I *could* make.

I took off at a run, ignoring the stares. I had to look a sight in my borrowed clothes and wild eyes. My cheeks were flushed with excitement, and maybe with a little exhaustion. I wasn't a fan of running anywhere, and I'd been doing a lot of rushing around lately. My legs were going to hate me in the morning.

Paul hadn't gotten far. He stood only a short ways down the hall, looking indecisive. I hurried up to him and then past him so he wouldn't grab me and stop me. I knew where those stairs led. "Her bedroom," I said, nodding toward the stairs even as I made toward them.

I heard him follow after.

I was panting by the time I reached Margaret's bedroom. The door was closed, and I could hear voices inside. Paul was right behind me and he wasn't even slightly out of breath. I really needed to start working out if I was going to keep doing this. Or maybe cut back on the cookies and ice cream.

"No!"

The shout came from the other side of the door. I recognized it instantly as belonging to Margaret Yarborough.

Paul didn't hesitate. He pushed past me and tried the door, which, of course, was locked. "Margaret!" he shouted, rattling the doorknob. When she didn't answer right away, he lowered his shoulder and opened the door by sheer brute force. I heard something snap in the lock and found myself out of breath for another reason entirely. I mean, he hadn't even backed up before using his shoulder to force open a locked door that had looked pretty darn sturdy to me.

His momentum carried him inside the room. I followed quickly after, not wanting to miss the confrontation.

Philip had Margaret by one wrist. His hat was lying on the bed, and his glasses were askew on his face as if he'd been slapped. He was red-faced, one cheek brighter than the other. Margaret's eyes were wide with shock.

"Let her go," Paul demanded. "Now."

Philip did as he was told. Margaret jerked her hand back and took two quick steps away from him. Tears burst from her eyes as she began rubbing at her wrist.

"I can explain," Philip said, his ever-present sneer in place. "We were just talking."

"It looked like a lot more than talking to me," I said.

"Krissy." Paul's tone was a warning to stay out of it. He kept his eyes on Philip and directed his next comment toward him. "Calmly move to this side of the bed, away from Mrs. Yarborough."

Philip raised both of his hands, pausing long enough to fix his glasses. He glanced down at his hat, which was lying on the bed, as if he was considering picking it up and putting it on. I noted the cats were missing, and hoped they'd found a safe hiding place and hadn't been hurt when Philip had attacked their owner.

"Okay," he said, moving slowly around the bed, away from Margaret, who was watching him with a strange expression on her face, as if she couldn't fathom he could be guilty of anything, even after what he'd been about to do. "There's no problem here. We just had a little disagreement, isn't that right, Margie?"

Margie? Even Margaret seemed taken aback by the nickname.

"I . . . We . . ."

"It's all right," Paul told her. "Everything is under control. We can figure this out later." He returned his focus to Philip. "Nice and slow."

The sneer never left his face as he moved slowly toward where Paul stood. His eyes flickered to me once, and I could see the understanding there. He knew we had him. He knew I was responsible.

Good, I thought with some satisfaction. It felt good to be this man's downfall.

Philip took another step forward; then he made his move.

The only martial arts I'd ever seen had come from movies like *The Karate Kid,* which pretty much meant I was clueless to what real karate looked like. Philip seemed completely at ease and willing to comply, when he suddenly burst into motion, aiming a palm strike straight for Paul's chest. It connected solidly, knocking Paul backward, into the wall, where he hit with a grunt and groan. The motion had been so fluid, so sudden, I'd barely had time to register what had happened before Philip was looking at me.

I might do some really dumb things sometimes, but this time, I did the wise thing. When Philip started toward me, I immediately darted to the side, out of his way. I could have tried to tackle him, but it was more likely I'd end up with a punch to the throat instead.

Philip ran past me, surprisingly light on his feet. I made a belated grab for his arm as he flew past, hoping to at least slow him down long enough for Paul to right himself and take over, but I missed completely. He was out the door and down the hall before I could even think of trying again.

By then, Paul had gotten back to his feet. He rushed past me, yelling "Stay here!" as he passed.

Who was I to ever listen?

I bolted after him, feeling only mildly guilty for ignoring his orders yet again. The real guilt came from realizing that my fear for my own safety was what might allow a killer to escape.

I couldn't let that happen.

Philip vanished around a corner, well ahead of both Paul and me. Just as we turned to follow, a door slammed, but neither of us saw which one. There were six doors along the corridor, ones I hadn't explored when I'd wandered the house earlier.

Paul gave me the briefest of annoyed looks and then started forward. He opened the first door, peeked in, and then closed it behind him. We worked our way down the hall like that, Paul in the lead, me trailing behind.

"Mr. Carlisle!" Paul called as he opened another door. "Give yourself up." He scanned the room and then closed the door.

As we moved, I kept checking behind me, certain Philip would leap out of one of the previously checked rooms and take us both out from behind. The man had proven he was more than he appeared, so it wouldn't surprise me if he was adept at hiding himself, too. It wasn't like Paul was entering the rooms and checking under all of the furniture, so he could be anywhere.

A sound came from one of the doors ahead. Paul glanced at me and then started toward the door. He didn't call out this time. He grabbed the doorknob, hesitated a second, and then pulled the door open. I had to shuffle back a step to give him room as he peered inside.

A white blur flew by as one of the Persians came tearing out of the closet as if its tail was on fire. It vanished down the hall, looking harried.

"A closet?" I asked, turning back. How had the cat ended up in the closet?

Before Paul could answer, the door behind us burst open and something heavy slammed into my back. I was propelled forward, unable to stop myself, and slammed into Paul, who was likewise off balance. We both staggered into the walk-in closet. Before I could so much as think to right myself, the door slammed closed behind us, followed by the unfathomable sound of the door being locked.

22

"Who puts a lock on a closet door?" I shouted, frustrated. We'd been beating on the door to no avail for a good five minutes now. Paul had already given up and was watching me as I pounded on the door as if I thought I could bust it down. He'd already tried forcing it open like he'd done the bedroom door, but this door seemed to be made of sturdier stuff.

"No one can hear us," he said. "We need to think."

"We don't have time to think! He might get away." I couldn't believe we'd come so close to catching the killer, only to be foiled by a closet as secure as Fort Knox.

"We know who he is," he said. "Even if he escapes now, we'll find him."

I sighed and stopped pounding on the door. He was right. Philip could run, could pack his things and try to escape, but they'd get him eventually. There was a chance he might flee to another country, sure, but how often did that really happen? It seemed like something you'd only see in the movies.

My shoulders sagged, causing my hand to bump up

against my leg. "Wait!" I reached into my pocket and pulled out my cell phone. "Crap."

"No bars," Paul said. "I checked while you were trying to smash your way through the door."

"Great," I grumbled. "Stuck in a locked closet with an impenetrable door, and no service. What does this thing double as, a bank vault?"

"Krissy," Paul said, his hand gently touching my shoulder. "Relax. Someone will come by soon."

"Then we should keep making noise," I said. "How else is anyone going to know we're in here?"

"We will," he said, calm as ever. "When we hear someone coming, we'll call out to them."

"And what if the door is soundproof?"

"We heard the cat."

Oh yeah.

I huffed and crossed my arms over my chest. I didn't like listening to reason, even when it made perfect sense. Maybe that was why I was always getting myself into trouble.

An uncomfortable silence fell between us then. The closet might be a walk-in, but that didn't mean it was gigantic. I could smell Paul's cologne and wondered if he reapplied it after his foray into the rain. No one should smell that good after being drenched and running after a suspected killer.

"I'm sorry."

The apology came so suddenly, I was struck dumb. I squinted into the gloom at Paul, who was an indistinct shape. The only light in the closet was coming from beneath the door, and it wasn't enough to see by. My phone would provide a little illumination, but I'd feel silly holding it.

We're in a walk-in, silly. They almost always had lights. And since this closet was built to withstand a nuclear assault, I figured it almost had to have a light somewhere. I began fumbling around for a switch or a cord as Paul continued talking.

"I was being stupid. I *knew* I was, yet I kept doing it, anyway."

My fingers bumped into a thin chain. *Bingo!* I tugged on it and a light came on, blinding both of us.

"What are you talking about?" I asked, rubbing my eyes. At least I'd had the presence of mind not to look up when I'd turned on the light, though I probably should have warned Paul.

He squinted his eyes at me a moment before answering. "You. Me." He sighed, sounding frustrated. "Us, I suppose."

"Us?" *Is he saying what I think he is saying?* My entire body broke out in a panicky sweat. *Oh God, not here!*

"It was my fault. I do really like you." He said it like I might contradict him. "Always have, but I let other things get in the way."

When he didn't continue, I prodded him. A part of me might not want to do this trapped in a closet, but a bigger part really wanted to hear what he had to say. "Like?"

He shrugged. "Like your involvement in the cases. I was scared you were doing it to impress me, and that you'd keep on doing it as long as you thought I'd like it."

I snorted. "Hardly. I did it because I like to help. Mysteries fascinate me. And I can't stand for murderers running loose, so I do what I can to stop them."

"I get that," Paul said with a smile. "I guess I sometimes wish they fascinated you a little less." His eyes met mine for a heartbeat before he looked down at his hands. "And then there was my mom."

Oh boy, that was a big one. Paul's mom, Patricia, was the Pine Hills police chief, which automatically made the situation a little more uncomfortable. I mean, it was bad enough Paul was a cop, but his mom, too? It made it look like I was in bed with the law, that I could do anything I wanted and get away with it. It was probably why Buchannan hated me so much.

And then there was the fact she'd tried to hook us up. It was both weird and flattering at the same time. She'd said she thought we'd be perfect together, a sentiment she was near recanting thanks to my actions as of late.

"She hound you about me too much?" I asked, knowing the answer already.

Paul laughed. "Every day. First, it was to give you a chance, asking if we'd gone out, for how long, what we did. I felt like a kid again. I didn't mind so much at first, but eventually, it started to wear on me, especially since we hadn't gone out other than that one time. And then, after that last murder, when you became a suspect . . ."

"She wasn't so eager to push us together."

"That's an understatement."

Patricia had told me as much when I'd been locked up for throwing a few harmless punches Buchannan's way. She'd started to doubt my character, which, in turn, made me doubt myself even more than I already did. Apparently, it had affected Paul, too.

"But you have Shannon now," I said, surprised by how much the words stung. *I'm over him,* I tried to tell myself. I was with Will now, or at least hoping I was. I didn't need to be mooning over more than one man, especially since I'd always struggled to get one to so much as look at me. This whole multi-guy thing was new to me, and I wasn't so sure I liked it.

Paul's smile turned wistful. "I do," he said, stinging me all over again.

"Have you been dating long?"

"A few months." He actually reddened at that. "When we started to drift apart, I couldn't stand it." He started to sound unsure of himself, like he was as confused as I felt. "We didn't really get to date, you and I. But I didn't want to be alone, and since our relationship was going nowhere, I thought it might be me. I felt like I was the problem, that I ruined everything, so I decided to give Shannon a chance." He paused and looked deep into my eyes. "I'm starting to wonder if I was too hasty."

"But you like her." It wasn't a question. I could see it in the way he talked about her, the way he looked at her.

"I do." He sighed.

My head was spinning. The closet felt as if it was shrinking, and before long, we'd be crushed together, unable to breathe. We'd die, clutched in each other's arms, suffocated by . . . what? A mutual affection turned sour? Our mistakes?

Why do I suddenly wish the murderer was back?

"Why are you telling me all of this?" I asked. My voice came out quiet, almost a whisper.

Paul shook his head and shrugged. "I don't know. We're here. No one else is around. It struck me that I'd screwed up, that I didn't give you a fair shake. I abandoned you when you needed me, all because of my own insecurities and fears. So, I'm apologizing. I see you with that other guy . . ."

"Will," I supplied.

"Will." Paul said his name with a sad smile. "He can

make you happy." He paused. "You do care about him, don't you?"

Was this a test of some sort? A legitimate question? Why did everything have to get so tangled up and confusing, just when I was starting to think I knew what I wanted?

"I do," I said. It felt like the temperature had risen a good twenty degrees since we'd first gotten trapped together. "But he's not the only one I like."

The silence that fell right then wasn't just uncomfortable, it was practically murderous. My breathing was fast, my heart was hammering. I couldn't see straight, and there was a ringing in my ears that was making me dizzy.

Paul didn't look any better. His hand was hovering between us, seemingly lost in the void that had grown there over time. He looked confused, scared. Basically, he looked like I felt.

"Paul . . ." I nearly choked on his name.

Here we were, trapped in a closet together, where no one could see us or hear us. We could say and do anything we wanted and no one would be the wiser.

The thought caused my heart rate to speed up. I felt myself move forward, an inch, maybe two. Paul looked up at me, longing and fear in his eyes.

"Are you sure they went this way?"

Buchannan's voice broke the moment. Paul and I stared at each other, wide-eyed, as if we'd never seen one another before. Buchannan's voice got louder, telling me he was coming our way. I sucked in a breath and, for a moment, was unable to speak or move.

Do I really want this to end? Paul had been completely honest with me, and it had been one of the best moments of my night. It felt like everything that had happened did so to lead me to this moment.

But was it really what I wanted?

Both Paul and I turned and started beating on the door at the exact same moment.

"John!" he shouted at the same time I yelled, "Buchannan!"

His voice cut off. There was a moment of silence on the other side of the door; then the lock clicked. A second later, the door swung open. Buchannan stood there, grinning like a fool, Margaret Yarborough at his side.

"Well, well, well," he said. "Taking a little time out for personal reasons, are we?"

"Can it," Paul said before I could formulate a response. He was much kinder than I would have been. "Our suspect got away."

"He locked you in a closet?" Buchannan asked, glancing past us into the small space.

"He shoved us from behind," I said, a bit defensively. "We couldn't help it there was a lock on the door." I looked to Margaret, who only shrugged.

"When Mrs. Yarborough found me, she told me you went after the killer?" Buchannan asked.

Paul nodded. "Philip Carlisle. Fedora, horn-rimmed glasses, long coat. He might have ditched some of the attire, so you can't go solely by that alone."

"I can't believe Philip would have done such a thing," Margaret said.

"Wasn't he assaulting you when we found him?" I asked, shocked that she could still want to defend him.

"We had a . . . disagreement. We all have them."

I gaped at her, shocked. The man very well might have been about to seriously hurt her, and yet she refused to believe he could have killed someone, might have even killed her. Either she was too trusting, or he'd worked her over pretty good.

"We need to find Mr. Carlisle," Paul said, taking control of the situation. "Buchannan, take Mrs. Yarborough and find somewhere safe for her. Once she is secure, man the front door. No one is to leave." He frowned. "We can't cover all of the exits, so if you can convince some of the help to guard the other doors, it would be appreciated. Tell them not to try to stop him, but to find you or me and tell us the moment they see him. This man is dangerous."

"I can assist with that," Margaret said. "They'll listen to me."

Buchannan gave a curt nod and then turned to his charge. "Mrs. Yarborough, if you would." She took his proffered elbow and they hurried down the hall, back toward the ballroom.

"Go with them," Paul said as I turned to ask him what he wanted me to do.

"What?" I gasped in shock. After everything that was just said, he was going to do this to me? "I can help!"

"You need to get somewhere safe. You saw what he did. You don't need to be wandering the halls where he can find you."

"But . . ."

"No." He held up a finger and gave me a stern look. "This is not your job. You need to go back to the ballroom and stay there. I don't want to have to worry about you while there is a killer on the loose."

My stubbornness kicked in then, and all of the good things we'd discussed in the closet became a distant memory. "I *can* help. You wouldn't even know about his past if it wasn't for me."

"Krissy, please." He gave me a pleading look. "Don't make this difficult. I'm thankful you helped identify the suspect, but leave the rest up to Buchannan and me. We'll take care of it."

I wanted to continue to argue but realized it would do no good. Besides, Paul was right; the man *was* dangerous. I saw him take Paul down with a single open-palmed punch. If he got hold of me, there was no way I was going to be able to stop him from doing whatever he pleased.

"Fine," I said, pouting. I might have realized it was the right thing to do, but it didn't mean I had to like it.

Paul looked relieved. "Thank you," he said. "Chances are good our suspect is long gone by now. There's probably nothing to worry about, but I want you to be safe."

I nodded, still unhappy. Paul gave me a smile and, shockingly, touched my cheek. "I'll see you in a bit." And then he turned and hurried down the hall, checking rooms as he went.

I stood there for a few long seconds before turning and doing what Paul wanted me to do. I'd done my part. I should be happy about that. For once, I'd helped without getting myself shot or choked. It was silly *not* to be overjoyed.

But if that was the case, why did I feel so crappy?

With a sigh, I trudged my way back to the ballroom to let the police do their job.

23

"I should be helping him look for him."

"No, Krissy, you shouldn't."

I was standing with my friends, who were doing their best to console me. Lance and Jules were giving me sympathetic looks, as if they completely understood how I felt, though they weren't willing to do or say anything to goad me into action. Mason and Will were mostly staying out of it, contributing a few words here and there. It was Vicki who was steadfastly refusing to let me give in. She knew how much trouble I could get in, especially if I found the killer on my own.

"You've done enough already," she said at my pout. "You've gotten yourself hurt by chasing after the bad guy. I don't think you should ever put yourself in that position again. It's hard on all of us, worrying about you."

I huffed and glanced toward where Buchannan was standing near the front door, giving anyone who came close to him the stink eye. Igor was off covering some other exit. I was worried someone was going to get hurt, someone who had no experience dealing with a murderer. *I* should be the one watching a door or a window, not one of the help, and especially not the girls wearing those old waitress outfits.

"But if two of us are looking for him, we can cover more ground," I said. "This can be over so much faster and everyone can relax."

"You said it yourself not but ten minutes ago, he might already be gone," Will said. "Don't stress yourself out over this. It isn't healthy." He put an arm around my shoulder and squeezed.

I looked down at his cane. He'd given it to me when I wouldn't stop wringing my hands. Now, my fingers were clenched tightly around the wood, so hard it was a wonder it didn't snap.

"Officer Dalton can handle it," Lance said. "And the other officer is watching the doors. We're safe in here. Together."

I knew they were right, but I was having a hard time sitting still and waiting. Margaret Yarborough was across the room, surrounded by people with hands over their mouths, as if in shock as they listened to her relay what had happened. Looking at her only made me angrier. She shouldn't have lied to us. If she'd come out and told the truth right away, we might already have Philip in custody.

"Krissy . . ."

I looked back to find Mason frowning at me.

"Let it go."

I wanted to scream, wanted to run out of the room and search every last corner of the house, but what good would it do? I didn't know where Paul was, where he had been. I'd be more likely to get myself killed than find the killer. Heck, finding Philip Carlisle was probably exactly *how* I'd get myself killed.

Staying here was safer. Smarter. The right thing to do.

"I'll be back," I said.

"Krissy, no." Vicki shook her head. "You are *not* going to go running around, getting yourself into trouble."

"I won't leave the room." *Yet*, I silently added. "There's someone I want to talk to. It'll keep my mind off what I'm *not* doing."

I'd noticed our resident Clark Gable, Terry Blandino, standing over by the refreshments. The food had stopped coming, so there wasn't much left for him to pick through, but he was trying.

"You sure, sweetie?" Jules asked. "You can always hang out with us." The twinkle in his eye told me he knew exactly what I was planning.

"I'm sure. I'll be right over there." I nodded toward the table.

Vicki crossed her arms over her chest but couldn't keep the crooked smile off her face. Like Jules, and apparently everyone in the room, she knew what I was doing. She might warn me off putting myself in dangerous positions, but she also knew it was in my nature to snoop. They'd have to tie me down to keep me away.

I took a few steps away from Will. He frowned and then followed me over. "Krissy . . ."

"I'll be okay," I said. "And I promise I'll be good."

He looked worried, but smiled. "Please, be careful."

"I will."

"And don't take too long, okay?"

"I won't." On a sudden impulse, I stood on my tiptoes and kissed him on the cheek. Then I hurried away, pointedly not looking at the faces around me, especially Will's. I didn't know if he'd be smiling or looking more worried than ever. I had a feeling it might be a little of both.

Terry was alone at the snack table, still picking through what little there was left. He had a plate in hand. A solitary grape rolled around on it, seemingly forgotten. He didn't notice me until I was standing right next to him, and even then, he didn't look my way until I cleared my throat.

"Did you need something?" There was no hostility in his voice, just a sad resignation. I wasn't sure if it was directed at me, or something else—his daughter perhaps.

"Hi, Terry," I said, putting on my best "We're buddies!" smile. "How are you doing?"

His brow furrowed. "Fine," he said, wary now. "Why?"

"You've heard about Philip Carlisle, right?" I asked, knowing he had. The entire ballroom was buzzing about it. "He's on the run, but should be in custody soon."

Terry's jaw clenched before he answered. "I'm not surprised he's involved."

"How well did you know him? I saw you two fighting a few times now. I'm guessing you didn't get along."

Terry slammed down his plate violently enough, the grape bounced onto the floor. "That is none of your business."

His tone was aggressive, yet I wasn't going to give in. I was positive Terry knew more than he was letting on. "I'm pretty sure he killed Jessica Fairweather, and might have been planning to do the same to Margaret Yarborough. Is that why you were arguing?"

"Philip and I had a disagreement."

"Over?"

"That is none of your business," he repeated, more forcefully this time.

Eyes were starting to turn our way, but I pressed on. "What about Elaine Harmon?"

Terry went still. "What about her?" His eyes flickered over my shoulder. I glanced back to see the girl in question standing against the wall, watching us while pretending she wasn't.

"She's your daughter," I said, turning back to him.

He didn't speak for a long moment. He stared at me hard enough, it felt like he was looking straight through me. He was breathing heavily, but in a controlled manner, telling me he was trying to rein in his temper. From what little I'd seen of him, I was guessing he had to do that a lot.

"What does she have to do with anything?"

"I don't know," I said. "But I find it interesting that she was wearing the same costume as Jessica Fairweather. And the man who murdered Jessica was seen arguing with you, not once, but at least twice. Tell me what you know. It could help."

"There's no connection." Harsh. Clipped.

"Are you positive about that?" I pressed.

"I am." He clamped his teeth together hard enough, I heard them click.

A new thought popped into my head. I'd assumed Terry had fought with Philip because he knew about the man's past and was looking to protect not just his daughter, but Mrs. Yarborough. But what if that wasn't it at all?

I took a step toward him, stepping on the lonely grape in the process. "Elaine doesn't know why she was invited here," I said, keeping my voice low. "She doesn't have the money or social standing to attend something like this." Neither did I, but at least I knew where my invite had come from. "She was wearing the same dress as the victim. That can't be a coincidence."

Terry's eyes hardened. "You don't know what you are talking about."

"Do you want to know what I think?" I asked, taking a quick peek at the table. There was nothing there Terry could use as a weapon, so as long as he didn't have a machine gun under his jacket, I thought I was safe. I did tighten my grip on Will's cane, just in case.

"Enlighten me." He crossed his arms.

"I think you invited Elaine to the party yourself. You haven't had a lot to do with your daughter, or your ex-wife, since the divorce. And then out of the blue, Elaine receives an invitation and is called and told to be here. So she comes to a party she has no business being at, with no one but you she knows, wearing a very distinctive outfit."

Terry glared at me then. I pressed on, hoping he would break and confess to something, rather than break and try to strangle me instead.

"You hired Philip Carlisle to kill her." I was as blunt as I could be, hoping it would surprise him and cause him to slip. "You knew who he was, what he was rumored to have done in his past. What you didn't realize was that he'd make a mistake. He saw Jessica dressed just as you described Elaine, and he took the opportunity to kill her. You were arguing with him, not because you were accusing him of murder, but because you were angry at him for killing the wrong person!"

"You're insane."

"Am I?" I asked, a satisfied smile quirking the corners of my mouth. "Am I really?"

"Yes, you are." Terry glanced around, cognizant of the eyes on us. "I didn't invite Elaine here."

"Oh?" I asked, not buying it for a second. "Then who did?"

"I don't know." He sighed. All of the strength seemed to go out of him then. Quite suddenly, he looked like a man tired of all of the pressures of his life—a man looking for a way out. "I was surprised when I saw her here," he said. "I never would invite her to this snake pit."

"But you didn't talk to her when you saw her, did you?"

He winced. "I wanted to, but didn't think she would want to have anything to do with me." He closed his eyes for a second, as if fighting back tears. "I saw her, and then when I saw Philip, I immediately thought something was wrong. I didn't know why he would want to hurt her, but feared he would. He isn't a pleasant man. Since neither of them should have been here, I knew it couldn't be a coincidence."

"So you confronted him about it," I said. Maybe I was wrong about Terry. I found myself believing his every word, though that could simply mean he was a very good liar.

"I did. I saw him talking to Margaret and, I don't know . . ." He shrugged. "I wanted to warn her off of him, to tell him to leave. Then, later, I confronted him about the death of that poor girl. He acted like none of it bothered him. I didn't know what his plan was, and still don't, but as long as he left Elaine out of it, I didn't care."

"If you were so worried about Elaine's safety, why didn't you go over to her? It's easier to protect someone if they are by your side."

"I . . ." His shoulders sagged. "I didn't want to fight with her. You have to understand, when I divorced her mother, I left them with nothing. I help out when I can, but I know it isn't enough. I don't know how to make things better between us; I wouldn't know where to start. How do you think she'd react if I suddenly appeared at her side and told her I was going to protect her after all this time? I'd be lucky if she only walked away."

There was real pain in his voice. I genuinely believed he wanted to have a better relationship with his daughter but didn't know how to begin. How *do* you go up to someone you'd left behind and make things right? I wasn't even sure you could.

"What about Margaret Yarborough?" I asked. I knew she had to fit into this somehow.

"What about her?"

"Were you two ever in a relationship?"

That caused a snort of laughter. "Hardly," he said. "I was never interested in her politics, or her way of life." As he spoke, his voice got angrier. "If it wasn't for the Yarboroughs, things wouldn't have gotten so out of hand." He glanced past me, to Elaine again. "If you wouldn't mind, I'd rather forget about all of this."

"I'm sorry," I told him. "I'm only asking because I want to know why Jessica was killed."

Terry gave a bitter laugh. "Ask Philip if you want to know that. She probably rejected him, much like she did her boyfriend. If it isn't obvious by now, Philip doesn't take the word *no* as graciously as others."

Could it really be so simple? Had Philip come across Jessica alone, angry over what she viewed as public humiliation, even though she'd been the one doling it out? What if he asked her out, or tried to kiss her? I had no doubt she would have told him off right then and there. He was a man of violence. He wouldn't take the slight softly.

But if he was a hired killer, why would he be here tonight of all nights?

Because of Margaret's list. They'd been lovers. He didn't have to have come with murder on his mind. It could have been something that had just happened.

"Thank you," I told Terry. "You've been a great help."

He grunted and then with a glance at his empty plate, he walked away.

Everyone who'd been watching us promptly lost interest and went back to their own conversations. When I turned, Elaine was still watching me, though. She looked sad, as if she'd wanted to join us but couldn't bring herself to take those fateful steps to reconciliation.

She turned away, looking heartbroken, and I realized she'd been hoping her dad would have been the one to send her the invitation. Just because their relationship wasn't great, didn't mean she didn't want to have one. It was human nature to care for family, even when things become strained.

Vicki glanced at me then. I raised a finger at her, telling her I'd be a minute more. She nodded and went back to the conversation with Will, Lance, and the others. I noted Darrin, Carl, and their wives had joined the group. I had no interest in listening to the two women complain. There were far more important things that deserved my attention.

I checked Buchannan next. He was smiling at a pretty young girl who was wearing a tiara. I think she was supposed to be a princess, but I couldn't tell for sure since her back was to me. Buchannan was shaking his head, even as he smiled. Chances were good she was trying to talk her way out the door, and he wasn't having any of it, though he did seem to appreciate the view.

It was now or never. Everyone was distracted. I moved slowly toward the hallway, eyes darting from Vicki to Buchannan, and back again. Neither looked up, but could at any moment.

I reached the hall and, for an instant, felt guilty for what I was about to do.

And then my usual sense of adventure kicked in.

"Forgive me," I muttered, knowing my friends would. I wasn't so sure about Buchannan and, really, couldn't care less if he did.

And then I slipped into the hall, on the lookout for trouble.

24

Plastic wrap blocked off the hallway leading to the pumpkin room where Jessica Fairweather was murdered. It was taped to the wall high enough I was able to easily duck under it. More plastic wrap barred the doorway. The door itself was closed.

Feeling like a criminal, I pushed open the door and then ducked under the barrier. With a quick glance down the hall to make sure no one had followed me, I eased the door shut and then turned to look for a clue that would help me understand why Jessica was killed.

She was still lying where she'd been found but was now covered by a white sheet. I assumed she was left there to preserve the scene for forensics or whoever would arrive once the driveway was clear. There were no little numbered papers or cones or anything marking off clues since the site had simply been secured to the best of Paul's ability. It wasn't like he had any equipment on him here at the party, so it was no wonder he hadn't tried to investigate the body for more than the basics.

I made sure to stick to the edge of the room so as not to disturb anything. The smashed pumpkins were still there, as were the scarecrows. Because of the sheet covering the deceased, a large portion of the actual crime scene was concealed. If there were any clues in the room, chances were good they'd be on or very near the body.

With a nervous glance back at the door, I crept forward, placing each foot carefully in front of the next. I was worried I'd knock something over, or brush away some important piece of evidence with my oversized borrowed clothing. But since I wasn't about to strip down to my undies to do this, there was no help for it. I hoped as long as I was careful, I wouldn't do anything to compromise the scene.

I reached the corner of the sheet, near where her hand lay. I was breathing fast, both from nervousness about being caught and by what I was about to see. I really didn't want to look at her body again. Jessica's was the first I'd ever seen outside a funeral, and I wasn't looking forward to doing it again.

"Calm, Krissy," I told myself under my breath. "You can do this."

I sucked in a deep breath and crouched down.

My hand trembled as I reached for the corner of the sheet. My fingers touched cloth and I shuddered as if I'd actually touched her cold flesh. *On the count of three.* Just one peek to see if there was some overlooked piece of incriminating evidence I could take to Paul and then I'd be out of there. I didn't want Philip to find a way to talk his way out of an arrest, though since he assaulted an officer, I was pretty sure he was in some serious trouble no matter what he said or did.

"One," I muttered, mentally prepping myself. "Two." This was going to be horrible. "Thr—"

"What are you doing in here?"

I shot to my feet, just barely releasing the sheet before I did. I spun, hands going behind my back, and gave Buchannan my best innocent smile.

"Hi!" I said, heart in my throat. "I'm checking the scene for you."

He frowned at me. "For . . . ?"

"Uh, clues?"

He crossed his arms over his chest and gave me a stern look. "I doubt Dalton gave you permission to be in here." His eyes flickered to the body before returning to mine. "Did you think we wouldn't have someone check in here every few minutes?"

"I was hoping you wouldn't."

Buchannan's frown deepened into his customary scowl. "Ms. Hancock, please step away from the victim."

I took a couple of quick steps toward him. "I'm sorry," I said. "I feel like there's something we missed that is vitally important to understanding why she was killed. I just wanted to peek to see if my suspicions were correct."

"Ms. Hancock . . ." I really wished he would stop calling me that. "You have no business in here. I could have you arrested for this. You know better than to walk all over a crime scene."

"It isn't official yet!" I said, gesturing toward the plastic wrap that separated us. "I only want to help."

"You can help by returning to the ballroom and staying there. I'll overlook it this time." He leveled a finger at me. "I won't be so generous the next."

I was so shocked that he was giving me a pass, I could only nod at him. I was speechless. I'd been certain he was going to zip strip me up, toss me in a room, and forget about me until it was time to run me down to the station.

"I don't ever want to see you in here again," he said,

continuing to scold me. "It might not look official, but this *is* a crime scene. You don't belong here."

"I suppose you're right," I said, lowering my eyes.

"I am." Buchannan took me by the arm and helped me past the first plastic wrap barrier. He started to lead me away, back toward the ballroom, when I stopped him.

"Maybe you should check to make sure I didn't disturb anything," I said, doing my best to sound as if I thought I might have. I knew I hadn't touched anything more than the corner of the sheet, so it was unlikely. I just didn't want him following me.

He gave me a suspicious look before glancing back. The sheet wasn't thrown off the body, but the corner did look as if it had been moved. It was laying over the edge of one of the undamaged pumpkins.

"Back to the ballroom," he told me with another finger jab. "I don't want to have to come looking for you."

I made an "X" over my heart and smiled.

Buchannan sighed and turned his back to fix the sheet.

I didn't hesitate, The moment his back was to me, I bolted down the hall, away from the ballroom. If I couldn't inspect the scene, well then, I was going to look elsewhere for clues. If Philip really was the killer, he might have gone into Margaret's bedroom or any number of rooms. He might have caught up with Jessica in the bathroom Quentin said she'd locked herself inside. Maybe there was something there.

I still had Will's cane in hand, for which I was thankful. Roaming the halls with a killer on the loose wasn't exactly the smartest thing to do, but I couldn't stand around waiting anymore. I'd been a part of this from the beginning and I planned on seeing it through.

I hurried down the hall, throwing glances behind me to make sure Buchannan wasn't coming after me. I reached a set of stairs that were blocked off by more plastic wrap. This time, it was done in a way that made it impossible to cross without tearing it down.

With a silent apology to Paul for destroying his hard work, I yanked the wrap from the wall and then took the stairs by two, leaving what was left hanging.

The mansion was a maze. There were more staircases than any house should rightfully have, and the same went for rooms. From what I could tell, no matter which staircase you took, you could eventually work your way anywhere you wanted to go . . . if you could figure out which direction to turn.

Having only been in the house for a few hours now, I wasn't sure how best to find my way around, other than to check in each and every room I passed until I saw something I recognized.

The first door creaked ominously as I pushed it open— more than likely by design. The room inside was dark, and seemingly windowless. The only light came from a strange, green glowing substance on the ceiling and in the corners. I closed the door before I caught a glimpse of an alien or some creature from an H.P. Lovecraft story.

I continued on down the hall that way, peering into rooms as I passed, looking only long enough to see if I recognized it before moving on. I wanted to start from Margaret's bedroom even though I'd already poked around there. I still felt as if there was something in there I'd missed the first time around and wanted to have another go at it.

But none of the rooms looked familiar. My first impressions of the house had been right; it was gigantic. I felt as if I could go on forever and never find the end of it, which wasn't entirely bad, though it would make finding Philip that much harder.

At least my chances of getting surprised by him are likewise tiny.

I opened the next door and poked my head inside, already bored with the horror themes.

A horrendous shriek startled me backward. Someone lunged forward from across the room, arm raised, knife glittering in hand. Strobe lights from behind my attacker made it impossible to see who it was, but my money was on Philip.

I screamed and hit the wall across the hall hard. I raised Will's cane to protect my face in the hopes of deflecting the first downward strike. I squeezed my eyes shut—not the smartest thing to do, but I couldn't help it. Seconds passed and nothing struck my upraised arm, or any part of my body. The shriek turned into a sinister chuckle. I opened my eyes as a faint whirring sound accompanied the dark shape's retreat back into the room.

I remained pressed against the wall, heart pounding in my ears. The door hung open. The strobe lights had shut off, casting the rest of the room in gloom. It took a moment for my eyes to adjust, and when they did, I could just make out the grinning dummy with fake knife in hand, waiting against the far wall. A barely visible track on the floor told me how it had been propelled forward. I assumed there was a sensor in the doorframe that triggered the whole setup.

"Are you kidding me?" I muttered. I was so done with this house.

I didn't bother closing the door, not wanting the thing to come charging at me again. I moved down the hall, looking for another staircase that would lead me back downstairs. If Paul wanted to look for Philip in this house of horrors, more power to him. I was finished.

The first staircase I found led down into a short hallway. A clank came from ahead, telling me I'd found my way to the kitchen. I was starving, and with the snacks no longer being served, maybe I could convince the chef, Mitchel, to make me a sandwich or something.

I followed the sounds coming from ahead, stomach grumbling. The clanks turned into a crash that sounded like someone had dropped an entire tray of plates and glasses. It was followed by a shout.

"Paul." My legs and feet, which were screaming from all the walking I'd been doing lately, propelled me forward without thinking. If Paul was shouting, it could mean only one thing.

He'd found Philip Carlisle.

I burst into the kitchen to find a few of the girls in the waitress outfits standing there, staring toward another exit in the room. Mitchel was there, too, hand over his mouth. I made straight for him.

"What happened?" I asked, out of breath.

He looked at me with wide eyes and licked his lips. "A fight. The police officer and another man." He motioned toward where all of the girls were looking. "They went that way; toward the back exit."

"Thank you." Despite the stitch growing in my side, I started running.

The kitchen opened up into what I took as a large pantry filled with canned and bagged goods, but it looked as big as a storage barn. A double-wide door, which was currently closed, gave access to delivery trucks so they wouldn't have to tramp through the entire house. I guess when you host parties of this size, you needed a place like this.

On the far side of the room, Philip stood, a long metal pole in hand. His chest was heaving, his hat and glasses missing. His coat hung off one shoulder, the undershirt ripped.

At his feet lay the prone form of Paul Dalton.

My heart just about stopped in my chest. Always before, I was the one who managed to get myself hurt and in need of rescue. Paul had always saved the day.

Now, with him unconscious, or worse, dead, I was the one who was going to have to do the saving.

But how?

Philip raised the metal pole above his head, ready to finish Paul off. There was no time to think, so I did the only thing I could.

I shouted at him.

"Don't you dare!"

Philip jerked as if he'd been shot, before lowering his arm and turning. "You." He laughed. "What do you think you are going to do?"

I hoisted Will's cane and tightened my grip. My hands were shaking, and I very nearly dropped it as I spread my feet in what I hoped was a close approximation of a fighting stance.

Philip laughed again, though his eyes never left me. "Please," he said. "Do us both a favor and turn around and scurry back to wherever you came from. You don't need to get hurt."

While it sounded like a fine idea to me, I couldn't

leave him alone with Paul. "No," I said, glancing at the shelving near me, hoping to find a weapon a little more suitable for taking down what was looking more and more like a trained killer. "It's over. We know you killed her."

Philip started toward me. There were a few cans and utensils on the floor. He stepped around them without looking down, as if he could *feel* them there. "You *think* you know," he said. "But you're just guessing."

"If you didn't do it, you wouldn't have run," I said, and then nodded toward Paul. "You wouldn't have attacked him."

Philip glanced back, and I very nearly charged at him. My brain wanted to, my fear that if I didn't do something, he'd hurt Paul worse than he already had nearly sent me careening forward. It was my legs that wouldn't work. They felt rooted to the spot.

He turned back my way, and the moment was gone.

"This is your last warning," he said. "Walk away now, or else you'll end up like your friend here."

Paul still wasn't moving. At least he was breathing. A trickle of blood trailed from his forehead and ran down over one closed eye. I mentally prayed he would suddenly wake and take Philip down from behind, but he gave no indication he was going to regain consciousness anytime soon.

I was on my own.

"Why'd you do it?" I asked, stalling for time. Maybe if I kept him from killing me long enough, Buchannan or Will would burst in and save me. I'd even go for Margaret Yarborough or one of the help, really. As long as it was just me and Philip, I had no doubt who would win.

Philip didn't answer like I hoped. He took a step forward, fingers tightening on his metal pipe.

I tensed and waited. I was either going to do this, or I was going to be knocked unconscious. I refused to run, not when it might end up getting Paul killed if I did.

Of course, now we both might end up dead.

It wasn't much of a comforting thought.

Philip lunged for me then. His pipe arced down toward my head, and I did the only thing I could. I brought up Will's cane to deflect the blow, much like I had when the dummy had come at me. Cane and pipe met with a jarring crash.

The pipe won.

Will's cane snapped in half as my hands both went numb. I dropped the shattered piece, unable to feel my fingers. Pain radiated from my fingertips, up to my elbows. I staggered back a step, one mirrored by Philip as he pressed his advantage. He swung again, and with nothing in hand to stop the blow, I dropped to my knees.

There was a loud clang as the pipe struck the metal shelving above my head. I hit my knees hard enough to cause me to cry out in pain, but I didn't let it stop me. I had a second or two before Philip would be able to rear back and strike me dead on the spot. There'd be no avoiding the blow this time.

I'd noted a serving platter on the bottom shelf during my hasty perusal of the shelves. I grabbed it then, and using every last ounce of strength I had, I swung it straight at Philip's unprotected shins.

The platter was an expensive one, built solidly, and to last. It struck him in the leg with enough force, I swear I heard it clang against his shinbone. He cried out and staggered back a step. The pipe fell from his fingers as he reached down to grab at his wounded leg. It was all by reflex, and it worked out perfectly for me. I came up from the floor, platter swinging, a scream of frustration ripping from my chest.

His face met the flat portion of the platter with the sound of a gong. With him moving downward, and with me going up, it added to the sudden stopping force of the impact. His head whipped back, and his feet went out from under him like he'd been standing on ice and I'd given him a quick shove. He hit hard, head cracking on the concrete floor. He moaned and went still.

I didn't wait around to see if he'd wake. I rushed over to Paul and dropped to my poor, abused knees. "I'm sorry," I told him as I patted at his waist until I found metal. I pulled free the handcuffs, thankful he'd included them with his costume instead of using what was his standard zip strips.

"Please don't be fake," I prayed as I rose and hurried back to where Philip lay. He hadn't moved since I'd last seen him, but I didn't trust it. I'd seen the movies. I was ready.

I reached for his right wrist, cuffs open and ready. Philip's eyes flashed open and he made a grab for me.

"Oh no, you don't." I brought the cuff down, right on his wrist. It snapped shut, just as his left hand grabbed hold of my hand.

"I'll kill you!" Philip roared. His eyes weren't quite right, as if he was still trying to regain his equilibrium. I think it was the only thing that saved me.

I slammed the other end of the cuff down on the metal

shelving, locking it in place. Philip's hand on my wrist tightened painfully, but he was trapped.

"Let me go," I warned him. His eyes were becoming focused and the rage was clear as day. He grinned, exposing bloody teeth.

So, as casually as you'd like, I picked up a broken fragment of Will's cane with my free hand, raised it above my head, and then clunked Philip Carlisle over the head with it as hard as I could. His light went out. I freed my hand and sagged against the shelving before rising and searching for help.

25

It was another two hours before we were allowed to leave. The crews had finally gotten Buchannan's car unstuck and had lain some hastily acquired gravel to give the cars some traction on the way out. The guests left in an orderly fashion, something that surprised me considering how unruly they'd been during the party.

Paul turned out to be okay after his encounter with the villain, suffering only a cut on his scalp and a wallop of a headache. He wasn't thrilled I'd been wandering around and had happened on the fight, but was appreciative. Apparently, he'd caught up to Philip just as the other man was making his way through the kitchen, toward the back exit. Mitchel had been assigned to watch that door but had been in the kitchen instead, getting something to drink, when it all went down.

Of course, it probably saved him from getting smacked upside the head with a pipe, so it worked out in the end.

After handcuffing Philip to the shelving, and checking to make sure Paul was still with us, I'd quickly gathered a grumbling Buchannan, who took control of the situation. Will took care of Paul's cut and made sure he didn't suffer a concussion, while Buchannan led Philip into the mock interrogation room. Not surprisingly, the killer refused to talk.

There was a buzz throughout the house as we lined up to leave. Margaret Yarborough looked exhausted, but relieved that it was all over as Will and I reached the door.

"Thank you," she said with a smile.

"All in a day's work." It came out sounding lamer than I'd wanted, but I was too tired to care.

Will led me to the car, hand on my arm as if he thought I might collapse at any moment. Then again, maybe he was making sure I wasn't going to run off again and get myself into even more trouble. My knees were killing me, and my hands still felt tingly, but otherwise, I felt pretty good. I was more tired than anything. The sky was going to start to lighten soon, and I wanted to get a few hours of sleep before the sun rose. I had a long day of work to face in the morning, something I was definitely not looking forward to.

"You okay?" Will asked once we were safely secure in the car and making the slow, muddy trek down the disaster of a driveway.

"Yeah." I tried on a smile, but it only made my face hurt. A wince worked much better instead. "He didn't hurt me. I did it to myself." I rubbed at my right knee, which I'd apparently smashed into the floor a little harder than the left. It was going to be black and blue tomorrow. *Maybe I'll have a legitimate reason to call off work in the morning.* If I couldn't walk, I couldn't work.

"You shouldn't have gone off alone."

I glanced at him out of the corner of my eye. "You sound like Paul."

A faint smile lit up his face. His mask was gone, removed sometime while I was off chasing after killers.

"Then maybe you should start listening. You could have been seriously hurt. If you were worried about him, you should have come to get me. I would have gone with you."

"I had your cane," I said, as if that made it all better. Then, remembering that the cane was now lying in two pieces, I added, "Sorry about that."

He laughed, though it broke up as he yawned. "Much better to lose the cane than to lose you."

I blushed and found myself smiling, despite how it made my face ache. It wasn't every day you found a guy like Will, someone who would drop everything to help you. If I would have asked, he would have roamed the house with me, even though he knew he shouldn't. Maybe next time he could be my partner in crime. I'd let him do all of the heavy lifting and wrestling with the culprit. Perhaps then I wouldn't end up hurting afterward.

I closed my eyes and leaned my forehead against the car window. Here I was, with a man who was absolutely perfect for me, and my mind and heart were still confused and uncertain. Did I want it to be Will? Or was it Paul my heart pined for? I couldn't believe how hard of a decision it was. I guess that's what happens when all your previous relationships fail and you suddenly have two perfect men in your life. How could anyone make such a difficult choice?

I must have dozed off at some point because Will was shaking my shoulder. I opened my eyes and found them heavy with sleep. I smacked my dry lips with a tongue that felt as if it was made of cotton.

"Krissy," Will said. "You're home."

"I see that." I yawned and fumbled for the door handle. "Are you coming in?" The question was out before I could think about what I was asking, and boy did it ever wake me up. I froze and broke out in a cold sweat.

Will's face cracked with a yawn of his own. "I'd better get back home before I fall asleep," he said, rubbing at his eyes. "But if you want me to walk you in, I can."

A way out or a rejection? I wondered, then decided it didn't matter. We were both exhausted and had gone through a pretty rough night. The next time someone invited me to a late-night party, I was going to take a pillow and a few snacks, just in case something like this ever happened again.

"I'll be okay," I said, deciding I didn't want Will to see my house, especially since Misfit had been left home alone all night, without dinner. I'd thought I'd be home in time to feed him. He was *not* going to be happy.

"All right." Will paused and cleared his throat. "Good night." Another pause. "Despite everything that happened, I had a good time."

"Me too," I said, and I meant it. Sure, chasing after a murderer and running around asking questions of strangers who couldn't care less about who I was, wasn't exactly the most pleasurable experience, but I'd still had some time with Will. And really, I didn't actually hate solving the crime; it was fun in its own way.

What did that say about me that my best dates usually ended with the police getting involved?

Will cleared his throat yet again and looked everywhere but at me. I considered leaning over and giving him a kiss on the cheek since we *were* on a date, but I was pretty sure if I tried, I'd end up passing out into his lap. That wasn't the way I wanted our evening to end.

"See you soon," I told him, then dragged myself out of the car. He waited until I'd unlocked my front door and was inside before he waved and backed out. A part of me wanted to chase him down and force him to come in for a little while, but I just didn't have the energy for it.

A meow caught my attention. Misfit was sitting beside his empty food dish, looking as if he hadn't eaten in a week.

"You're fine," I told him. "It's not like you'll starve to death." I trudged my way to the cabinet where I kept his food, removed the bag, and poured half of it on the floor when he shoved his head under the bowl, just as I tried to fill it. I was simply too tired to care, so I returned the bag to its cupboard and then headed for the bedroom.

Thankfully, it appeared Misfit had behaved himself. There'd been times when I'd forgotten to feed him on time and he'd destroyed the place. If I'd come home to a shredded pillow or a broken lamp, I would have exploded.

Well, maybe not right away. I would have grumbled about it for a bit and then fallen asleep. His reprimand would have had to wait until morning.

It wasn't until I reached my bedroom that I realized I hadn't grabbed the trash bag containing my dirty costume. My phone and keys were in the pocket of my borrowed pants, so other than my shoes, I didn't care what happened to my lost things. I suppose I'd ask about them when I returned Margaret's clothes.

I stripped out of said clothing and climbed into bed. I was out in seconds.

Even though I was bone-weary, my sleep was restless. Something deep in the back of my mind nagged at me, causing my dreams to be unsettled. We'd caught the killer, yet I was sure we'd missed something. And it wasn't just Philip Carlisle's motive. I was pretty sure the police would eventually get that out of him, or figure it out on their own, so it wasn't that. I felt like I'd stared at something important that was right under my nose and had completely missed it.

I didn't want to, but I was up and out of bed after only four hours of rest. I took a shower, got dressed, and then dragged myself to the coffeepot to start it. I dozed as I waited for the coffee to be done, added my cookie, and sipped slowly as I waited for my mind to kick into gear. I still had a couple hours before I needed to be at work and wanted to use them to think.

Misfit was sitting by his bowl—empty, yet again. I filled it, and this time, he waited until there was some food in the dish before shoving his face inside.

What am I missing? I thought, sitting down at the island counter. I considered grabbing a puzzle to see if working on one would jog my memory, but decided against it. I'd probably only mess it up in my current state. A yawn that swallowed my face proved my point.

I glanced at the clock. It was only eight in the morning. I didn't have to be in to work until noon. I needed more sleep and thought I could set my alarm for ten or eleven and still make it to work on time, possibly refreshed enough to actually do some work.

I stretched out my legs and winced. My knees weren't black and blue, but they still hurt. I so wasn't looking forward to standing on my feet all day.

But the thought of going to bed just wouldn't fly. My mind was too abuzz with whatever it was I'd missed. I'd end up lying there, staring at the ceiling, wishing I was doing something else.

So, instead of getting much-needed sleep, I grabbed my purse and keys, and left Misfit to gorge himself on food. I had a feeling I'd return to a mess on the floor;

the cat didn't have an off button when it came to food. He'd often eat until there was simply no room left.

I got into my car, started it up without checking to see if Eleanor Winthrow was watching me from her window, and then headed to my sanctuary.

Death by Coffee was busy when I arrived. Lena was manning the register, and the new hire, Jeff, was running around, filling orders. I was surprised to see Vicki upstairs, selling books, looking fresh and vibrant, as if she'd just stepped off a runway.

I tried hard not to be jealous. My eyes were puffy, and my entire face felt about two sizes bigger than normal. There was no runway for me; scraping myself off the highway maybe, but definitely no runway.

I slouched my way to the back of the short line. Two yawns later, I reached the counter, where Lena beamed at me.

"Have fun last night?" she asked.

"It depends on what you mean by fun."

She laughed, and I wasn't sure if it was because she'd heard about what had happened, or if she thought I was joking. Either way, it appeared nothing would mar her good mood, something I wished I could manage more than I did. Somehow, something always seeped in.

"So, why are you here so early?" she asked. "I didn't think you were supposed to be in yet."

"I thought I'd come in and see what it was like to be on the other side of the counter."

"Oh! Well, what can I get you?" her grin was infectious.

"Black coffee and a chocolate-chip cookie." As if she didn't know.

Jeff fetched my order as I stepped aside to let the next

customer in line order. I watched him nearly drop the cup twice as he filled it, noting that his eyes kept darting my way. When he finally brought me my coffee, I gave him a reassuring smile.

"Don't be so nervous," I told him. "You're doing fine."

"Thanks, ma'am," he said, not meeting my eye.

"Call me Krissy, okay?"

He nodded vigorously before hurrying away to fill the next order. I watched him fondly, thinking that despite his nervousness, he was going to work out. He was going to be a keeper.

I carried my cookie and coffee to an open table in the back of the room. I plopped the cookie inside and gave it a moment to sop up some coffee and begin to break down before taking my first sip. I wanted to check in with Vicki, to make sure she was really okay, but she was pretty busy upstairs. I could catch her when it slowed down. Instead, I pulled out my phone and dialed, knowing that if I didn't call now, I'd hear about it later.

The phone rang twice before there was a *click*. "Buttercup?"

"Hi, Dad."

"You okay? I saw the news."

My dad had begun to check the Pine Hills news reports online ever since I'd started getting myself in over my head with murder cases. He'd probably seen something about Jessica Fairweather's death there. Chances were good my name was attached to the article somewhere.

"I'm fine," I told him, taking a sip of coffee. Bliss. "It was pretty scary, but I think that had more to do with the house than anything."

He chuckled. "I saw a few photographs of the place. It would be an interesting place to visit."

Sure, as long as no one got murdered while you were there.

"Are you sure everything is okay?" Dad asked. "You sound strange."

"I'm not at home," I said, knowing that wasn't what he'd meant. "And, well, I feel like I missed something."

"Such as?"

I sighed. "I don't know. I'm positive we got the right guy, and even if he tries to fight the murder charge, he nearly killed a police officer, so he's going to be in some serious trouble no matter what."

"But . . . ?"

"But what was his motive? The killer is rumored to be a hired hand. I don't see him showing up to a party just to kill some random girl. There has to be more to it."

There was a long stretch of silence while my dad thought. James Hancock was a semiretired mystery writer, and this sort of thing was right up his alley. It was likely the reason I was so interested in murder mysteries. I always felt like I needed to do whatever it took to prove I could be just as creative as Dad. He'd never pressured me to it; my own competitive nature did that instead.

"Did you see him interact with anyone?" Dad asked. "Argument? Heated or otherwise?"

I opened my mouth to speak when the door opened and two people I didn't know walked in. Nothing about them was all that interesting, yet I found myself watching them anyway. My subconscious prodded at me, though I had no idea why.

The man looked to be in his mid-forties. His hair was dark, combed back and tucked behind ears that were heavily lobed, so much so that they hung comically low around his jaw. It might be mean, but *Dumbo* immediately came to mind.

The girl at his side looked as if she was no older than twenty. Her hair was blond, but it was obviously a dye job. He said something to her, causing her to laugh. She reached up and tucked her own hair behind her ear.

An ear that was identical to her father's.

"Krissy?"

My dad's voice came from a long ways away.

"I have to go," I told him, mind working overtime. I clicked off, not thinking about how it must have sounded to him.

Why were these two so fascinating? I watched them approach the counter and order their coffees. They got them to go and, after paying, carried them out. I watched them walk down the sidewalk and out of sight.

It was their ears, the way it made it obvious they were related, I realized. But how did that fit in with Jessica Fairweather's murder? There were people who were related at the party, sure. I even knew a few of them. Heidi and her mom, Regina. Mason and his dad, Raymond.

But that wasn't it. Whatever it was, it was right under my nose and I couldn't see it!

I froze, mid-thought.

Nose.

I knew what I was missing.

I shot out of my seat and rushed for the door, leaving my mostly full cup behind.

26

"Woah there, Ms. Hancock."

I stopped just outside the Pine Hills Police Station and turned as Chief Patricia Dalton approached. She was holding her hat, as if she'd been in the process of putting it on when she'd spotted me. The top button of her shirt was undone, telling me she was more than likely just now arriving.

"Chief," I said, breathing heavily. I'd practically sprinted across the parking lot.

"What has got you in such a tizzy?" she asked, eyeing me. "You look harried."

"We've got the wrong guy." My mind was whirling. I wanted to see Paul, to talk to him directly. He would understand where I was coming from; he'd been there.

"What wrong guy?"

I slowed my breathing and forced myself to calm down. If I continued running around like I'd lost my mind, people would start treating me that way. "The killer. At the party. We have the wrong guy."

"Philip Carlisle, you mean?" Patricia frowned and crossed her arms. "He's already confessed to killing

Ms. Fairweather. He even took something from her body. It was still on him when we took him in."

I shook my head as she spoke. "I know he killed her."

"So, if he is our man, how exactly do we have the wrong guy?"

"Where's Paul? I really need to talk to him." I was dancing from foot to foot in my excitement.

"Not until you tell me what you're trying to say." Chief Dalton moved to stand between me and the door. One look at her told me she wasn't going to budge until I told her what she wanted to know.

"Philip killed Jessica," I said. "But you don't know why, do you?"

"He didn't give a reason. A man like that rarely needs one to kill someone. He not only confessed to her murder, but at least three others. I spent most of the night listening to him."

Which meant she was running on fumes by now. I imagine she'd gotten only a few hours of rest before coming back in, more than likely to continue questioning Mr. Carlisle.

"It's because he was hired to kill her," I said. "That's why he didn't say why."

"By whom?"

"I . . ." Some of the oomph went out of me. "I'm not sure."

"Then how do you know he was hired?"

"It's all in the nose!"

Skepticism flashed across her features, and maybe a little bit of pity. I wasn't doing a very good job of sounding sane. "Now, Krissy, we can't have you running all over town, accusing every suspicious person of wrongdoing, all because you have a hunch. You need to provide solid evidence. Facts."

"It's more than a hunch," I said. I was already regretting coming to the police station. I should have called Paul, told him where I was going, and went ahead and gone on my own. It was what I would have done before everyone started telling me to be more careful. See what I get for listening?

Chief Dalton still didn't look impressed, so I pressed on.

"I saw a photograph. The more I think about it, the more certain I am that it is the key to this whole thing. If I can just talk to Paul, he'll understand. He'll believe me." The last came out at a near whimper.

"I'm not saying I don't believe you." Patricia sighed. "But we have to follow protocol here. Do you have any evidence that Mr. Carlisle was hired for the murder? What photograph are you talking about?"

"Chief?" To my relief, Paul strode out of the police station in full uniform. He appeared as tired as his mom, which was as tired as I felt, but boy did he look great right then. "What's going on?"

"Ms. Hancock here believes we have the wrong guy in custody."

"Not the wrong guy," I said, clarifying. "Just not all of them."

It was Paul's turn to give me a skeptical look. "What are you trying to say? He confessed, and never once mentioned someone else."

I took a deep breath and let it out in a frustrated huff. I'd hoped to keep much of what I thought I knew to myself. If I told them everything, then I was positive I'd be left behind when it came time for the interview I was hoping to be a part of. This wasn't the mansion where Paul had little other choice.

"We need to talk to Terry Blandino."

"Terry?" Patricia asked. By the sound of her voice, I could tell she knew him personally. I'd need to be careful here. "Why?"

"I think he knows more about Philip's motives than he let on before."

The Daltons shared a look and then as one, turned to me, neither looking as if they were about to jump into a car and drive me to the man's house.

"Please, Paul," I said, focusing on him. "If you take me there, I'll explain everything on the way."

"Krissy, I don't know. . . ."

"If I'm wrong, you can arrest me for interfering or disturbing the peace or whatever you want. But I'm not wrong. I know it!"

Paul scratched the back of his head and looked to his mother. "She's been right before."

"And wrong just as many times," she said, deflating my hopes. After a short pause, she added, "But I think it might be worth checking out, especially if it earns us a motive. If Mr. Carlisle backtracks on his statement, I'd like to have some more proof, just in case."

My knees just about gave out in my relief. "Thank you," I said to both of them. "You won't regret it."

"We'll see about that." Patricia smiled as she said it.

I started for my car, but Paul veered off toward his own. I followed after, figuring it was probably a better idea, anyway. I didn't know where Terry lived. I hadn't thought to look it up before I came.

"Shouldn't we take your cruiser?" I asked as he opened his car door.

"I haven't been home," he said. "Once we do this, I'm going to get myself a little sleep."

Paul got into the driver's seat and allowed me to ride up front with him. His costume sat in the backseat in a rumpled pile. He gave me a long, steady look before starting the car and saying, "I hope this is worth it."

"It is," I promised him.

We started down the road, and he immediately started in. "Now, tell me what you know."

I told him pretty much everything I told his mom, but little else. Call me paranoid, but I didn't want him to drop me off at the side of the road, or worse, make me sit in the car, just outside Terry's house. This was my epiphany, so I thought I deserved to be involved in the questioning.

He wasn't happy, but at least he didn't pull over and force me to tell him what I knew. It was why I wanted to go with Paul Dalton, rather than any of the other cops. For whatever reason, I found him easier to manipulate, though I didn't like to think of it as manipulation. Easy to convince to my way of thinking sounded far better.

After a fifteen-minute drive, we entered the hills that gave Pine Hills its name. Another five minutes and we pulled into a long, paved driveway. The house sat on a hill overlooking a man-made lake. Unlike the Yarborough driveway, the Blandino one was graded properly. A dock sat in the lake, and another small house sat on its shore. A small boat leaned against it. It looked dry from where we sat, but I could imagine Terry taking the boat out daily, enjoying the sun and breeze.

I was insanely jealous.

"Does everyone living in the hills have a place like this?" I grumbled as we got out of the car.

Paul snorted. "Seems like it, doesn't it?"

I let him lead the way to the front door. He rang the doorbell and stepped back, hands behind his back. It took only a few seconds before the door opened and Terry Blandino appeared, dressed as if he was about to go horseback riding. He even carried a riding crop in one hand. I hadn't seen horses on the way in, but then again, I hadn't seen the back of the property, either. As far as I knew, he had an entire stable back there, along with a racetrack and meadow.

"May I help you?" he asked, eyes flickering toward me before firming on Paul. It was obvious by the downturn of his mouth, he wasn't happy to see us.

"We'd like to ask you a few questions," Paul said. "Would it be all right if we came in?" He didn't flash his badge like they did on TV and the movies. He spoke in a friendly manner, as if we were all going to have a nice little tea party.

Terry didn't seem soothed by his tone. "What is this regarding?"

Paul looked to me since I hadn't fully told him why we were here.

"It's about Elaine," I said. And then, after a brief pause, I added, "And her relationship to Howard Yarborough."

Terry Blandino wasn't a dark-skinned man, so seeing someone so light pale so completely was actually a little frightening. He took a step back, as if he might faint, before catching himself and turning it into a smooth step to the side.

"Well, I guess you'd better come in then."

We followed him into the quiet house, down a short hall, and into a sitting room. There was a fireplace, but no fire. He motioned toward the couch and took a chair of his own. He practically collapsed in it.

"Is anyone here with you, Mr. Blandino?" Paul asked. He'd noticed the tomb-like silence, too.

"No," Terry said. "I wanted time alone, so I sent everyone out. I thought it would help me clear my head, but the silence got to me. I was about to go for a ride when you knocked."

"We're truly sorry to disturb you," I said. "I'm sure this won't take long."

Terry waved off my comment. He shifted to sit at the edge of his chair, seemingly unable to sit back and relax. It was a wonder his leg wasn't jiggling up and down. If I'd been in his shoes, I wouldn't have been able to sit still at all.

"What did you want to ask me?" he asked. From the tone of his voice, he already knew what I was going to say. "You wanted to speak about Elaine?"

"She's your daughter, right?" I took point since I was the one who knew why we were there. "From your former marriage?"

His eyes held mine steadily. "That's right."

"Why did you get a divorce?"

A slight pinching at the corners of his eyes told me he wasn't thrilled about this line of questioning. If Paul hadn't been there, I imagine he would have told me to take a hike.

Instead, he answered, "Irreconcilable differences."

I let it pass. "When I found out Elaine was your daughter, I was surprised," I said, sitting back. "She looks nothing like you."

"So?" Terry said, stiff as a board. "Not every child takes after both parents."

"But I think Elaine did."

Paul leaned forward. "Is this going somewhere, Krissy?"

I nodded. "Of course it is." I focused back on Terry. "When I needed to change out of my costume, thanks to an unfortunate trek through the mud, Margaret Yarborough let me use her personal bathroom to clean up in. She left the clothes I was to wear in her bedroom. As I was getting changed, I noticed a photograph on her dresser, one of her late husband, Howard."

Terry shifted in his seat, all the world looking like a rat who realized he was already caught in the trap.

I went on when he didn't respond right away. "Howard had a, shall we say, a very distinctive facial feature. When I saw it, I was bothered because I swore I'd seen it somewhere before, yet I couldn't place it. I thought he'd come in for a cup of coffee or I'd seen him around town somewhere, but that wasn't it, was it?"

Terry closed his eyes for a long couple of seconds before opening them again. When he did, there was resignation in his gaze. "No, it wasn't."

"Elaine," I said. "I talked to her at the party. She's very nice, but was confused as to why she'd been invited to a party where she knew no one but you." I paused a heartbeat before going on. "I couldn't figure it out. I didn't even know why you would invite her since she was living with her mother, a woman you left without much to her name."

"She's provided for, as is Elaine," Terry said, defensive. "I didn't abandon them, despite what she says." He ground his teeth together and spoke the last through them. "What she did."

"And what did she do?" Paul asked.

Terry's head moved glacially slow as he turned to look at Paul. "She cheated on me."

The air felt heavy as silence stretched on for a few moments before I said, "With Howard Yarborough."

Paul tensed as if he thought Terry might leap across the room at us, though the other man seemed only to sag in on himself. "You didn't think to tell us this before?"

"At the time, I wasn't sure it was relevant," Terry said. "And this is the sort of thing you don't want to get around if you can help it. My wife's infidelity wasn't something I reveled in, not like these other fools who thought screwing around with someone else's loved ones was perfectly acceptable behavior."

That was something we could both agree upon.

"So you were embarrassed by it," I said. "You didn't want people to know your wife cheated on you, that it was the reason you left her. You didn't want it to get out that the daughter you supposedly had together wasn't really your daughter at all."

Terry sighed. "I don't know how no one else saw it," he said. "It was as plain as . . ." He trailed off and frowned, so I finished for him.

"As the nose on her face."

He nodded, clearly bitter. "I couldn't take it. I tried, but every time I saw her, it reminded me of what happened. Margaret knew about the affair and about Elaine, as did Howard. But otherwise, we kept it our secret. Not even Elaine knows who her real father is." A panicked look came into his eyes then. "Please don't tell her. It would ruin what little relationship we have, and I fear it would crush her mother."

"We may have to," Paul said, before turning to me.

"How does any of this relate to Jessica Fairweather's murder? That's why we're here, right?"

I kept my focus on Terry. "I saw you argue with Philip Carlisle at the party. It was about Elaine, wasn't it?"

He hesitated a moment before nodding. "We talked about it before. I had my concerns about him." He gave me a smile that was very nearly a sneer. "Because of what my wife had done, and with Howard's recent death, I was concerned. Think what you want, but I don't want anything to happen to Elaine."

Paul looked confused. "Why would you think that?"

"The costume," I answered for Terry. "Both Jessica and Elaine were wearing the same Marilyn Monroe outfit."

"As was Margaret Yarborough," Paul added, as if I might have forgotten.

"I don't know why Elaine was there," Terry said. "I swear to you, I had nothing to do with it. I was as surprised as anyone when I saw her. I thought maybe Margaret invited her because Howard had died, but when she didn't even go over to say hi to her, I began to wonder."

I frowned. If Terry hadn't invited Elaine, then who did? I knew it had to be related to Jessica's death. There were far too many coincidences for it not to.

And then it hit me like a ton of bricks. When I wanted Paul to bring me here, I'd thought we were going to be confronting the man who hired Philip Carlisle to kill Elaine. I thought Terry had invited her because he'd found out she really wasn't his daughter and had decided to have her killed. Since there was a good chance Philip didn't know what his victim looked like, he could easily have made a mistake since both women had worn the same costume.

But Terry had already known about Elaine. So what other motive would anyone have had to kill Howard Yarborough's illegitimate daughter?

"The will," I said, breathless.

"What will?" Paul asked.

Terry nodded, slowly. He'd figured it out already. I could tell by the look on his face. I even knew why he hadn't said anything. If he would have come forward, his secret would be out, something he didn't want.

I turned to Paul, excited again. "We have to go."

"Why?" He seemed genuinely confused.

"Terry didn't hire Mr. Carlisle to kill his daughter like I originally thought." I glanced at the man in question, and added, "Sorry about that," before turning back to Paul. "I can't believe I didn't see it until now!"

"Okay?" Paul frowned. "I assume you know who did then?"

I stood and started for the door. Paul could either follow or I'd walk all the way there and confront Philip's accomplice on my own. I refused to let this one get away.

"Who else?" I said as he leapt up to follow. "Margaret Yarborough!"

27

This time, I told him everything in the car.

"The Yarboroughs had no children, and as far as I know, no other family."

Paul glanced at me for a brief moment before returning his attention back to the road. "So, how does that help us?"

"Howard died. He would have left a will." I still couldn't believe I never saw the connections before now. It was all right there in front of me the entire time I was at the party. "In that will, Margaret would more than likely receive some of his money." I was guessing they held separate accounts. My dad had once told me that people with money often kept their earnings separate, just in case the marriage didn't work out. And if one of them were to unexpectedly die—especially if foul play might be suspected—it prevented the other partner from inheriting until everything was cleared up.

"Okay?" Paul said, still confused. "I get that. But how does that lead to Jessica Fairweather's murder? As far as I could discern, she had nothing to do with either of the Yarboroughs. She was an acquaintance that got invited to the party because she had money."

"The costumes!" I nearly shouted it in my excitement. When he didn't immediately get it, I went on. "Someone, more than likely Margaret Yarborough, invited Elaine Harmon, Howard's illegitimate daughter, to the party. Margaret found out what Elaine planned on wearing, probably by recommending it to her and making sure the costume ended up in her hands. Then she told Philip Carlisle to look for it, hiring him to kill her."

"But why do it at the party, rather than somewhere that wouldn't put Margaret and Philip both at the scene?"

I shrugged. "To make the party livelier? To create a situation where there would be more suspects? I don't know for sure. She might have wanted to have it take place close to her so she could witness it firsthand." Which made her a lot more diabolical than I would have pegged her for, but who was I to judge levels of insanity? "All I know is that Philip made a mistake. He saw someone dressed as Marilyn Monroe and killed her, thinking it was Elaine."

"Mrs. Yarborough was wearing the same thing," Paul said. "Why would she do that if she was going to have Mr. Carlisle kill someone wearing that specific dress?"

"It might be how Philip knew who to kill. If Margaret did indeed tell Elaine what to wear, she could have bought the same thing, telling Philip that whoever was wearing the Monroe costume was his target. Then, once the deed was done, she could change into something else, claiming she was doing it because she didn't want to wear what a murder victim had been wearing. She couldn't have known Jessica was wearing the same costume until it was too late. And then when she tried to talk to Philip before the murder, Terry Blandino interrupted."

"Yeah, but . . ." Paul fell silent for a few seconds and then a lightbulb seemed to go on. "The will."

"Exactly!" I wanted to hug him, but since he was driving, held off. "Howard knew about Elaine, had probably provided for her in some way. Margaret didn't approve, so whatever he was doing had to be kept quiet. If he made it public that Elaine was his daughter, it would cause a scandal. Even Terry, who knew about the affair and knew his daughter wasn't really his daughter, didn't want that."

We were already racing toward the Yarborough mansion faster than was safe, yet Paul managed to put on more speed.

"What if Margaret realized Howard was going to leave a substantial amount of his fortune to his illegitimate daughter? She might have snuck a peek at the will—which she said hadn't been processed yet—or had their lawyer tell her. From what I understand, she was pretty tight with him. Since she didn't want anyone to know about Elaine, and she wouldn't want to have so much money go to a girl she'd never raised, never cared to get to know. She couldn't have been happy."

"So she had her killed."

I nodded. "She hired Philip Carlisle, a man rumored to have killed for hire, who very well might have had a hand in Howard Yarborough's death, if the rumors are to be believed. She had him kill a girl who was about to take a rather large piece of the pie Margaret thought belonged solely to her. When she talked about the women who'd come asking for money, it was obvious she viewed them with scorn."

"And Elaine had a legitimate claim on the money where these other women didn't."

"Exactly. So, in comes Philip."

"Who killed the girl," Paul said, sounding sad. "Jessica Fairweather died for no reason. It was all a mistake."

"And Elaine could still be in danger," I said, realizing it for the first time. "Just because Philip failed, doesn't mean Margaret won't try again some other way."

Paul didn't hesitate. He snatched up his phone and pressed a button without looking. He slammed it to his ear hard enough, it had to hurt.

"Buchannan," he said when he picked up. "Get someone over to Ms. Elaine Harmon's place as soon as possible. If she's at work, find her there. She could be in danger." A pause while Buchannan spoke. "No, now." He clicked the phone off.

"Will he do it?" I asked, knowing how stubborn Buchannan can be.

"He will. John can be difficult sometimes, but he's good at his job. He won't let his personal feelings about me cloud his judgment."

I wasn't so sure about that when it came to me, but I let it go. Buchannan seemed to be trying, and I owed it to everyone to do the same.

"How did you figure it out?" Paul asked. We were almost to the Yarborough mansion, so I had to talk fast if I wanted to get it all out before we confronted Margaret.

"I saw a photograph of Howard in the bedroom," I said. "He has a very distinctive nose. His daughter does as well. When I saw it, I didn't put it together right away, but it hit me today. I figured they had to be related."

"Which Terry confirmed."

"And while I was asking questions at the party, I'd heard all sorts of things about the Yarboroughs. They had no kids, which called into question about who would inherit once Margaret was gone. No one was asking about who would get *Howard's* money, which I bet Margaret was counting on. And then when I learned that Philip might have killed Howard, how he might have once been a hitman, it all sort of tumbled together."

"Good work," Paul said, sounding impressed.

"I should have seen it before now," I said. I was thrilled by the compliment, but it wouldn't mean anything if Margaret were to get away, or worse, Elaine ended up dead.

We reached the driveway, which was still a muddy mess, but at least now there was enough gravel we were able to get up it with little trouble. Paul parked right outside the house and was out of the car nearly before he'd put it in park. He muttered, "Stay here," but I think we both knew I wasn't going to listen. I had my door open and was coming around the front end almost before he finished speaking.

He gave me a resigned sigh as we approached the front door. He knocked, and when no one answered right away, he started pounding harder. "Mrs. Yarborough! Open up. It's Officer Paul Dalton with the Pine Hills Police Department. I'd like to ask you a few questions."

It took a few more seconds before the door opened and a man I didn't recognize right away peered out. He was wearing a pair of jeans and a white T-shirt—not something you'd expect to see someone wearing in a mansion like the Yarborough place.

"Officer Dalton?" the man asked. "How can I help you?"

I blinked at him. I finally recognized him by his voice, and yet still couldn't see it in his face. He had cleaned off the makeup and wasn't wearing his costume, but it was Vince, Margaret's butler, the man I'd known as Igor.

"I need to speak to Mrs. Yarborough," Paul said, not thrown off by the change in the slightest. "Can we come in?"

"You can," Vince said. "But Madam Yarborough isn't here, and I don't think she's coming back." He looked down at his tennis shoes and sighed. "She let the staff go this morning and left with many of her bags packed."

Paul gave me an alarmed look before turning back to Vince. "Do you know where she's gone?"

Vince grinned as he leaned forward and lowered his voice, though I don't think there was anyone in the house who could have overheard him even if he'd shouted. "I heard her speaking on the phone early this morning when she thought no one was around. She said she needed to stop at the bank and then would meet someone at his office afterward. I believe she was talking to her lawyer, Christian Tellitocci." He glanced at his watch. "She left ten minutes ago."

"Thank you," Paul said to Vince, before turning to the car. "Let's go." That to me.

"I hope you get her," Vince said. He sounded so sincere, I think he actually meant it. My observation at the party that the help didn't seem to enjoy working for Mrs. Yarborough seemed pretty accurate now.

Paul was on the phone when I slid into the car next to him. He backed out, cursed, and then tossed the phone down. He turned the car around in the parking lot at the side of the house and then sped down the driveway, slipping and sliding everywhere. I held on for dear life, certain we'd end up off the road and stuck in the mud, but we somehow made it down without crashing.

If there were any doubts that I'd gotten it right, they'd fled right along with Margaret Yarborough. Why else would she be on the run if she didn't have anything to do with Jessica Fairweather's murder? Chances were good she was afraid Philip would cave and turn her in, so she was getting out while she still had time.

Of course, that brought up the question as to why he *hadn't* given her up. Love? Stubbornness? Some sort of killer's code that prevented him?

"Look up Christian Tellitocci for me," Paul said, gesturing toward his phone. "I think I know where his office is, but I want to make sure."

I grabbed his phone and brought up Chrome. A quick Google search and I knew where we were going. I told Paul the address, which earned me a nod, but little else. I could tell his mind was elsewhere, probably running through all of the facts, or prepping himself for what was inevitably going to be a confrontation.

I was too excited to make much in the way of conversation, anyway. Paul looked intense and I didn't want to shatter his focus, either. I wished we would have taken his cruiser so he could turn on the siren and lights. We were forced to slow down a few times because cars didn't get out of the way, something that would have happened if we'd been in the correct vehicle. And there was no radio in here he could get in touch with the station, on Paul or in his car. I think he'd taken that stuff off before leaving the station, and I assume his failed call was him trying to get in touch with someone at the station, meaning we were on our own.

Again.

"When we get there, I need you to stay in the car," he said. We were on Rosebud Avenue, a stretch of road on the far side of the downtown area where most of the buildings were filled with lawyers, tax consultants, and other niche jobs. There were no coffee shops or candy stores here. Everything was brown, and rather boring, which was sad in a way. Much of Pine Hills was so rich and vibrant, and here, there weren't even any clever names. I was surprised to find I missed the strange business names of the main stretch.

"I will," I promised him, not wanting him to lock me in the car or handcuff me to the door. While a part of me wanted to be in the middle of the action, I knew where that would get me. Although a trip to the local doctor's offices wouldn't be such a bad thing if Will was around.

A blush came unbidden to my cheeks, but thankfully, Paul was too busy parking to take notice.

A Lexus sat idling two cars ahead. No one was inside, but since it was running, I doubted that would last long. Paul shut off the engine and got out of the car, hand already near his gun. He jogged toward the front of a building with TELLITOCCI AND SONS written in white on the glass window. He reached for the door just as it burst open and a rather large man came barreling out, slamming into Paul, taking them both to the ground.

Paul rose to one knee, his gun in hand, and aimed at the big man on the ground—Christian Tellitocci if I didn't miss my guess—who was holding both his hands above his head in surrender. He was babbling nonstop, as if he could talk his way out of an arrest. I hoped he was confessing and giving up Margaret Yarborough, but knew it was unlikely.

Paul lowered his gun as the man continued to talk. He grabbed zip strips from his pocket and moved to secure the lawyer.

Movement near the corner of the building caught my

eye. Paul missed it because he was distracted with the lawyer and his steady stream of words. While Christian might have given himself up, he wasn't making it easy, moving his hands and wrists so Paul couldn't get a grip on them.

Margaret Yarborough stepped out onto the sidewalk, back slightly hunched as if she thought that if she crouched down, no one would notice her. Her eyes were locked on Paul. She didn't see me, thankfully. She was making for the Lexus, a briefcase in hand. I was pretty sure it was filled with a large portion of Howard's money.

Paul had said to stay in the car, but he hadn't anticipated this. I threw open the car door and grabbed the only thing I saw in the immediate vicinity I could use as a weapon. I darted toward the fleeing woman and held it up like a gun as I shouted, "Margaret! Stop!"

She froze less than a yard away from the front of the car. She glanced at me, then to the Lexus, before finally looking past me to Paul, who cursed loudly just as Christian started screaming, "Run, Margie, run!"

From the scuffling sounds that followed, I knew I was on my own.

"Margaret," I warned as she took a step toward her car. "Don't make me."

She snorted. "Make you what, dear? Text me to death?"

My grip tightened on Paul's phone. "Don't do this," I said. "I know about Elaine, about Howard's will." Or least, I thought I knew. I was mostly bluffing, hoping Paul would secure Christian before Margaret got away.

Her jaw clenched and she pulled the briefcase closer to her. "He gave her everything!" Barely suppressed rage made her quake. "I stuck with him despite everything. The house. The women. And he gives it all away to

some . . . some . . . *child* he made with a tramp who didn't
understand the basic concept of contraceptives."

"So you decided to have her killed."

Margaret's eyes narrowed. I think she was trying to
determine if Philip had turned on her, or if I was simply
guessing. In the end, she must have decided it didn't
matter either way.

"This is all Howard's fault." She started for the car.

"Margaret!" I shouted, but this time, she didn't stop.

The struggle was still going on behind me, Paul cursing nearly nonstop. Even partially zip-stripped, Christian
was putting up a good fight. It meant he wasn't going to
be able to help me, and since Buchannan—and more
than likely most of the small police force—were busy
keeping Elaine Harmon safe, I had to stop her by myself.

Knowing no help was on the way, I did the only thing
I could think of.

"Catch!" I shouted, throwing Paul's phone at Margaret's
head. She ducked, surprised by the heave, and the phone
sailed harmlessly past her.

It was a good thing hitting her hadn't been my intent.

The moment her eyes were off me, I charged forward.
With a primal scream, I went to dive over the hood of the
car to tackle Margaret. I, of course, didn't put enough
oomph behind my leap and landed on the hood instead of
on the fleeing woman. I slid a few inches and then *rolled*
down and on top of Margaret. We went down in a tangle of
limbs, and I cracked my chin a good one on the concrete.

"Get off of me!" Margaret shouted, but I remained
where I lay, mostly because my head was spinning, and
partly because I was afraid she'd take off running the
moment she was free. There was no way I was going to
chase her down, age difference or not.

When I didn't move, Margaret sank her teeth into my right arm.

I screamed, surprised by how hard she'd bitten me. This wasn't your typical feeble old lady. She bucked under me, causing me to partially roll off her. I grabbed her by the arm and started to reach for the briefcase when she swung it.

I tried to duck, but I was already low to the ground as it was. The briefcase hit me upside the head hard enough to cause my neck to jerk back, slamming the back of my head into the front bumper of the Lexus.

My grip on her loosened and she tried to slither away, but I grabbed her again and reapplied my weight to keep her down. She wasn't going to get away, not as long as I was conscious.

Margaret opened her mouth as if she was going to bite me again when a shadow fell over us. She looked up, savage snarl forming on her lips, and then just like that, it all died away. She went limp beneath me and released her grip on the briefcase.

"It's not fair," she mumbled before bursting into tears.

"It's okay, Krissy," Paul said from above me. "You can get off of her now."

I didn't think I could stand, so I rolled off her, once more hitting my head on the pavement. "Ow," I grumbled, closing my eyes as Paul began to read Margaret Yarborough her rights.

28

There were children everywhere.

Rita stood beside me in the parking lot of the local church, talking nonstop about my discovery of not just the killer, but the person behind the entire fiasco. She was impressed, as she always was whenever I do something. I imagine I could have baked a batch of cookies and gotten a round of applause from her.

I nodded in all of the right places and did my best to answer her whenever she had a question, but my heart wasn't in it. I was so over Margaret Yarborough and the mess she caused because she didn't want to give up what she viewed as her inheritance to a girl who was deserving of it.

Andi and Georgina stood on one side of Rita, listening raptly to her as she gushed over my involvement in the case and how her tip led to the arrest of Philip Carlisle, who still insists he committed the crime of his own volition. Even after she'd all but abandoned him, the guy was loyal to Margaret. True love? I suppose even killers needed someone to care about.

"Trick or treat!" A pair of miniature ghosts appeared before me.

"Terrifying!" I said with a mock shudder as I deposited a piece of candy in each of their bags. They giggled and ran off.

As soon as they were gone, I rubbed at the bandage on my arm where Margaret had bitten me. It still itched. I hadn't realized it at the time, but she'd broken skin. My head hurt, but not as much as the darn bite. With the way it was starting to itch and burn, I was afraid it might get infected.

Will won't let that happen. I smiled, thinking of how he'd bandaged me up, tsking over and over again, though I could see the pride in his eye.

"Here you go," Lena said, handing candy to a ten-year-old priest. The girl was as cute as could be, and her grin caused even the normally somber Adam to smile where he stood at the back of the group.

The trunk or treat was going better than I'd expected. Parents were happy to let their children run free as they retrieved candy from the groups present. There were games on one end of the lot, things like pin the tail on the werewolf, that had many of the children screaming in laughter. I didn't even know there were that many kids in Pine Hills, though I suppose many of them had come from nearby towns.

My car sat behind us, trunk filled with candy. While all of the other cars in the lot had candy in them, most were using bags to hold it. Rita had insisted on dumping the candy out into the trunk, claiming it was tradition, which was supposed to make it all right. I knew I was going to find rotten candy hidden in the corners of the trunk for the next ten years.

My eyes traveled along the parking lot as a break in the kids appeared. The church itself had its own car. The local preacher and a few old ladies were handing out candy, smiling and treating everyone with kindness, even the kids dressed as demons and devils. No one was left out here, no matter race, gender, or religious beliefs. It was enough to make me smile. The sense of community was overwhelming.

"There's Officer Dalton!" Rita said, waving at him. "He's the arresting officer, you know?" she told Andi and Georgina, who nodded knowingly.

I really didn't want to look, but my eyes betrayed me. Paul was with a few other cops, including John Buchannan, who was actually smiling as he passed out candy. Paul looked up at nearly the exact same moment I glanced over, as if he'd heard Rita's exclamation. Our eyes met. We both blushed. And then the moment was gone as we both looked away to focus on the latest beggar.

"Here you are," I told a boy who had to be at least eighteen, dressed like Cinderella. He curtsied and then moved on.

I looked past him to the pink car parked two spaces away. It was the most popular, and with good reason. Jules was dressed in full-on super candy mode. He wore a red-and-white-striped suit, with matching hat and tie. And the candy he was giving out put everyone else's to shame. I wished we would have been placed next to each other because I really would have liked to talk to him, rather than listen to Rita extoll my virtues.

"And then she tackled her, without worrying about hurting herself. Look over here a second." Rita grabbed my chin and turned it so a pair of middle-aged women I didn't know could see the scab there from where my chin had struck pavement. "And here." She let go of my chin and nearly yanked my arm out of its socket to show the bandage.

"I'll be right back," I said as the women oohed and aahed. "There's something I need to do."

"Don't be too long!" Rita said, before going back to her story.

I scurried away and headed for the police car. While I knew they had the killer and his accomplices, I still didn't know what had happened to them, or to Elaine for that matter. Had Margaret sent someone else after her? Or had she and her lawyer taken the money and were going to make a run for it? I was determined to find out.

"Hi, Krissy."

I froze as Will approached, leading a little girl by the hand.

"Will," I said, face flaming as if he'd caught me smooching Paul Dalton in the closet. "What are you doing here?"

He smiled. "My niece." He turned to the girl in question. "Gemma, say hi to Krissy."

"Hi, Krissy!" She was six at the most, and cute as a button. She was wearing a Batgirl costume and holding a bag with Wonder Woman on it.

"Hi, Gemma," I said. "Are you getting a lot of candy?"

"Yeah!" She sounded excited, which was understandable. I would have loved going to something like this when I was a kid. "See!" She opened her bag so I could peek in.

"Wow," I told her. "That *is* a lot!"

She giggled and went sorting through her bag, adults forgotten.

I turned my attention back to Will. "I didn't know you had any siblings."

He shrugged. "It never came up. My sister would have been at the costume party, but she was out of town for work. I'm glad she didn't come, though. It was bad enough my parents were there for that." He looked glum for a moment before smiling. "But we all made it through it okay."

"Yeah." Other than Jessica Fairweather, that was.

"Come on, Willy." Gemma tugged at his hand. "I want to see the funny man." She was looking at Jules, who was tap dancing in front of his car, Lance looking on fondly.

Will smiled and gave me a helpless shrug. "I'll talk to you later, okay?"

"Sure. Have fun."

He let himself be led away. I watched him go with a contented sigh. He was good with kids and looked natural with Gemma. I could see him as a doting father someday.

My stomach tightened at *that* thought, and I turned to find myself looking at the police car where Paul was busy handing out candy. I no longer wanted to go over and talk to him, afraid that Will might take it the wrong way. He knew we'd gone on a date, which means he knew we might still care for one another. I really didn't want to screw up a good thing.

"Torn, huh?"

I jumped and turned to find Chief Dalton dressed in full uniform smiling at me.

"I don't know what you are talking about," I said.

"Sure you don't." She laughed and then tipped back her hat. "You are becoming quite a celebrity around here. One more solved murder and we might have to build you a statue."

I blushed. "It's nothing."

"Right." She sighed and shook her head. "I don't know what I'm going to do with you. Sometimes, I want to kiss you, others, I want to smack you so hard upside the head, you get whiplash."

"I'm just a coffee shop girl." Lately, it was starting to feel as if I was anything but. "How is Elaine?"

Chief Dalton rubbed at her chin as she scanned the mass of children. "She's good. Inherited everything apparently. Since Mrs. Yarborough is going to be spending the rest of her life in a cell, she'll even get the house."

"Is that legal?" I paused, thinking how stupid it sounded to ask a cop that. "I mean, wouldn't Margaret still have control of the house, even locked up? She's not dead."

"That, she isn't," she agreed. "But she never did have any real claim to the house. Apparently, it was solely in her husband's name and he had a provisional clause in his will that stated that if anything were to happen to her— including incarceration, if you can believe it—Elaine was to receive everything."

"Wow." I thought about that a moment. "I guess he never really trusted his wife, did he?"

"Not at all. She was left almost completely out of the will. If she would have left well enough alone, she would have lived comfortably, but not as comfortably as Elaine and her mother. She couldn't stand for it, though. She hired Mr. Carlisle to kill the girl who was standing in her way of a fortune."

"Where do you find a hired killer, anyway?"

Patricia snorted. "She didn't. As far as we can tell, the

only person Mr. Carlisle has killed was Ms. Fairweather.
Everything else was just boasting and rumor."

"Huh." Go figure. "I would have thought the Yarboroughs being married would have meant Margaret would
have a bigger say in the fate of the estate."

"It was all part of the prenup she agreed to when they
were first married. And with everything that happened,
you can bet Mr. Yarborough knew what his wife was capa-
ble of and made precautions against it."

"Krissy."

I groaned and turned to see the last person I wanted to
talk to standing nearby, a sheepish grin on his face.

"I'll let you two chat," the chief said before walking
away with a knowing chuckle.

"What do you want, Robert?" I'd thought he'd left
town—*hoped* for it, actually—but apparently he hadn't.
"I'm kind of busy right now."

"I won't take up much of your time."

I resisted the urge to say, "Too late." But there was no
sense in starting a fight. I crossed my arms and waited
for him to tell me what he had to say so he could go away,
preferably for good.

"I just wanted to tell you I'm sorry. I shouldn't have
stalked you like that."

Surprise warred with my distrust. "No, you shouldn't
have," I said, and then added, "but thank you."

"And I shouldn't have cheated on you." He looked
down at his feet. "I was wrong to lie to you about it. I
should have owned up to it right away."

Darn it. I was finding it harder and harder to hate him,
the jerk. "It's okay, Robert. It's all in the past now."

"I guess I just want to know if you'll ever see it in your

heart to give me another chance?" He looked up, trying his best to look like a sad puppy, begging for his master's forgiveness.

I wasn't buying it. I'd seen that look before and it always led to no good. "Robert, I have no interest in dating you. I'm sorry, but I just don't."

The puppy-dog eyes cracked and turned hard. "You'll change your mind," he said. He looked around the church parking lot, nodding as if in approval. "I like it here. I think I might stay."

And with that grand declaration, he turned and walked away.

"Great," I grumbled, heading back for my car. Just what I needed, Robert hanging around, hounding me to get back with him. Maybe I could sic Buchannan on him.

I resumed my place at Rita's side and proceeded to hand out candy to the smiling faces. Even after everything, I found myself smiling right back. Despite Robert, despite the recent murder, and despite my indecision over two great men, things were looking up for me. Life was good.

Please turn the page for an exciting sneak peek of
Alex Erickson's next Bookstore Café Mystery

DEATH BY VANILLA LATTE

coming in June 2017!

1

A contented sigh slipped through me as I finished the last page of the book I'd spent the entire morning reading. My orange cat, Misfit, was curled up in my lap, purring softly. A now-cold mug of coffee sat just out of reach on the coffee table where I'd left it about two hours ago. The soggy cookie inside would end up in the trash, but I was okay with that. This was about as close to bliss as I could come.

My eyes strayed to the wall clock and I sighed. "I'm sorry," I said, running a hand down the soft length of my cat.

He glanced up at me and gave me a silent "please don't" look.

"I wish I could stay forever," I told him. "But I have to work." I picked him up, causing him to make a meow of protest, and then deposited him on the warm spot on the couch where I'd just been sitting. He glared at me once, swished his tail, and then jumped down. He then stretched, gave me one last angry look, and then padded his way to the bedroom where he'd pout for the rest of the day.

I didn't let his sour grapes shake my good mood, however. Whistling to myself, I rinsed out my coffee mug, put it face down in the sink, and then grabbed my purse and headed out the door.

Afternoon sunlight warmed the inside of my car on a day that was just shy of being chilly. I drove, music blaring, and sang along like a fool, even when I really didn't know the words. I passed by Phantastic Candies and waved to Jules Phan who'd poked his head out the door to see what all the ruckus was about. He returned the wave with a bemused smile.

A few minutes later, I was parked down the street from Death by Coffee, having struggled to find a spot closer. I wondered if there was any way we might buy one of the nearby lots and turn it into a parking lot, but after only a moment's thought, I decided it would probably cost too much. The shop might be doing better than ever, but that didn't mean we could up and spend however much we wanted, even if it might help the business grow.

Besides, the short walk would do me some good. I kept promising myself I'd work out, yet it seemed the only exercise I got these days came in the form of work. Maybe I'd start doing sit ups next week.

And maybe I'd hit the lottery while I was at it. Both were just as likely.

I pushed through the front door only slightly winded. Lena Allison and Jeff Braun were both behind the counter, hard at work. The line was short, but most of the tables were full, telling me it had been a pretty busy morning. Upstairs, Vicki was talking to a pair of middle aged women near the bookshelves, using her charms to sell a book or two.

"Mrs. Hancock!" Lena said as I came around the counter. "It's a great day, isn't it? A really great day." Her grin was a little too wide and she was dancing from foot to foot.

I cocked an eyebrow at her and then turned to Jeff, who just about tripped over himself spinning away. He started filling a cup even though no one had ordered anything to drink.

"What's going on?" I asked.

"What do you mean?" Lena ran her fingers through her short purple hair and refused to meet my eyes.

"You called me Mrs. Hancock. You never do that."

She shrugged. "Thought I'd try it out. A little much?"

"A little."

She spun around as a customer came to the counter and let out a big sigh before saying, "Welcome to Death by Coffee! What can I get you?"

I watched her a moment, perplexed, and then with a shrug of my own, I went into the office to deposit my purse. I snatched the apron off the wall by the door, and then headed back to the front to start what was starting to look like a very peculiar day.

"How did opening go?" I asked Jeff, who was still standing by the coffee pots. Today was the first day he'd worked open with Vicki and I was curious to see how he liked it.

"It was okay, ma'am," he said, lowering his gaze.

"Krissy," I reminded him. "Call me Krissy."

He nodded, still not meeting my eyes. "Sorry."

I patted him on the shoulder. "Go ahead and clock out."

He scurried off, seemingly relieved I hadn't kept him

there any longer than I had. He'd never quite gotten over his shyness, but I was slowly trying to break through to him. He was a hard worker despite being something of a slow learner. He was working out just fine, which was a relief, considering how the last guy I hired turned out.

I spent the next half hour making sure the coffee was fresh and replacing the cookies in the display case with fresh ones. I whistled while I worked, though I was still worried by Lena's strange behavior. I'd had to run inventory all last week, and boy, let me tell you, that wasn't something I enjoyed. No one had ever told me how hard owning your own business could be, especially when it came to making sure you were fully stocked. I'm forever thankful Vicki handled most of the behind the scenes bits because if it had been left to me, we'd have closed within months of opening. Let's just say, money and paperwork aren't my strong suit.

The front door opened and a thin man with flyaway brown hair and glasses entered, carrying two heavy looking boxes. He was sweating profusely from the weight and looked as if he was seconds from collapse. His eyes flickered my way, but he didn't come to the counter. Instead, he went straight up the stairs to where Vicki was waiting. She relieved him of one of the boxes, and together, they carried them to the back.

"Who's that?" I asked.

"Stock delivery?" Lena replied, though she winced as she said it.

"We get our books shipped," I said. "He's not our usual delivery guy."

"Maybe he's new."

"Okay, where's his uniform then?" I glanced out the front door. "Or his truck?"

Lena shrugged, and then spun on her heel to walk straight into the back.

What in the world is going on here?

I was about to head upstairs and ask Vicki about it when the door opened again and my answer strode through.

"Hey, Buttercup."

I sucked in a shocked breath and staggered back a step. "Dad?"

James Hancock, retired mystery author, and father to yours truly, smiled as he walked over to me. His beard was trimmed, as was what was left of his hair. He was smiling and I swear I saw a tear in his eye when he held out his arms to me.

"What are you doing here?" I asked, coming around the counter to give him a hug. "Not that I mind that you came. You never told me you were coming!"

He chuckled—a dry raspy sound that resonated through my entire body and brought memories of long nights sitting around a crackling fire, him typing away on his typewriter, and then later, laptop, and me reading a favorite novel.

"I had business and I wanted to surprise you." His voice was gravelly from years of trouble with his throat. I always found it fit him just right, made him sound like one of those old time detectives with a cigarette hanging loose from his lips, calling all the women dames, much like quite a few of his creations.

"Well, I'm definitely surprised!" And then realization dawned. I turned to find Lena grinning from behind the counter. "You knew!"

She rolled her eyes. "Of course I knew." She was practically beaming.

I turned back to Dad, not quite believing he was actually there. When I'd moved to Pine Hills, I'd left him behind, knowing how much it would hurt to be away from him, but needing the fresh start. It was surprising how good it felt to have him here now, even though I'd been blindsided by his sudden appearance.

"Why are you here exactly?" I asked, suddenly worried something was wrong. "Are you sick?"

He looked surprised for an instant before his smile returned. "No, I'm not sick." He cleared his throat, rubbed at his beard. He looked down at his hands for a second, before looking up and giving me a sideways smile. "I sort of have a new book coming out."

"You what?" I blinked at him. "But you're retired!"

"Semiretired," he countered. "You know I couldn't just up and quit. The story was burning in me for a while now, so I decided to go ahead and write it down." He took me by the arms and looked me in the eyes. "I swear I took care of myself this time. No fasting or skipping showers just to finish up a page."

His health was part of the reason he'd retired in the first place. I got my obsessiveness from him. He would forget to eat, forget to change clothes, or sleep, just so he could finish one last chapter. He never mistreated us or totally abandoned his family, though there were some days you could tell he wanted to get back to writing. His dedication is what made him such a good writer, though it definitely took a toll on his well-being.

"When's it coming out?" I asked, and then remembering the boxes that had come in a few minutes before, I added, "Is it out now?"

"No, not now," he said with a laugh. "I'm here to announce the book and sign some of my old novels. Rick thought it would be a good idea to make an event of it, and where better than right here, in a store that bears the name of one of my books?"

At mention of Dad's agent, my mood darkened just a little. "Rick? Is he here?"

As if summoned, the door opened and in walked Rick Wiseman. He was wearing a suit that looked as if it had come off a bargain bin rack, worn until it was little more than rags, and then tossed into a trash bin. His hair was much thinner than when I'd last seen him, but that didn't stop him from trying to conceal the spreading bald spot with a bad comb over. When he saw me standing next to my dad, he grinned, exposing his crooked left front upper tooth. He was holding a travel coffee mug with his name written on it in big black letters.

"Kristina!" he said, holding out his arms for me. "I'm so glad to see you."

"Rick," I said, not budging from where I stood. One glance at my dad and I forced myself to turn my scowl into a friendly smile. He'd just gotten here, so there was no reason to sour the festive mood with my distaste for the man.

"You've grown up so much," he said, seemingly oblivious to how I felt about him.

"I have." I hadn't seen Rick for at least ten years now, and I'd hoped to go another ten or twenty before I ever saw him again.

"We should get together and catch up sometime," he said, glancing around the coffee shop. "Somewhere nice."

I caught the implication and my smile grew even more strained. "Want a refill?" I asked, nodding toward his coffee mug. "What are you having?"

He shook his head and grimaced. "Vanilla latte. Made it myself. Brought the machine with me so I wouldn't have to drink something from a package."

I bit my lip hard enough I very nearly drew blood.

"It is quite a quaint little place you have here," he said. "Could use some paint, but I think it'll be fine." His attention snapped over my shoulder. "Cameron! There are five more boxes outside and they aren't going to walk themselves in here."

I glanced back to find the man who'd carried in the boxes hurrying down the stairs, and away from Vicki, who he'd obviously been talking to. "Sorry, Mr. Wiseman."

"Don't Mr. Wiseman me." Rick sighed. "Come on. Let's make sure you don't mess something else up . . ." He turned back to me. "Nice to see you again. We'll definitely have to talk."

Rick strode out ahead of Cameron, who kept his head down all the way out of the store. The poor guy looked as if this sort of thing happened all the time.

"Why is he here?" I asked Dad, who was watching the display with a frown of his own.

"He wanted to come. I told Rick it wasn't necessary, but he'd insisted."

"That poor man." I hoped Rick wasn't loading Cameron down with all five boxes of books at the same time. "Is he Rick's son?"

Dad laughed. "No, not his son. I guess you'd call him his assistant. Cameron Little has been working at the agency for the last year now, though I'm not sure what all he does."

"Why does he put up with him?" I wondered out loud.

Dad gave me a look. "Now, Buttercup, Rick works

hard. He can be abrasive, but his heart is in the right place.
I'm sure they both get quite a lot out of their working
relationship."

I wondered about that, but kept my opinion to myself.
Rick only cared about one man, and that was Rick. If my
dad stopped earning him money, I'm sure he wouldn't
hesitate to drop him and move on to the next sucker.
Sure, it's cynical, but I had a feeling it was the truth.

The door opened and I braced myself for another
interaction with Rick, but instead, I was broadsided by
something far, far worse.

Rita Jablonski made it all of two steps inside before it
registered who was standing just inside the door.

"Oh!" It came out as a surprised sound as her eyes
widened. Then, her hand fluttered to her chest as she realized exactly what she was looking at. "Is it really . . ."
She sucked in a breath and for a moment I thought she
might let out one of those screams teenaged girls make
when they see their favorite pop star.

"Rita," I said, hoping to stem the tide before she
started gushing, but it was too late.

"James Hancock! It's really you." She started breathing
in and out like she might hyperventilate. She fanned herself off as she hurried over to where we stood. "I can't
believe it. You've finally come after all this time. It's a
blessing, I tell you. A downright blessing straight from
Heaven, sent to me on this most blessed of days."

"Hi," Dad said, holding out a hand, polite as ever. "I
am James. You are?"

"Dear me." Rita was flushed as she took his hand.
"Rita Jablonski. I'm your number one fan."

I just about choked. We went from overexcited teenager straight to *Misery*. Could this get any worse?

"It's very nice to meet you, Rita," Dad said, practiced smile in place.

"We've met before," she said with a wave of her hand. "I got your autograph from a signing you held a few years back. I traveled quite a ways to meet you then." Her eyes widened. "Are you doing a signing here in Pine Hills? Please tell me you are! I can't imagine what other reason you'd have to come to our little town."

I cleared my throat, but I might as well not have been there.

"I am," Dad said, his smile turning amused. "It won't be until this weekend, however."

Rita just about glowed with excitement. "That means you'll be here all week!" I could see the wheels spinning behind her eyes and knew whatever she was thinking couldn't be good.

"Rita," I said, forcing her to look at me. "Dad and I haven't seen each other for a few months now. We'd like to have a few minutes to catch up, if that's okay?"

"That's fine, dear," she said, actually shooing me away. "You'll have plenty of time to catch up, I'm sure."

Behind her, the door opened and Cameron came in, three boxes in his arms this time. Rick trailed behind, carrying only his coffee mug. The least he could have done was to offer to carry the last two boxes, but apparently, physical labor was beneath him.

"I have an idea!" Rita said, clapping her hands together and startling me half to death. "We hold a writers group meeting every Tuesday night. You should come and talk to our members!"

"I wouldn't want to intrude," Dad said, for the first time sounding uncertain.

"Nonsense!" Rita patted him on the hand. "It will be a special meeting, one held in your honor. I'll let everyone know you're going to be there and they can prepare for it. I bet we'll have at least three times as many people show up, all because of you! It's going to be fantastic!"

And before my dad could protest, Rita spun away. Her cell phone was in her hand even before she reached the door. As she stepped out on the sidewalk, I could hear her say, "Georgina! You won't believe who I just ran into!" And then the door closed, and she was gone.

"What just happened?" Dad asked, a bemused expression on his face.

"You don't have to go," I said. "Rita gets overexcited at times and forgets that people sometimes like to make up their own minds about what they do."

"She seems nice enough."

"She is," I said. "But if you let her, she'll have you paraded all over town. You won't have a moment's peace."

Dad patted me on the arm. "I'm in town, so I might as well go. I'd like to get to know the people here and the writers group seems like the perfect place to start."

"Are you sure?"

"I am."

A crash and a pained yowl caused us to turn. Cameron lay sprawled on the floor, the boxes of books spilled before him. The store cat, Trouble, sat a few feet away, licking his back foot, and glaring at the poor assistant like he'd stepped on him on purpose.

"Be more careful with those!" Rick shouted. "What is wrong with you?"

Connect with 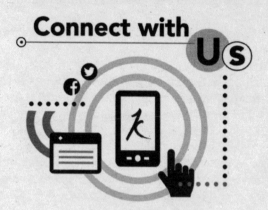U(s)

Visit us online at
KensingtonBooks.com
to read more from your favorite authors, see books
by series, view reading group guides, and more.

for sneak peeks, chances to win books and prize packs,
and to share your thoughts with other readers.

facebook.com/kensingtonpublishing
twitter.com/kensingtonbooks

Tell us what you think!

To share your thoughts, submit a review,
or sign up for our eNewsletters, please visit:
KensingtonBooks.com/TellUs.